MINE TO KEEP

CYNTHIA EDEN

This book is a work of fiction. Any similarities to real people, places, or events are not intentional and are purely the result of coincidence. The characters, places, and events in this story are fictional.

Published by Cynthia Eden.

Cover art and design by: Pickyme/Patricia Schmitt

Proof-reading by: J. R. T. Editing

DEDICATION

I want to dedicate MINE TO KEEP to all of my wonderful readers. Thank you so much for all of the notes and emails that you've sent me about Skye and Trace. You have been absolutely incredible!

CHAPTER ONE

She couldn't get free. No matter how long or how hard she struggled, Skye couldn't escape from the handcuffs.

Or from the basement that she knew would be her grave.

The place smelled of blood and death. Fear. Her fear.

Skye's breath sawed in her lungs. Hunger gnawed at her, twisting her stomach. The darkness was so complete.

She was trapped there. Skye knew that she would die there.

"Weston is dead." The brutal words came to her in the darkness.

Weston. Trace Weston. Her Trace.

He was gone, and, soon, she would be dying, too.

Because there was no escape from the darkness. Or from the monster that waited there with her.

"Skye! Dammit, wake the fuck up!" Hard hands grabbed her. Shook her.

Tore her right out of the nightmare.

Skye Sullivan's eyelids flew open. Light surrounded her, flooding from the nearby lamp and spilling onto the rumpled bed.

Trace leaned over her. His hands were wrapped tightly around her upper arms. His blue eyes — so bright that sometimes it almost hurt to look into them — blazed down at her. "You come back to me," he demanded, his voice a low, deep growl. "You come back *now.*"

Her heart thudded in a frantic rhythm against her ribs. She couldn't suck in a breath that was deep enough, and Skye realized that her cheeks were wet with tears.

Because that hadn't just been a nightmare.

It had been a memory.

Four weeks ago, her ex-lover, Mitch Loxley had kidnapped her. He'd kept her captive in a basement. Starved her. If it hadn't been for Trace, Skye knew that she would've died in that stinking pit.

"I'm back," she said, but the words were hoarse, as if she'd been screaming.

When Mitch had taken her, she'd screamed for hours. Days? Until her voice broke.

"He can't hurt you anymore," Trace said. The faint lines around his eyes tightened as his gaze swept over her face. "Baby, that bastard is rotting in the ground. He won't hurt *anyone.*"

Thanks to Trace. Because Trace had killed Mitch.

Memories can't hurt you.

Lately, that had become her mantra.

Trace bent his head. His lips brushed over her cheek. "I don't want you crying because of that SOB."

But she hadn't been crying for Mitch. She'd been crying because...in that twisted memory, Trace hadn't come to save her.

Trace had been dead.

She wet her dry lips and stared into his eyes. In one way or another, Trace had been the central point of her life since she'd been fifteen years old.

He'd saved her the first night they met. Her foster brother had been attacking her. Skye had been so certain that no one would hear her cries for help.

Trace had heard her.

Without him, sometimes she feared that she would be lost.

And that scared her to death.

"Make love to me," she said, the words coming out in that same hoarse, husky tone.

His hold tightened on her.

"I need you," Skye told him, and it was the truth. Trace was real and strong, and she wanted him to banish the fear that twisted within her.

"Skye..."

Her hands rose up. Her fingers sank into the thickness of his midnight black hair, and she pulled his head toward her. Her lips met his. Open. Hungry. Desperate.

She licked his lips. Licked his tongue.

They were in bed. She was naked, tangled in the sheets. She needed—

"I'll give you anything you want, you know that," Trace said, biting off the words against her lips. Then he yanked the sheets away from her. Flesh met flesh. He was warm and hard, his body strong with muscles, and he was *alive*.

His fingers slid down her body. Parted her legs. His fingers stroked her. Eased up and—

"No." Skye was surprised by the clipped denial that broke from her, but she wasn't looking for seduction.

She needed pleasure. Release. Fast. Hard.

His jaw tensed.

"You," Skye whispered. "I need to feel you."

Her hands curved around his shoulders. Her short nails raked over his flesh. Down, down she went. Her hand slid around his sides, pushed across his rock-hard abs.

Then she was touching his cock. Heavy and full, thrusting toward her. "I don't want to wait," Skye said as she stroked him. "I need you, *now*."

"You're not ready, Skye." His words were a rumble.

"Yes, I am." She arched toward him. "Trace, please!" She tried to urge him toward her, but Trace was too strong, and he pulled back.

Her heart stopped then.

"Not like this," he said, the words hard and sharp and—

He kissed her. Deep and long even as he caressed the center of her need. She pushed against him. Because she didn't want to go slow. She needed fast. One hundred miles an hour. Too fast to think. Too fast to do anything but feel—

He thrust a finger into her. Stretched her.

Not enough. Not even close.

His mouth trailed down her neck. He kissed her throat. Licked her sensitive flesh.

His fingers kept stroking her. Desire built, pulsing through her. But the desire wasn't enough. It wasn't going to be enough, not until he was *in* her. Skye arched toward him. Her legs wrapped around his hips.

But Trace's hands caught her legs and pushed them back down.

No, she wanted *him.*

Trace slid down—

And he put his mouth on her.

Pleasure came then, surging through her and a moan broke from her lips.

"Much fucking better," Trace growled. "*Now*, we do this."

He positioned his body and drove into her. Deep. So deep. She stared into his eyes, those bright, glittering eyes. Stared right into that blue even as the bed shook beneath her. He thrust, again and again. Harder.

There was no more thinking. Only feeling.

Meeting him. Thrust for thrust.

Sweat slickened their bodies.

She couldn't look away from his gaze.

His hands had locked around her hips. He lifted her up, holding her easily, as he thrust. Every muscle in her body tightened. She was so close to release. So close—

Pleasure exploded. The release burst over her with an impact that took her breath away. She shuddered and quaked, and he was there. Trace stiffened against her. Held her even tighter. The hot surge of his release filled her.

Alive.

Tremors shook her sex. Shook her.

But the memories of fear and death were gone. Pleasure surrounded her.

Because Trace surrounded her.

In that moment, Skye could almost convince herself that she was safe.

Almost.

The thunder of her heartbeat slowly eased its mad drumming. She became aware of other sounds then. The rush of waves, the pounding of the water against the shore.

The scent of the ocean.

She wasn't in Chicago. Not New York. They'd escaped together, and Trace had taken her down to the Florida Keys.

She wasn't supposed to be cold there. She wasn't supposed to be afraid.

His lips feathered over her cheek. "Do you want to talk about it?"

Skye shook her head.

"He's dead. I won't ever let anyone hurt you again."

Her lashes lifted, and she found herself staring up into Trace's eyes once more. She'd always felt like Trace could see straight into her soul.

Past the pretenses that she gave to others.

Right to her core.

Trace Weston. His face was hard, strong. Slashing cheekbones. A square, tight jaw. Lips that were cut in the faintest of cruel lines.

One look, and a smart woman knew he was dangerous.

Skye knew, and she didn't care.

He'd killed for her. She probably *should* have been afraid of him. She wasn't.

Because, deep down, Skye knew the truth.

I'd kill for him, too.

With each day that passed, she was discovering a new darkness within herself.

Maybe that was why she'd always been drawn to Trace. They were the same.

He slowly withdrew from her. Stood. He stared down at her, his legs brushing against the side of the bed. "You have to talk to someone."

No, she didn't. What she had to do was shove the memories into the deepest, darkest part of her mind.

And move the hell on.

That was what she'd done before, when her parents had died. Burying the pain and the dark memories—that was the way she survived. Her coping mechanisms had gotten her through life.

One stumbling step at a time.

"The nightmares aren't stopping." His hands clenched into powerful fists as he stared down at her. "You need to—"

"I have what I need," she said, and she rose from the bed, too. Skye pulled the sheet with her, letting it cover her body. Trace had never cared for modesty. She shouldn't either, but Skye still found herself pulling the sheet closer. "Talking to some shrink isn't going to magically fix me."

"Skye..."

A loud, insistent ringing cut through his words.

Saved by the bell.

Skye glanced to the right. Trace's phone waited on the small nightstand.

"It can damn well wait," he muttered. "You should—"

But she'd leaned forward to see the screen. "It's Reese. You'd better talk to him." Because Reese Stokes was Trace's right-hand man. A bodyguard, a friend—one of the few confidants that Trace actually had in the world.

"Go ahead," Skye urged him. "It could be important." She headed for the bathroom. Took the silken robe that waited on the hook behind the door. "I'll be outside."

The ringing stopped just as she opened the balcony door.

When she heard Trace answer the call, Skye stepped outside. The pounding of the surf was louder. The salty scent of the ocean filled her nose.

A private island.

Trace didn't do things half-way. Since the guy was a freaking billionaire now, he could have anything or anyone that he wanted...with just a snap of his fingers.

The wind blew her robe back against her, molding the silk to her body.

Skye headed for the churning waves. The light of the moon glinted off the water, making it look almost black.

She walked toward that beckoning darkness.

One foot, in front of the other.

These days, that was the only way she could get through life.

The waves hit her feet, and they washed away the foot prints that she'd left behind.

***

"Reese, this had better be damn important," Trace Weston snarled as his fingers tightened around the phone.

He'd jerked on a pair of jeans and then followed Skye out onto the balcony. He stood now, watching her as she walked along the shore. The waves crashed against her feet.

Skye. His beautiful, lost Skye.

The nightmares weren't stopping, and the pain in her green eyes seemed to be getting worse with each passing day.

The trip to the Keys had been designed to heal her wounds.

Not make them worse.

"Boss, you're not going to believe who dropped by for a little visit today." Reese's voice flowed easily over the line.

Trace kept his eyes on Skye. Was she going into the water?

"Ben Sharpe was here, looking for you."

A hard breath blew from Trace. The name was from his past, a blood-soaked past that he'd tried to bury. "What the hell did he want?"

"The guy said he had a message. One that he could only give to you."

Figured.

"But, there was…there was something about his eyes…" Now hesitation had entered Reese's voice, and that in itself was damn unusual. "The man's been unstable for years, hell, I know that, but this was different."

Trace didn't take his eyes off Skye. Her scent was on him. She'd marked him in ways that went far beneath the skin.

"He was afraid," Reese added. "Terrified."

"Everyone is afraid of something," Trace murmured. He'd learned to fear recently. Before, he tried to fool himself into thinking that he was invulnerable.

Then a bastard had tried to take Skye from him.

No one takes her.

She'd waded into the water. She looked so small out there.

And her robe was getting soaked.

"He came to the penthouse," Reese told him, "not the security agency."

Weston Securities wasn't just an agency. It was the biggest private security firm in the United States. Trace had built it with blood and sweat. And with the aid of secrets. So many deadly secrets.

"Tell me you have a man on him," Trace said. Because Reese would understand how important—and volatile—Ben could be.

Reese had been in hell with Trace. They'd both survived.

As had Ben…

Well, Ben had *mostly* survived.

The waves crashed into Skye. She stumbled.

Trace surged forward.

"Yeah, a guy's on him," Reese said, sounding annoyed now. "Jeez, boss, what do you think this is? Amateur hour? I'm calling because I thought you'd want to know. I thought this news might make you get your ass off that island. You have to come back home sooner or later."

Yes, he did.

He'd let Skye hide long enough.

The nightmares aren't going away. This place doesn't make her feel any safer.

"We'll be coming back on the jet tomorrow."

Reese's breath rustled over the line. "Good. Good, but…is she…okay?"

The waves crashed into her again. This time, Skye didn't stumble. She stood strong. "She's not going to break." Because he wouldn't let her.

I need her too much.

"Make sure the guards are in place," Trace directed. Because he wouldn't be taking any chances.

"They're ready and waiting."

Good. Trace ended the call. He tossed his phone onto the hammock near the edge of the balcony, then he hurried down the wooden steps that would take him to the beach and to her.

She didn't turn at his approach. Trace wasn't even sure that Skye could hear him, not over the rough pounding of the surf.

Her long, dark hair trailed over her back. Her hands were lifted up, as if she'd touch the waves. Her body was delicate, lithe, a true dancer's body, but she'd become too fragile since her abduction.

"Skye."

She didn't look back.

He followed her into the surf, not caring that his jeans got soaked, but he did say, "Baby, you're getting your robe wet, you—"

She glanced over her shoulder at him.

The moonlight fell on her face. Her high cheekbones. The gentle curve of her jaw. The straight line of her nose.

Her fuck-me lips.

The woman had a mouth that always made him think of sin. A mouth that made him need.

Her stare held his. It was too dark for him to see the green color of her eyes or to read any emotion in her gaze.

"We're going home, aren't we?" Skye asked.

Home. Back to Chicago. He nodded.

"Then let's go out in style," she said, and she slipped off the robe.

"Skye—"

She tossed the robe toward him. He caught it, his hands flying up in a reflexive action.

Skye's laughter teased his ears. He loved that sound. Happy. Free. She hadn't sounded that way in so long.

His fingers fisted in the robe.

Naked now, Skye dove into the waves.

He tossed the robe onto the beach behind him.

"Come and get me…" Her words taunted him when she broke through the surface of the water.

That was exactly what he planned to do.

Trace stalked into the water.

She won't break.

Her laughter reached him once more, banishing the chill that had crept over him when he'd awoken to the sound of her screams.

Skye was stronger than most people realized.

Her arms reached for him.

He held her tight and knew that he couldn't let her go.

***

Ben Sharpe hunched his shoulders as he turned and hurried into the alley.

He knew he was being followed. He'd known for a while now.

Death was coming. Stalking him with slow, certain steps.

He had a debt to repay before he died. His father had always taught him that a man had to pay his debts.

One way or another.

He owed Trace Weston. He'd pay him.

Warn him.

The faintest shuffle of a footstep reached Ben's ears. His gaze flew to the mouth of the alley.

Death had been after him for years now.

After him. After Trace.

You could only run for so long.

The faint shuffle came again.

Before the past catches you...

His fingers curled around the knife that he always kept close. Death wasn't going to have an easy time taking him.

He planned to fight for every moment that he had left.

And if he had to, he'd kill to keep living.

He knew how to kill. He was good at it.

Thanks to Weston.

And I'll repay that debt...

Even if it was the last fucking thing he did.

CHAPTER TWO

The limo pulled to a slow stop in front of the Chicago high-rise. The building stretched so far up that it seemed to blend with the clouds.

Skye glanced at Trace. "You just assumed we'd be going back to your place?"

He put down the papers he'd been reading. Some thick manila file. His gaze locked on her. "I want you to move in with me."

She tried to keep her face expressionless. "And *this* is how you ask me? We were on a white sand beach for days, and you couldn't find some nice, romantic moment there to—"

"I suck at romance, Skye." He heaved out a hard breath and reached for her hand. His fingers smoothed over the big, gleaming diamond that she wore on her left hand. *His ring.*

He'd asked her to marry him after he'd saved her from Mitch. He'd never said they would move in together *before* they got married.

"Skye, look, we probably only have ten seconds before Reese opens that door and—"

They had less than five seconds. There was a soft click of sound, and Reese opened the door.

"His timing is shit," Trace muttered, sounding disgusted.

Skye climbed from the car. Reese was frowning at her, more than a hint of concern on his face. Reese's face was just as hard as Trace's—maybe even harder. All angles and rough planes. Reese's hair was cut brutally short, and his dark eyes glinted. "Is there a problem?"

Skye looked up at the high-rise once more. Trace's penthouse waited all the way at the very top.

He'd sure come a long way in the last ten years. Once, they'd both barely had enough money for food. For clothes.

Now, it seemed that Trace could buy the whole world.

Is he trying to buy me? Sometimes she wondered if that could be the case. She was highly conscious of the weight of her ring around her finger.

"Have the doorman get the bags, Reese," Trace directed as he exited the vehicle.

But Skye put her hand out, stopping Reese. "Not yet." Because their living arrangements weren't settled. She straightened her shoulders. There was something about this city that got to Skye. Chicago was home for her. The noise. The people. The activity.

She was starting to feel stronger already.

"Skye…"

She turned to face Trace. "Why?"

He blinked at her. "Why what?"

Skye sighed. "Why do you want me to move in with you?"

"Aw, hell," she heard Reese mutter as the faint Alabama drawl in his voice deepened. "He's right. Shit for timing…" He edged back.

Trace growled.

Skye didn't move.

"Here?" Trace demanded as his brows shot up. "Now? *This* is where you want us to talk?"

Cars honked around them.

"You picked the place," she pointed out. "Now tell me why."

Trace was tall, easily hitting over six foot three, and his body seemed to dominate hers as he curled his hands over her arms. "Because I want you close. Always, right beside me."

And that was where she wanted to be. His answer was also the one that she'd needed to hear.

"Then you can have my things brought over," she told him as she turned away and headed for the building's gleaming entrance. The doorman hurried to meet her.

"I already did," Trace said. His words followed her. Froze her.

Skye glanced back at him. "Confident, were you?"

His head tilted as he seemed to assess her. Then, taking his time, Trace headed toward her. His hand lifted, and his fingers slid over her cheek. "When it comes to you," his voice dropped. "Yeah, I am. Because you were either going to spend the night with me, or I was going to move in with you in that little apartment over your dance studio. Either way, we were going to be sleeping in the same bed tonight."

Blunt, wasn't he? But, that was Trace. Dominant, fierce. Always in control. Always—

"Weston!"

Trace moved in a flash at that shout. He caught Skye and pushed her behind him. She saw Reese moving quickly, too. Reese had a gun in his hand in less than two seconds' time, and he lunged toward Trace.

No, not toward Trace. Toward the man who was rushing down the street and heading straight for Trace.

"Weston!" The guy cried out again.

His hair was long, brushing his shoulders, disheveled, and a dark beard lined his jaw. The man was tall, with broad shoulders. He ran toward them, his gaze intent on Trace.

"*Ben*," she heard Trace growl.

Reese lifted his weapon. "You need to stop right there, Sharpe."

The guy staggered to a stop. His jeans were dirty, torn. His shirt was black and ripped at the side. He ignored Reese and the weapon Reese had pointed at him. The man's eyes focused on Trace with a feverish intensity. "I owe you," he mumbled, shaking his head. "I'm here to pay."

Skye's heart raced in her chest.

"Reese," Trace's voice snapped out, "I want you to take Skye inside."

The doorman peeked out at them, eyes wide. *Henry.* Skye had met him a few times before Trace had whisked her to the Keys. Henry was a nice guy, but totally not equipped to deal with the situation out there.

"Take her inside and stay with her every moment," Trace ordered.

Reese glanced back at him, hesitating. "You sure, boss?"

Skye wasn't sure what in the hell was going on. She reached for Trace. "What's going on?" Who was this guy — this Ben?

At her words, the man's gaze jerked to her face and his stare locked on her.

"She's the one," the stranger whispered. He shook his head, "Weston, she's going to destroy you."

What?

Trace caught Skye's hand in his. "Go to the penthouse. Unpack. I'll be there soon."

Reese hurried to her side. "Come on, Skye."

She was just supposed to leave Trace there?

"No!" The cry came from the other man as he leapt toward Trace. His fingers grabbed Trace's shirt. "It's not safe out here. *He's watching.*"

A chill skated down Skye's spine. She'd been stalked before. Hunted. She knew just what it was like to feel as if someone was out there, watching.

Every minute.

She studied the man again. This time, she clearly saw the fear in his brown eyes. "I think we should all go upstairs," she said, hoping her voice didn't show her own fear.

But she wasn't just going to walk away and leave Trace alone in that street. Something was wrong, very wrong, and she didn't want to abandon him.

Trace's jaw locked, but, after a brief moment, he gave a hard jerk of his head.

They all headed for the gleaming doors. The doorman's eyes were huge as he studied them all. "Uh...Mr. Weston?"

"Have all the bags brought up." Trace had an unbreakable grip on Skye's arm. He barely spared the doorman a glance but he did push a very nice tip toward him.

"Y-yes, sir."

Maybe the tip would help Henry get over the fact that he'd just seen Reese draw his gun.

The doorman's gaze flickered to Skye. "Good to see you, Ms. Sullivan."

"Hi, Henry," she whispered back.

They all loaded into Trace's private elevator. It seemed to fly up to the penthouse. She tried to glance over at the man Trace had called Ben, but Trace had put his body in front of hers. Shielding her or blocking her view — she wasn't exactly sure what his intent was.

The ride was over quickly, and the group strode toward the penthouse door. Trace led her inside, but then, before the others could follow, he spun back around. "I'll be needing your knives, Ben."

Wait, knives? Plural?

The man bent and pulled a knife from his right boot. Then his left. He put them in Trace's open palm.

"All of them," Trace snapped.

Ben pulled another knife from his waist. The sheath had blended perfectly with his belt, and Skye would've never even noticed the weapon.

"You remembered," Ben said, giving a little nod. "Can't stop being a soldier, can you?"

Reese took the knives and shoved them all inside a drawer in the den.

Skye stood there, uncertain, as the others filed into the den.

"He can't watch us up here," Ben said as he glanced over at the large windows that overlooked the city. "Fuck me…" he marched toward the glass on the right. "You're a damn rich bastard now, aren't you?"

Trace's fingers brushed against Skye's jaw and she jumped. She hadn't heard him move toward her. Sometimes, he did that—moving so soundlessly that she didn't know he was there until he touched her.

"It was a long flight," Trace said, his gaze searching hers. "We're all secure up here. You should go rest, baby. I know the trip back wasn't easy for you."

Because she was still afraid of flying. No, it wasn't so much fear as the fact that she just *hated* it.

While there might have been a hint of sympathy in Trace's eyes, she knew he wasn't just trying to get her in the bedroom because she was tired.

Trace wanted to get rid of her. Too bad. She wasn't in the mood to be dismissed. If Trace was in some kind of danger, she wanted to know about it.

She glanced over at Ben once more. His gaze was on her. That brown stare was unnerving. The fear was gone but…

Her breath caught.

I know that look.

She knew that look because she'd seen it in her mother's eyes before.

Insanity.

Skye instinctively took a step back.

"She's the reason, you know…" Now Ben seemed almost musing, but his eyes burned with an intensity that frightened her. "You revealed too much with her. The story was splashed in all the papers. It was on all the TVs. She's your mistake, and she's going to destroy you."

In a flash, Trace was across the room. He'd shoved Ben back against the big, picture-frame window behind the couch. "You sure as hell had better not be threatening her." His forearm thrust under Ben's throat.

"Trace!" She rushed forward, but Reese stepped in her path.

"Not...me..." The words wheezed from Ben.

Trace lifted his arm.

Ben sucked in a deep gulp of air.

Trace's shoulders tensed. "I let you up here because of the past. Reese told me you'd come by before. That you had a message for me. Deliver it, now."

A rough bark of laughter escaped Ben as the redness slowly faded from his cheeks. "The past...that's what we have to worry about. It's not dead. It's coming back, and it's going to burn us all."

The man wasn't making any sense.

But Reese's body had turned to stone beside her. So maybe the cryptic words made sense to him.

Skye could be the only one in the dark.

"Do you believe in ghosts?" Ben asked as he blinked up at Trace.

"No." Trace's response was instant. "The dead are in the ground. They can't hurt us anymore."

"Don't be too sure." Ben's lips twisted. "You took from him, and now he knows what to take from you. He's coming after us all, and he won't stop, not until he's destroyed us...the same way we tried to destroy him."

"Ben..." Now Trace's voice had roughened. Deepened. "Have you been taking your meds?"

At that question, Ben's eyes flashed angrily. "I don't need them! I don't need the fuckin' things!" He shouldered past Trace and staggered across the room. "I know what's happening. He's here. Watching. I *know!*"

Skye bit her bottom lip to hold back the instinctive cry that wanted to break free. The way this Ben was acting...*it's so familiar.*

"Have you been hearing the voices again?" Trace asked.

Tears stung Skye's eyes. This was too much like her own past.

"Sometimes," Ben said, his voice hoarse, as he turned back to stare at Trace. "But they're just trying to warn me. Death is coming for us, Weston! We have to be ready." He ran a hand through his hair. "Kill or be killed. Just like in the old days."

Trace hadn't told her about his "old days" in the military. He hadn't talked about the military at all.

"You need to take your medication," Trace said.

Her heart was aching.

Trace paced steadily toward Ben.

Ben shook his head. "It makes me…weak. Dulls my senses. I have to be ready." He jabbed a finger toward Trace. "*You* have to be ready. He's gonna make you suffer more. You're the one who killed her. I-I wasn't."

Her?

Trace put his hands on Ben's shoulders. "You're confused again. The past is over. You need to let it go."

Ben sucked in a sharp breath. Then he jerked away from Trace. His accusing finger pointed right at Skye. "She'll die."

This was *not* the homecoming that Skye had anticipated.

"No, she won't." Trace was certain. "Because I will destroy *anyone* who ever tries to hurt her."

Goosebumps rose onto Skye's arms.

"And that includes you," Trace told the man. "Don't ever come near her again, do you understand?"

Ben blinked. "I-I was warning you." Confusion seemed to thicken his words. "Paying my debt."

"Consider it paid." Trace's gaze flickered toward Reese. "Now Reese will escort you out. He can take you back home—"

"I don't have a home. Don't got nothing." Again, a lost tone had entered Ben's voice. "Maybe…you ever think you should've just let me die? Instead of dragging me out—"

"Reese will make sure you get set up at a hotel tonight. We'll contact the VA." Trace's expression was grim. "They'll get your meds going again."

Ben's mouth tightened. "Then I'll be a dead man." He turned on his heel. Hurried for the door.

Reese was right behind him.

But, before Ben left, he cast one last glance toward Skye. "You still look the same," he told her. "Just like the picture Weston kept. An angel in hell..."

"I-I don't understand," Skye began.

"I hope you don't die," Ben said. "He's coming and you need to be ready."

"*Out.*" Trace snarled, his patience seemingly gone.

And...just like that...the mysterious Ben was gone. Reese followed him out, and Trace secured the door behind them.

Skye was left alone with Trace.

Only...

Trace was different.

He stalked toward her, his steps sure, but his eyes shone with an emotion that she couldn't decipher.

"Wh-what was that about?" She hated the stutter in her voice as much as she hated the nervousness twisting her guts in knots.

"Ben Sharpe had a...hard time during his enlistment. The last mission went wrong, and he came back—"

"Broken?" Skye finished because that was how the man had looked.

And it's the way my mother had appeared. So many times. There'd been no mistaking the look in Ben's eyes.

"He wasn't the same," Trace said instead. Then he rolled his shoulders, as if trying to push the past away. "Reese will see to it that he's taken care of. Don't worry."

"But Ben said someone was watching him." And, not too long ago, she'd gone to Trace and told him the same thing. *Someone is watching me.* She'd been afraid that Trace wouldn't believe her. The cops sure hadn't bought her story.

But Trace had.

He'd protected her. Saved her life.

"When he's off his meds, Ben has hallucinations. He talks to people who aren't there. He *sees* people who aren't there."

Just like her mother. Skye swallowed. "But are you sure—"

He kissed her. His lips—so warm and sensual—pressed to hers. "Don't worry about him," he whispered against her lips. "You don't have anything to fear from Ben."

It wasn't Ben that she was afraid of. It was his warning that wouldn't stop playing through her mind.

He'd said death was coming. "Are you safe?" Skye asked Trace, lifting her lashes to look into his bright gaze.

"Always," he told her, and she wanted to believe him.

After all, Trace wouldn't lie to her...

Would he?

His hands closed around her shoulders. He seemed so warm and solid, so incredibly strong before her. "I don't want that part of my life ever touching you."

She shook her head. "That's not going to work. We can't be that way."

Trace stilled.

"No secrets," she heard herself say. "That's the way it needs to be. You know everything about me..." Every fear she had.

Every desire.

He let her go. "There are some things that you're better off not knowing."

"Trace..."

He lifted his hand. "Let it go, baby. Just...let it go. The past is buried, and all I care about is my future with you."

"But that man—"

"He's crazy!" Trace exploded.

She flinched. Not because of the anger in his voice, but because his words hit far too close to home. "And what if I am, one day? What if—"

She didn't get to say more. Because Trace had her in his arms, holding her so tightly that she knew she might bruise, but Skye didn't care.

"You aren't. You *won't* ever be."

So easy for him to say.

But Trace hadn't lived in a home with a mother who lost her hold on reality a little more each day. A woman who talked with people who weren't there. A woman who hurt her daughter and never remembered doing it.

The doctors said her mother had been psychotic. Sometimes, too many times, Skye wondered if there was a ticking time bomb within herself.

That's why I won't go see the shrinks. I don't want to know...

"You survived that sick bastard's kidnapping. You're the strongest woman I've ever met." He'd lifted her up against him and buried his face in the curve of her neck. "I know crazy, Skye, and it's not you."

She could barely breathe in his grasp. Skye pushed against him, and Trace let her toes touch the floor once more. "I came to you," she said, searching his eyes, "with the same story that Ben just told. Someone was watching me. You believed me." *What if he hadn't?* "Are you so certain that man wasn't telling the truth?"

"Ben...he has a problem with reality. For the last few years, he's been convinced that someone was after him." His lips thinned. "He thought his past was chasing him."

"What if it is?" He'd seemed so desperate.

Her mother had been desperate that way, once.

Her desperation had led her to take her own life—and to take the life of Skye's father in the process.

"I'll have another talk with him, okay?" Trace said. "If he's being hunted by anything other than his own demons, I'll find out."

Relief had her shoulders slumping.

"Your heart's too soft," he growled, and Trace sounded angry. Odd, he didn't usually get angry with her.

Everyone else? Oh, yes, but not her.

"You can't be so trusting, Skye." He let her go and stalked across the room. The marble floor gleamed beneath his feet. He stopped at the bar. A bar that took up half the left wall. Trace grabbed the decanter of whiskey and poured a sloshing glassful. "That trust can get you into trouble."

Even though he wasn't looking at her, Skye's chin hitched up. "Trouble? You mean the kind where I trust the wrong man and nearly get killed because of it?"

He whirled around. "Skye—"

"Been there, done that," she snapped at him. Her hands fisted. "I've got to say, this is one hell of a moving-in party."

She spun on her heel and marched down the hallway. Her heartbeat sounded like drums in her ears and—

"I don't…want it touching you."

Skye paused a few steps away from their bedroom. Then, *crap*, she found herself storming back toward him. "What are you talking about?"

He drained the glass. Slammed it back on the bar. "I've done things that weren't good, Skye. Things that—if you knew about them—they'd give you even more nightmares."

He headed toward her with slow, determined steps. A predator, stalking his prey.

I'm the prey.

"I don't want you to know about the things I did while we were apart. I want us to go forward. Fuck the past." He stopped just a foot away and gazed down at her. She couldn't read the expression in his eyes. "What we have is good. I'd damn well die for you, and you know that."

She did. She also knew…

He'd kill for me.

The world saw Trace Weston as a suave businessman. A charmer who'd exploded onto the security scene. He'd amassed billions in record time.

But no one knew about his past.

Once, Skye had thought that she knew everything about him.

Now she was realizing that Trace had secrets he didn't intend to share with her.

"Nothing can come between us now," he told her.

Why did she feel like he was making a vow?

Trace smiled. The smile that had always made her breath come a little faster.

He advanced toward her. "You were right when you said this wasn't the way to celebrate your moving in..."

"Trace."

But he'd scooped her into his arms. He carried her to the bedroom. The room was dark. The sun was setting, and the light barely spilled through the curtains and onto his massive bed.

But...something was shining on his bed.

Skye glanced over, frowning, even as her arms tightened around Trace's neck. "What is that?"

"It's your welcome home present." He kissed her and slowly lowered Skye to her feet.

Then his hands went to the back of her dress. A flick of his fingers unhooked the button near her nape, and the dress slid to the floor with a soft slither of sound.

She was left in her high heels, her black panties and her matching bra.

Trace was fully dressed.

"Don't move," he told her.

Then he reached around her, and, yes, the sparkle on the bed seemed even brighter now.

Diamonds. A necklace full of glittering diamonds.

He put the diamonds around her neck. They were cold, and she let out a little gasp.

A fortune. That's what he just put around my neck.

She knew exactly how much those diamonds had cost him. In another life, she'd been a prima ballerina in New York. Before her car accident and her stalker, before the nightmares—

"*Skye.*" Her name was a sharp demand.

Her gaze flew to his face.

"Stay with me," he ordered.

He always knew what she was thinking.

But do I know him?

The diamonds chilled her skin.

He lifted her hair, brushing it back over her shoulder. "You're so beautiful."

And he was the only man she'd ever loved.

At fifteen, he'd burst into her life, saving her from an attack. He'd been her hero then.

Her world.

But he'd left her. Gone away, and for ten years, they hadn't seen one another.

What happened to him during those years?

He lowered his head and he kissed her neck. Her breath rushed out because that spot was so sensitive, and Trace knew that.

Just as he knew everything about her.

He lowered her onto the bed. Came down with her. Surrounded her.

"I'll make you happy," he promised. "We can have everything."

Skye shoved her doubts and fears away. This was Trace. They'd survived hell before.

They could survive anything that came their way.

"I already have everything," Skye said softly, and she didn't mean the necklace that seemed to be such a heavy weight against her skin.

Trace didn't strip. She expected him to, but he didn't. His hands became harder, rougher on her. He pulled her to the edge of the bed.

His fingers slid between her legs. One yank, and her panties were gone. He stroked her, caressed her, had her own fingers twisting in the bed covers as the need grew within her.

But…

He's too careful.

Since the attack, he'd always been that way when they had sex.

She didn't want care.

She wanted fire.

Lust.

Need.

He unzipped his pants. Put his cock right at the entrance of her body. Trace leaned over her. "Forever, Skye."

Her eyes locked with his. Her hands grabbed him, and her nails dug through the fabric of his shirt, sinking in with a sensual bite.

"Forever," she agreed, and her hips surged toward him just as he thrust into her.

She lost her breath then. He stretched her, filled her so completely. He tried to pull back, to go easier.

"I won't break," she said, panting out the words. "Faster, Trace, *harder.*" Because it was what she needed.

His gaze never left hers. He gave her what she wanted.

Fast.

Hard.

But *he* was in control. Every moment. She could feel it in the tight movements of his body. See it in the hard clench of his jaw.

She wanted him out of control. Wild.

But he wasn't letting go.

"Trace!" His name was a demand.

His head bent. He jerked her bra out of the way and put his mouth on her breast. Licked. Kissed.

She felt the light edge of his teeth on her.

Skye erupted. Pleasure blasted through her, and she held him as fiercely as she could.

His movements roughened. His hips pistoned against her. Close—close—*he was almost losing his control.* Skye just needed to push him over that edge.

She wrapped her legs around him.

He came with a shout. His eyes flashed, seeming to go blind for an instant. He shuddered, his body curving over her. He was still standing at the edge of the bed.

Still dressed.

Still holding all the control, even in his moment of release.

Skye stared up at him, lost.

She'd been lost with Trace from the beginning.

There was no going back. Not for her.

Not for him.

He pressed a tender kiss to her lips. "I knew you'd be gorgeous in diamonds."

The diamonds *were* beautiful, but Skye didn't care about them. *I only care about him.*

He withdrew from her. Tenderly took care of her and even tucked her under the covers.

But he didn't join her.

"Get some rest," he told her, voice gruff. "You're safe, and you're home." He smiled down at her. "Our life is just starting…"

***

His life was ending.

Ben Sharpe ran down the busy Chicago street. Rain beat down on him, the storm erupting suddenly from the sky.

Weston hadn't taken his warning seriously.

He'd tried to help the man, but Weston hadn't wanted to hear his words.

Weston hadn't wanted him there at all.

He didn't want me near her.

It was just as bad as Ben had feared. Weston's weakness was right there, and the man didn't even realize it.

Skye Sullivan would be his downfall. Weston needed to protect himself, to back the hell away from her.

Before it was too late.

***

Trace shut the bedroom door.

He could smell Skye's scent on his skin. Sweet vanilla. He could feel her silken flesh beneath his fingers.

He wanted to go back in that room, to wrap his arms around her and hold her through the night.

But first, he had to take care of some unfinished business. Business that would *not* be allowed to touch Skye.

He hurried down the hallway. Grabbed his phone. In seconds, he had Reese on the line. "Where is he?" Trace demanded.

Lightning flashed outside of his windows. The storm had come up so suddenly.

"He's about to hop the train. I tried to get the guy to stay at a motel." Disgust and anger thickened Reese's voice. "But the fool took a punch at me."

Trace's back teeth clenched. "Keep your eyes on him until I can meet up with you. I'm leaving now." He glanced toward the hall. Skye's soft heart would be a problem. Because she looked at Ben Sharpe, and she saw her own mother.

But Skye's mother had been dangerous.

And so was Ben.

You won't get near Skye again.

Reese was still talking, giving Trace intel about the train and Ben's location.

Trace left the penthouse. The elevator descended quickly to the parking garage.

Once upon a time—a lifetime ago—he'd saved Ben Sharpe's life.

Once upon a time...

***

Thunder crashed.

Skye jerked up in bed, her heart racing.

She was alone.

"Trace?"

He didn't answer her call.

She rose, grabbed for her robe.

She still had on the diamonds. They still felt too cold.

Her fingers closed around the bedroom doorknob. She twisted it, and the door opened with a creak of sound. "Trace?" She tip-toed down the hallway.

He didn't answer. Lightning flashed just outside of the windows, long jagged streaks of light.

Trace wasn't there.

Skye stopped in the den, then she turned to the big-picture window, and she watched the storm rage.

                              ***

Another alley.

Ben ran forward, his boots hitting the rain puddles and sending mud flying around him.

He's tracking me. The bastard is coming after me.

He had to run faster.

His breath sawed from his lungs. For an instant, the buildings around him vanished.

When the thunder rolled, he heard it as gunfire.

Another place, another time.

He looked down, and the mud was gone. The pot-hole filled alley was gone.

He saw snow. Blood. Death.

"You shouldn't have come here."

The voice whispered from the darkness.

His head jerked up. He reached for the knife at his belt. *Gone.*

Weston had taken the weapon. He hadn't given it back.

Ben reached for his ankle sheath.

Her lips tilted up and her eyes seem to warm. "I love you. You know that, don't you?"

He did. Skye's love was his certainty in life.

Sometimes, he felt like it might be his *only* one.

He smiled back at her. "Of course, you do. What's not to love?"

And she laughed. A true, beautiful laugh. Light and free. He could see it then — see her coming back to him. Skye was pushing past her fear and trying to be happy once again.

He would do anything, everything, to make sure that she stayed happy.

"Arrogant," she teased.

His head tilted in acknowledgment. He was. Arrogant. Controlling. Trace was well aware of his many faults.

And Skye still loved him? He was a lucky bastard, and he knew it.

"It's a good thing you're sexy," she said, giving him a wink. "Something has to balance that arrogance." And she left him, giving a saucy roll of her hips as she walked away.

He didn't move. Just watched. Enjoyed the view.

I will always love you, Skye. Always.

When she gazed at him, love was in Skye's eyes, too. Yet Trace couldn't help but wonder…if she ever learned the full truth about him and all the things he'd done, would Skye still look at him the same way?

***

Trace had done more than a little bit of work at the fire station. "Upgrades, my ass," Skye whispered.

He'd completely renovated the place.

Skye stepped inside the converted fire station, her gaze darting to the left and the right.

The hard-wood floors gleamed. Barres had been placed to run the length of the right wall. Floor to ceiling mirrors circled the main room, throwing her reflection back at her.

And there were—there were even storage lockers down the narrow hallway that snaked back from the main room. Shining, silver lockers for her students to use.

When she actually got her students to start attending her new dance studio.

"He said he'd installed new security here," Skye said.

"Uh, well, you know the boss," Reese replied from beside her. "The guy doesn't believe in doing things half-way."

No, he didn't.

"He knew you'd want to come back here," Reese continued. "And he told the crew that everything had to be ready for you." He walked forward and motioned to the speakers that had been mounted on the ceiling. "Surround sound, you know, for that full dance experience."

She'd come in, ready to get her hands dirty and her muscles aching, as she tore this place into shape.

But, in true Trace fashion, he'd done it for her.

"I can't tell if you're pissed or pleased," Reese said, his drawl deepening as he scratched his jaw. "Kinda hard to determine from your expression."

She stepped forward. "I think I'm both." Pissed because he'd done all of this without her input but pleased because he'd cared enough to try and give her the dream she wanted.

Pissed or pleased? She still wasn't sure.

Skye turned around and marched out of the main studio room. Trace's crew had knocked out some walls, opening up the space. Columns secured the ceiling. The place looked *huge*.

"He left the fireman's pole," Reese said as he followed after her.

She glanced to the right. The fireman's pole gleamed.

"The boss thought you might like it so he left strict instructions for the workers."

Her gaze followed that pole upstairs. "What about the apartment up there?" Her hands had come to rest on her hips. Had Trace organized the apartment, too? Or had he been so sure that she'd move in with him that he hadn't even bothered to touch that place?

"Uh…" Reese coughed. "Security was set up there, but I don't think much else has been done."

"Then I'll do it," she said, giving a firm nod. Because that upstairs area was still *hers*. She might be living with Trace, but she could use the upstairs apartment area as a refuge from the dance studio. She'd decorate every inch of it herself.

"He wanted to make you happy."

Her attention shifted to Reese. He shrugged. "Trace…you know the boss doesn't think like most people. He knew if you came back here, the way this place was…you'd work like a fiend to get it in shape. He wanted to help."

"Trace likes his control." *Even in the bedroom.* "But this time, it's all right." Because the studio's condition meant that she could get her business up and running faster. She already had clients scheduled from weeks ago. She could contact them and get this place going—

And then she'd pay Trace back for the work he'd done. Every cent.

Because the studio is mine. She needed it to be.

Skye rolled her shoulders. This was going to happen. A smile spread over her face. "We'll count this as a tentative pleased," she said, "but if—"

A knock sounded at the main door. Skye turned, frowning. She hadn't told any of her students-to-be that she was back in town yet.

"This way," Reese said. He directed her to what *had* previously been a closet, but when she opened the door, she saw the area had been expanded. Four television screens were mounted on the wall. One showed the rear exterior of the old fire station, two showed the sides of the building, and the largest screen showed the entrance—and the man who stood there.

"Like the boss said," Reese told her, "he upgraded your security."

She leaned toward the big screen. "That's Alex—Detective Griffin." The one cop who'd finally believed her story about a stalker.

She turned away from the screen and hurried toward the front door. She hadn't seen Alex in weeks. *Before my abduction.*

Because Mitch had taken her to New York, the NYPD had taken over the case. They'd closed the file on Mitch Loxley.

After quickly unbolting the door, Skye swung it open. "Detective Griffin!" A broad smile split her face. "It's good to see you."

He blinked at her, and an answering smile slowly stretched across his handsome face. Alex Griffin was just a little shorter than Trace, and his shoulders weren't quite as wide, but the cop was fit and smart. And he'd *been there* for Skye when she'd been at the end of her rope.

Sunlight glinted off his blond hair, and his gaze swept over her. "It's good to see you, too." He surprised her by pulling her into his arms and giving her a big hug. "Damn good. Because the last time I saw you…" A rough sigh broke from him as he eased back a bit and stared down at her. "You were lying unconscious in a hospital bed."

That response surprised her. "You came to see me in New York?" The time after her abduction was a blur for her. She'd gone too long without food. Spent too much time in the darkness.

She'd come too close to death.

Alex nodded. "I needed to see for myself that you were all right." Now he frowned. "Weston didn't tell you I was there?"

No. He hadn't.

Alex dropped his hold. Stepped back fully. This time, when his gaze swept over her, his attention locked on her left hand.

Or, more specifically, on the ring there.

"I'm sure..." Reese cut in, clearing his throat from behind them, "that Trace was more concerned with Skye here healing...and not giving her a full visitor listing."

Alex didn't glance at the other man. "Should I congratulate you, Skye?"

Her throat felt dry. There was something about his tone. A hard edge that worried her. "Yes," she said, straightening her shoulders. "Trace and I—we're together now and—"

"As if he'd have it any other way." Alex's growled words definitely held anger.

"Watch it," Reese warned him. "Cop or no cop, you—"

Alex shook his head and kept staring at Skye. "As good as it is to see you—awake, aware, and not looking like death anymore—I'm actually here on business."

They were still standing in the doorway. Skye backed up and bumped into Reese. "What kind of business?"

"I transferred to homicide."

Uh, okay. She circled around him and shut the door. Her fingers flipped over the lock.

"Thought it was time for a change."

"Congratulations." That was the right response, wasn't it? From the sound of things, he'd taken a new job, so she was supposed to congratulate him.

Just as he *should* have congratulated her.

Alex's gaze cut to Reese. "Can your guard give us a minute? We need to talk, *alone*."

"I don't think—" Reese said.

"It's fine, Reese." She walked toward him and patted his arm. "Why don't you just go and—well, take a few moments to relax?" Right, like the guy ever relaxed. She'd sure never seen it.

One brow lifted, but Reese gave a curt nod. "If you need me, I'll be close." Then, after one last, measuring glance at Alex, he was gone.

Alex didn't speak, not at first. After a few tense moments, he exhaled and asked, "Still under guard duty?"

Because she'd thought the exact same thing, Skye's words held bite as she told him, "It's just a precaution, only for a few days. We just wanted to make sure there wouldn't be any trouble from the press."

"And the fact that Weston has a shitload of enemies? *Deadly* enemies? That has nothing to do with the bodyguard detail?"

His tone was scaring her. "You said you had business to talk about..." And he was *homicide* now. Oh, damn, this couldn't be good.

"Does the name Ben Sharpe mean anything to you?"

Ben. The man's face flashed before her. The feverish intensity of his eyes. The certainty in his voice.

He's here. Watching. I know!

"You know him," Alex said, apparently reading the truth on her face.

"We met last night," she said as she rubbed at the knot of tension in the back of her neck. "Briefly."

He stepped closer to her. "And was Weston there for this little meeting?"

"Ah, yes. He was. Trace and Ben knew each other from—"

The front door swung open with a creak. Her gaze flew to the door. She'd been sure that she locked it—

Trace stood in the doorway.

Of course, he'd have his own key.

"Griffin." Trace bit out the cop's name. "You moved fast."

Alex's eyes narrowed. "Guess you heard, huh? Or did the bodyguard call you and tell you to haul ass over here?"

"I was just a few blocks away. I didn't have to haul ass that much." Trace closed the distance between them. He put his body next to Skye's but kept his attention on the detective. "You shouldn't be questioning Skye. She doesn't even know Ben."

Alex's brow shot up again. "Really? Because she was just telling me that she did. Skye said that she met him last night, with you."

The tension between the two men was palpable.

"What is going on?" Skye demanded as she threw her hands up in the air. "Why are you asking these questions about Ben?"

But she already knew. The twist in her gut told her the truth, and she didn't really want to hear it. She didn't want to hear Alex say —

"Ben Sharpe's body was found this morning, tossed away like garbage in an alley."

Her hands fell to her sides.

So it would seem that Ben hadn't been so crazy after all. "He said someone was watching him," she whispered.

"Did he now...?" Alex drawled.

Her knees were trembling. "How did you know we were connected to him?"

"It was pretty easy to follow the dots." Alex inclined his head toward her. "The guy had a picture of you — some grainy shot torn from a newspaper — in his pocket."

She's your mistake, and she's going to destroy you. Ben's words replayed in her mind.

"And, of course, there was the business card." Now Alex's attention shifted to Trace. "*Your* business card, Weston. A card that was gripped tightly in the dead man's hand."

Her heart raced in her chest. "Wh-when did Ben die?"

"The medical examiner says it was last night, sometime between midnight and two a.m."

Trace had been gone after midnight.

"Now…see…that's not really the question that I expected you to ask," Alex said, and his gaze was right back on her. "Maybe something like…how did he die? But jumping straight to *when*…that's not what most folks usually do. Unless, well, unless they're trying to work out an alibi." He paused a beat. "Are you doing that, Skye? Are you trying to work out some kind of alibi?"

"Of course she isn't," Trace snarled. His fingers caught hers. Twined with them. Squeezed lightly. "We appreciate you notifying us of Ben's death, Detective Griffin."

"Cut the bull," Alex suddenly demanded. "You and I both know I'm not here for some kind of *notification*." He advanced on Trace until the men stood toe-to-toe. "What the hell is going on here, man? Did you have something to do with the guy's death?"

Skye sucked in a sharp breath. Trace glanced back at her. He stared into her eyes, then he lifted her hand. He brought it to his lips and lightly kissed her knuckles. Her ring caught the light, gleaming even brighter.

Trace was still looking at Skye when he said, "No. I had nothing to do with Ben's death."

She had the feeling he was trying to convince her of that fact, not Alex.

"Don't *you* want to know how he died?" Alex pushed.

Trace kept his hold on Skye's fingers, but he looked at Alex once more. "How did he die?" Trace asked.

"Someone carved him up with a knife."

Skye flinched. Instinctively, she tried to jerk her hand away from Trace. He didn't let her go.

"What the hell was the guy doing in that alley?" The question erupted from Alex. "Why was he —"

"Ben Sharpe was a very disturbed individual. He suffered from severe PTSD. He had hallucinations, delusions." Trace's voice was flat. "And I'd recently learned that he had stopped taking his medications. My card..." He exhaled on a hard breath. "He had my card because I wanted to help him, not because I was the man who took his life."

It felt like her thundering heartbeat was shaking Skye's entire chest.

The floor creaked behind her, and she turned to see Reese standing there, watching them.

"And Skye's picture?" Alex asked as he glared suspiciously at Trace. "Why'd he have that?"

Trace's fingers tightened on hers. "I'm afraid that Ben would need to be the one to tell you about that."

She's your mistake, and she's going to destroy you.

Alex watched them in silence. It was the thick and hard and uncomfortable type of silence.

Finally, Alex said, "Let's just get this out of the way. I'm going to assume you were both together last night? She can alibi you, Weston?"

"Yes," Trace said. "I was home with my fiancé."

The lie rolled so easily off his tongue.

But even as Trace said the words, Alex's gaze was on Skye's face.

Did I flinch? Did I show any sign that Trace just lied?

Alex inclined his head. "Then I guess that will be all...for now." He stepped back. Paused. "It *is* good to see you again, Skye." His gaze seemed to warm. "You scared the hell out of me in that hospital, and I'm damn glad you survived that bastard's attack."

"Thank you," she whispered.

Trace motioned with his hand. Immediately, Reese advanced and escorted the detective back outside.

Skye waited a few seconds, making sure that both Reese and Alex were out of ear shot. Then she jerked free of Trace's hand and rushed into the main studio. Her reflection stared back at her—eyes too wide, skin too pale.

"Skye..."

She turned to confront him. "What in the hell was that about?"

"Probably a robbery." He shook his head. The faint lines near his eyes had deepened, making him appear grim. "Ben was in the wrong place and—"

"You lied to Alex."

At her words, every bit of emotion vanished from Trace's face. "What do you mean?"

"I woke up last night. You were *gone*. That's what I mean." And she was shaking. Nausea tightened her stomach. "Tell me you didn't go after Ben. Tell me—"

He shot forward and grabbed her forearms. "I wanted to help him."

She didn't want to hear this. Hadn't she just said for him to tell her that he *didn't*—

"I found Ben. I tried to get him to come with me so that I could *help* him, but the guy refused. He ran away from me. He left, and I went back home, to you."

She stared up at him.

"It was storming and the lightning lit up the bedroom." His pupils expanded, swallowing some of the bright blue in his gaze. "You were wearing the diamonds and the black robe I bought for you."

She'd fallen asleep in that robe, and she'd kept the diamonds on—for him.

"You were curled up in my bed, looking so sexy you made me ache. I climbed into that bed with you. I held you because I didn't want you to have another nightmare. I wanted you to know that you were safe with me." His voice thickened. "I was with you. When Ben was killed, I was with you."

There was a raw edge to his voice. Almost a desperation, but there was still no emotion on Trace's face. She searched his gaze and believed him. "Find out who killed him." Trace could do it. His company, Weston Securities, had nearly limitless resources.

Trace had found her when she'd vanished.

He could find Ben Sharpe's killer.

"I will," he promised her, and he let her go.

Her heartbeat was starting to slow down. The ache in her chest had eased.

Trace glanced around the studio. "Are you pissed?"

What? She blinked. He was going to ask that *now?*

"We can change it." He straightened his tie. Not that it needed straightening. "Anything that isn't right, the designers can fix. I just wanted the place to be ready for you. A-a wedding present." His lips thinned. "But Reese called me...said you were angry."

"I'm not." Not any longer. "I like my present."

The tension eased from him. She could see it vanish.

"But next time," Skye added, "*ask* first."

He nodded.

He started to walk away. Skye wasn't having that. She grabbed Trace and pushed him back against the mirror.

His gaze widened in surprise.

Ah, there it was. Real emotion.

She pressed up onto her toes and leaned into him. "I don't want you lying to me." Her voice was a whisper.

"Skye..."

"It's you and me. Us. Forever. No secrets and no lies."

His hands closed around her hips. Now he was the one holding her in place. "What happens when you don't like my secrets?"

"How do you know what I'll like?" Her voice had gone husky.

He was too controlled, even then. There was a wall between them, one that she was determined to break. Skye wanted it to shatter, just like the mirrors around her could shatter.

One hard punch — *shatter*.

"I know who you want me to be." The words seemed torn from Trace. "Let me be that man."

"I want *you*." Good and bad and everything in between.

In her darkest moment, he'd been there for her.

Couldn't he see that she wanted to be there for him?

"You have me," Trace said. "Always."

Then he moved, lightning fast. He spun them around, switching their positions so that she was the one penned against the cold pane of the mirror. And his mouth was on hers, crushing down.

Not with careful restraint. Not with studied passion. But with wild, driving lust. His mouth was hard. His kiss demanding. His tongue thrust into her mouth and took.

He wasn't treating her like a delicate china doll — the way he'd been treating her since the attack. Wasn't holding her carefully.

The fire was there, exploding between them. The fire that she needed and wanted so badly.

She'd been cold, until then.

Lost, until then.

He lifted her up, holding her easily and pressing her back even harder against the mirror's surface. His tongue thrust into her mouth again. His arms and scent and body surrounded her.

She wanted him naked.

Wanted to take and take until they were both lost.

Wanted *everything* —

Then she heard it. The shattering of glass.

One hard punch — shatter.

Her eyes flew open even as Trace jerked her away from the mirror.

"Fuck! Skye!"

The mirror had shattered behind her. No, not behind her, but beneath Trace's hand.

He'd hit the mirror? She hadn't even realized—

His hands were running all over her now. "Where are you hurt?" A feverish intensity thickened the words. "I see the blood. Tell me where, baby, tell me-"

Skye caught his hands. "It's not my blood. It's yours." She turned over his right hand, showing him the knuckles and the red slashes courtesy of the broken mirror.

He stilled. Stared down at the blood.

Skye licked her lips, and she tasted him. "They're just scratches. We'll go wash the blood off and get you cleaned up." She tried to tug him toward the bathroom.

Trace didn't move.

"I want you so much."

His deep, growling words made her heart jump.

"Sometimes, I can't control myself. I'm strong—too rough for you. If I'm not careful, I'll break you, the same way I broke the mirror."

Skye shook her head. "No!"

But he wasn't listening. Trace had pulled away from her.

"I wanted you," he said, but he wasn't looking her in the eyes. "And I was about to take you. I was so rough I broke the damn mirror." He stormed away.

She stood there, staring after him, aching.

He's leaving.

"You broke the mirror, but you didn't break me!" Skye called.

Trace stilled.

Okay. She sucked in a couple of deep breaths. "I'm not a mirror or a doll or anything—I'm a woman." *Your woman.* "But you keep seeing me as a victim, and it has to stop." The words were pulled from deep within her.

And they were true.

She was trying to heal.

He was still seeing her as the broken woman that he'd carried from the basement.

Shaking his head, Trace looked back at her. "That's not true."

Wasn't it? "Then lose control with me. Stop holding it so tightly." She stepped forward and the broken mirror crunched beneath her feet. Screw the mirror. "I don't want the fancy tycoon. I don't want the suave gentleman." She'd seen him play those roles too easily. "I want the man beneath the mask you wear."

A muscle flexed in Trace's jaw. "Be careful what you wish for, baby."

Another step. The mirror crunched again and—

He had her in his arms. "The mirror could cut through your shoes. You could get hurt."

He was always protecting her.

Even from himself.

He put her down a few feet away. "I'll send a crew over for repairs."

She looked over at the mess. His blood had dripped onto some of the broken shards.

"Skye…"

She tilted her head back to study him.

"I know you're not a fucking victim. I know…" He put his forehead to hers. *"That you're mine."*

***

Alex Griffin eased into his car. His gaze locked on the old fire station just across the street. Skye's studio.

Reese Stokes stood outside, a guard who was watching Alex with an avid stare.

There was no sign of Skye or Weston.

Alex's fingers drummed on the steering wheel.

Trace Weston was a very dangerous man. He was also a man used to being in total control—both of himself and of those around him.

When Weston had said that he had an alibi, that he'd been with Skye, those words had rolled so easily from the man's mouth. His expression had been set. Seemingly open.

But Skye…her eyes had widened. A small movement, but one that Alex had caught because he'd been watching her so closely.

When it came to lying, Skye wasn't as good as her lover.

In Alex's experience, there was only one reason a man lied about an alibi.

Because the man was guilty as sin.

His gut had told him that Trace Weston was a threat, right from the very first moment that they'd met.

But Weston had saved Skye so he'd thought…

Screw what I thought.

He was going to keep following this case. He'd see where the evidence took him. And if he found out that Trace Weston was responsible for Ben Sharpe's death, he would take the man down.

He didn't care how much money Weston had.

Justice came to everyone, and the guilty — they *paid*.

CHAPTER FOUR

Trace stared down at the bandage on his right hand. Skye had insisted on bandaging him up. Hell, he guessed it was a good thing that he'd told his men to stock a first aid kit at the dance studio.

She'd carefully applied the bandages, her fingers so soft against his hand.

No one else had ever cared about him, not the way that Skye did. Hell, his mother had spent more time inside a bottle than out in the real world with him.

He'd bounced from foster home to foster home. He hadn't felt any connection with anyone. He'd wondered if he *could* even connect.

Then he'd met her.

Trace stared at the stark white bandages. He'd lost control for a moment. Wanted her so badly...

He'd driven his hand right into the mirror.

Shattered it. *But I won't shatter her.*

"Ah...boss?"

Trace stood just outside of Skye's studio. The sunlight glinted down on him, and Reese waited a few feet away, studying him with cautious eyes.

Trace strode toward the other man. Skye was still inside. The clean-up crew would be arriving there soon.

"Is the cop gone?" Trace asked, getting right to business.

Reese nodded. "He just left but, you should know, I don't think he bought your alibi."

"It doesn't matter. He's not going to be able to tie me to Ben Sharpe's murder." *Ben, why the hell did you seek me out? Why didn't you just stay hidden? You could have stayed alive then.*

"The detective's gonna dig." Reese thrust his hands into the pockets of his pants. "Are you worried about what he'll find when he starts poking around in Sharpe's past?"

Sharpe's past was linked to Trace's. "He'll see the official records, nothing more." Because there were things that Uncle Sam wanted covered up, too.

Some blood and death didn't need to ever see the light of day.

"You went after Sharpe." Reese's voice was hesitant. "Is the ME gonna find anything on his body that will link back to you?"

Trace remembered the instant back at his penthouse when he'd shoved his forearm under Ben's jaw. Rage had burned through him in that moment, and he'd reacted purely on instinct. "I think I'm clear."

Trace glanced back at the fire station — no, it was a studio now, her studio. "Stay close to her." He pulled out his keys.

"Boss?"

He glanced at Reese.

"There something that you want to tell me?" Reese's gaze was steady. "You pulled me off Sharpe's detail last night. Told me that you could handle things."

Reese thinks I killed him. Trace shook his head. "There's nothing else you need to know. Not yet." Not until Trace had done some digging of his own.

Reese gave a grim nod.

Trace looked down at his hands. The tanned flesh. The callused fingertips. Sure, he wore the thousand dollar suits. He sat in the boardrooms. He played the games.

But there was more to him than that. And there would always be blood on his hands. One way or another.

***

Alex Griffin paused outside of the nondescript apartment. He heard the rumble of the train outside the building, the scream of sirens.

He was following a hunch that he sure hadn't shared with his new captain. Because when it came to Trace Weston, the captain would let fear rule him.

Fear of money and power. Alex had seen that same shit go down before. It wasn't happening again.

Alex raised his hand and pounded against the door. He had little to lose—so why worry about fear?

Footsteps shuffled toward him, then the door opened, and a man stared out at him with bleary eyes. Thick stubble lined his jaw, and his eyes, a muddy brown, widened as he took in Alex.

"You again?" the man demanded as he shoved back his dirty blond hair.

"Yeah, Parker, it's me."

"Hell." The guy definitely didn't sound happy to see him, but Parker Jacobs backed up and let Alex into his apartment.

The place was a dump. Not because of its location, but because Parker Jacobs was a slob. Half-eaten food and old newspapers littered the area. A pile of dirty clothes hid the couch.

Parker shoved the dirty shirts and jeans away and slumped on the faded cushions. "Why the repeat visit?" Parker ran a hand over his face. "I told you everything I knew about Trace and Skye last time."

Alex didn't sit. He crossed his arms and stared down at Parker, carefully studying the other man. There was a heavy bump in the middle of Parker's nose, from an old break. A break that Alex knew Trace Weston had caused.

"Your parents took in Trace and Skye as foster kids when you were sixteen," Alex said. He figured it was better to start back at the beginning.

"Shit." Parker exhaled heavily. "If we're going over all of this crap again, then I need a drink." He lunged up from the couch.

Alex shoved him back down. He'd already smelled the alcohol on the guy's breath. His breath, his clothes, his skin. The guy reeked. "You've had more than enough already."

Parker's eyes narrowed into angry slits.

He'd heard this story before, but Alex needed to hear it again. So he said, "They took them in, but the first night Trace Weston was there—"

"The asshole attacked me!" Parker's trembling hand slid over his nose. "He pounded my face, again and again. The jerk is crazy. Fuckin' insane!"

"And why did he attack?"

"I *told* you last time, when you came sniffin' around—"

"Tell me again." He kept his voice flat.

"Because that slut Skye was playin' us both! He caught us together and freaked the hell out."

"Playing you both," Alex repeated.

"Don't buy her innocent act." Now disgust thickened Parker's voice. "It's bullshit. She wanted me, and she came after me."

Alex cocked his head. "If Trace had just arrived at the house, then how was Skye playing him? How did she—"

"I think he knew her from before. He had to." Parker's breath blew out on a hard sigh. "The way he looked at her. The way he acted...it was like she was already his. I should've read the signs. I should've stayed away from that cock tease."

"But you didn't," Alex murmured.

"And he nearly beat me to death." Fury was there. Reddening Parker's cheeks and snapping in his words. "Trace deserves payback, *that's* what he deserves."

"Why did he stop?"

Parker shook his head. His hair was thick and matted, and it sagged over his eyes.

"Why didn't he kill you, Parker? Why did Trace Weston let you live?"

Parker seemed to think about that. Thinking didn't exactly look easy for the guy. "Because…because Skye told him to stop." The memory was there. Alex could see it on Parker's face. He also saw the flash of rage that followed that memory. "He always has been her dog, tied on her leash."

Alex hated talking to the jackass, but Parker Jacobs was the one person who was actually linked to Skye and Weston. He knew their past—and he was willing to talk about it.

Now, with calculation, Alex threw out, "Both Trace and Skye told me that you were a liar. That you fed me a story of bull about what really happened that night."

Parker glared up at him. "What happened…I kissed his precious Skye. He went psycho, and I wound up in the hospital." Once more, his fingers slid over his nose, as if checking the old wound. "When it comes to Skye, Trace isn't exactly the controlled kind of guy. Some women are like that, you know. They can push a man too far."

"Did Skye push you too far?"

And there it was. The faster breathing. The gaze that darted nervously around the room.

"Did she push you," Alex asked softly, "and you decided that you just had to take what she was offering?"

"I was just *kissing* her—"

And Alex took a stab in the dark. "Then why'd she cry out for help?"

Parker jumped to his feet once more. "Because she wanted to set me up! She was a cock tease, I told you! She wanted me to kiss her, but when things got rough, she started crying and begging me to stop. I had to put my hand over her mouth, but it was too late. Trace had heard and—"

Parker grabbed him and shoved the guy against the nearest wall. "So that's what the truth sounds like from you."

When Skye had been stalked, Alex had questioned the guy. Cleared him because the man had plenty of people to back up his alibis. And Parker had been too happy to tell him about Weston's dark side.

No wonder Weston attacked you. You were hurting Skye.

Alex had come to realize that Weston didn't let *anyone* hurt Skye. The last man who had—the bastard who'd kidnapped her—Weston had sent him to hell.

Alex's muscles were hard with his own fury. "You were hurting Skye, and Trace stopped you."

"He tried to beat me to death!" Parker heaved against him.

Alex just tightened his grip. "Yet you're still breathing."

"Only because of Skye. She pulled off her attack dog, that bitch—"

"Sounds to me like you should be grateful to her, instead of calling her a bitch." He stared into the man's eyes, and Alex saw his own past.

His sister...she'd been hurt. She'd trusted the wrong man and—

"Trace Weston is psychotic." Spittle flew from Parker's mouth. "He's a ticking time bomb, and that man's gonna explode."

Alex sucked in a deep breath. Then another. And he forced himself to back away from Parker. "When was the last time you saw either Trace Weston or Skye Sullivan?"

"I haven't seen them in years." Parker's thumb jerked toward the TV set. "Except on the screen. Their faces have been splashed plenty there."

Yes, they had.

Alex had one more question for the asshole. "What do you know about Trace Weston's time in the military?"

"Nothin'. I was hoping the guy would get his ass blown to hell." Parker rolled back his shoulders. "Instead, he came home to a freakin' fortune."

Yes, he had.

Ben Sharpe had been in the military, too. When he'd been found dead, the man had still been wearing his dog tags.

He suffered PTSD. That had been Weston's line.

Just what had happened to Sharpe during his days in the military?

Weston and his secrets...the man was going to drown in them.

Alex marched for the door.

"But at least the bitch got hers, didn't she?" Now there was smug pleasure in Parker's voice. "That doc took her and held her in that basement. I bet he did all kinds of things to her...*all kinds...*"

Alex slowly turned back to stare at Parker. "You're a sick fuck."

Parker smiled. "You didn't say that the first time we met, Detective Griffin. Back then, you were so eager to find out dirt on Trace. You keep digging, and you'll find plenty."

He was already staring at dirt. "Skye should've pressed charges against you when you tried to rape her."

Parker flinched.

Sonofabitch — that's exactly what he had done.

Alex's hands fisted so hard they ached.

But Parker...he recovered fast and his smile grew.

Alex knew he was staring right into the eyes of a monster.

***

She danced until her muscles trembled. Until her calves clenched and the balls of her feet knotted.

Then Skye danced some more.

Sweat gleamed on her body. Her hair was in a bun, but loose tendrils had escaped — they were slick and clung against the side of her face.

The music kept pounding.

She flew up onto her toes. Grabbed the barre. Stretched —

And saw Trace's reflection behind her.

He stood there, just watching her. For an instant, Skye faltered.

He'd left over eight hours ago. Left after making her ache—and leaving her unfulfilled. Reese had been keeping guard from the other room. Her music had driven him away.

And the music had covered Trace's entrance.

"Don't stop." She didn't hear those words from him, but she saw his lips move and form them.

Her breath eased from her. Skye lifted her hands over her head, stretching. Her left leg came up, moving easily, fluidly, despite the injury that had sent her running from dance.

An injury that had changed her life.

She'd been in a car accident one rainy night after a performance. For hours, she'd been trapped in that car. Her leg had been savaged.

But she'd recovered. One painful step at a time.

She'd walked again. She'd danced.

She turned then, fully facing Trace. Her eyes locked on his face. *My spotting place.* He would be her constant as she danced. It was a trick most dancers used. Focusing on one object to maintain control and balance during turns.

He is my constant.

Skye straightened her shoulders, balanced, focused on him—and she turned. Once. Twice.

Her gaze locked on his.

Again.

His face.

She spun, moving fast and furiously so that her body would almost appear to be a blur, and he was what she saw. He was her only focus.

Always.

He was—

Trace caught her, stopping her spin. Bringing her close against him.

"I-I thought you wanted me to dance," she whispered as her breath blew out in a frantic gasp.

He smiled at her. "I never understood how you could spin that fast, that much, without getting dizzy."

"It's easy," her voice was soft, breathless. "I just look at you."

His pupils expanded, the darkness covering more of that amazing blue.

"You're my center. My focus. For every spin, a ballerina needs a focus."

But she wasn't just talking about dancing.

They both knew it.

She glanced down at their bodies. She was covered in sweat and his suit, well, she didn't even want to know how much it cost. Hurriedly, Skye backed away from him. "I-I need to shower real fast and get changed. Give me just a minute."

The music had died away. The end of her routine. The spin was the end.

Her steps were soundless as she walked across the floor.

"You don't limp."

Her stride faltered.

"I've been watching you carefully for weeks now, and I never see you limp."

"I-I hadn't been doing much dancing during those weeks, either. After today, my muscles will feel it." Particularly the muscles in her left calf. Her left leg would always be weaker. Her constant reminder of the life that was gone now.

But I don't miss the bright stages or the crowds. The stage hadn't actually ever mattered to her. Neither had the crowds. It was the dancing that she loved.

"You left New York because you didn't think you could dance as well again. Not after the crash."

Skye glanced down at her leg. Her tights covered the scars there. Her leg had needed surgery—so many surgeries—to recover. She'd been in therapy for months.

The scars were still there. They always would be. And her dancing...

"I'm not dancing for the stage anymore. That's over. I'm dancing for *me*." She'd said good-bye to her life in New York. She'd come back to Chicago to start over.

And she'd found Trace.

Her head lifted and she glanced toward the now-repaired mirror. She could see Trace's reflection. He stared at her and said, "I think you're the most amazing dancer that I've ever seen. When I watch you, I forget everything else. You…make me forget."

She wrapped her hands around her stomach. "I should…I'll be just a moment." Then she fled.

Skye stripped and hurried into the shower area. The water blasted onto her, and she glanced down at her body once more. Without the clothes, the tights, there was no hiding.

Her gaze hit her left leg. The scars weren't an angry red any longer. Pale, white. Twisting on her skin.

Before the accident, her dancing had lit up the stage. Prima ballerina. She'd worked toward that goal for years.

After the crash…she'd had nothing. All of her money had been used to pay the medical bills, and the first time she'd tried to dance—

I fell. Again and again, I fell.

Her hand flew out, and she jerked off the water. She shivered, standing there, dripping wet, with the past around her.

Maybe Trace was right. Maybe looking at the past was wrong.

She grabbed a towel. Dried off. Dressed as quickly as she could. Jeans. A loose top. Sandals. She hurried back to Trace. "I'm done," Skye called out. "We can—"

He wasn't in the studio. The lights were on, but there was no sign of Trace.

She made her way to the front of the building. Skye found him, sitting in one of the new chairs that had been brought over. His gaze was directed out of the window, staring at the night.

"If I came out here," he said, not glancing her way, "I figured I'd be less likely to jump you in the shower."

Her lips curved at that. "I wouldn't have minded a little jumping."

She saw his hands tighten along the arms of the chair. "My…self-control isn't what it needs to be tonight. Not for you."

They'd better not be back to that.

He rose then and offered her his arm. "I want to get you home."

Home. She liked the way he said it. Did Trace realize that the only home she'd really had, since she'd been fifteen — well, it had been with him? Trace was her home.

They left the studio. The streetlights were on, spilling light onto the pavement. There was no sign of Reese, but Trace's dark Jag waited near the corner of the street.

He led her to the passenger side door. Started to open it, then stopped.

She looked up, wondering what was wrong, and Skye saw that he was staring across the street. Trace was looking at the figure that stood — waiting, watching — just beneath the street light.

A baseball cap was on the man's head. His shoulders were hunched, so Skye couldn't see him clearly. He had on jeans, and, even though the weather had warmed, he wore a light coat.

"Get in the car," Trace ordered her. In a flash, he'd yanked the door open. Pushed her into the seat.

And then he rushed across the street.

What the hell? Skye jumped from the car and ran after him. "Trace, stop!"

The man in the baseball cap was lifting something from his coat. Something small and dark.

A gun. Dear God, what if it's a gun?

"Trace!" Skye yelled.

He leapt up onto the curb. Grabbed the man's hand. Light flashed. The guy screamed. His baseball cap slipped to the ground.

"Let me go!" The streetlight fell on his face.

An angled jaw. A hawkish nose. High forehead.

A stranger. Skye had no idea who this man was.

"You can't attack me, man!" The fellow snarled. "I'm Press! I've got rights, you can't—"

The flash of light. Skye glanced down and saw the shattered remains of the camera on the ground.

"This-this is assault," the guy sputtered. "You *can't* do this to me—"

"I just did." Trace's voice was cold and hard. "Want to know what I'll do next?" His hand shoved into the man's pocket, and Trace yanked out a wallet. He flipped it open, thumbing through the contents.

"Stop! *What. The Hell!*"

She saw that Trace had found the guy's ID.

"I'll call your boss, Clyde Jones. I'll get your ass fired." Trace tossed the wallet back at the man. "Because what kind of *Press* hides in the shadows, stalking a woman? What were you going to do if she'd come out alone?"

"J-just take some pictures." Clyde swiped the broken camera from the ground. "It would've been an exclusive."

"Screw the exclusive," Trace spat. "You're done." He caught Skye's hand, linked his fingers with hers, and marched back across the street.

A few moments later, he spun out of the lot with a squeal of the Jag's tires.

Adrenaline beat in Skye's blood. "I-I couldn't tell that he had a camera. I thought it was a gun."

The Jag's motor revved. "And you still chased after me, knowing the jerk could have a weapon?" Trace spared her a glittering glare. "I told you to get in the car!"

"And I didn't feel like waiting for you to fight my battles!" The words burst from her.

Silence.

"That's what you're doing." The scent of leather filled the car's interior. "Giving me guards. Trying to protect me, twenty-four, seven. You can't do that. I've told you already, I won't live in a prison. Not even for you."

"I want you *safe* – "

"There's no guarantee of safety. Not for any of us." Ben Sharpe had discovered that truth. "The guy on the street was a reporter. He would have taken some pictures and been done. He's not going to be the only one who comes wanting a story, and you can't attack reporters every time they show up."

He slowed at a red light.

"He could press charges against you," she whispered.

"Let him try."

The wildness was there again. In the slightly cruel curve of his lip. In his eyes as he glanced over at her.

Trace was balanced on a razor's edge – he'd been that way for weeks, and Skye couldn't help but wonder what would happen when he fell over the edge.

Her hand lifted and curved around his. His fingers were clenched tightly along the wheel. "You saved me, Trace."

His eyelids flickered.

"You got me out of that basement. I'm alive. You're alive."

A car horn honked behind them.

Swearing, Trace accelerated.

She didn't let him go.

"Everything is going to be okay," she told him. She wanted to soothe him, to just hold him.

But Trace gave a hard shake of his head. "You don't know..." His words faded into silence.

"What? What is it that I don't know?"

"You have your nightmares. I have mine."

"What happens in your nightmares?"

He was staring straight ahead, at the dark road. "I don't get to you in time."

Her heart seemed to stop.

"And without you, I go fucking insane."

***

Every man had a strength.

And every man had a weakness.

When it came to Trace Weston, the man's greatest weakness was Skye Sullivan.

From the shadows, he watched as the reporter stomped away. The guy was clutching his camera. Muttering about lawsuits.

Interesting.

He crept up behind the man. He'd overhead their conversation easily enough. Trace had been so focused on Clyde Jones that he'd never looked around for another threat.

His mistake.

No, his weakness. The woman seemed to consume Weston, and when a man fell that hard—

It was the perfect moment to strike.

He pulled out his weapon, and his fingers curled around the handle of his knife.

It would be so easy to take out Clyde Jones. A fast swipe of his knife. The guy was a leech. A vulture who made his living by feeding off the pain of others.

If he killed Jones, then he'd probably be doing the world a favor.

But he's not my target.

Jones swore and headed toward the busy intersection. "Taxi!" Jones shouted.

He put up his knife. He'd learned to control his impulses long ago. Jones could keep breathing.

But Weston? Soon enough, he'd be dying.

CHAPTER FIVE

He grabbed her, his fingers closing tight around her arm. Trace yanked Skye against him, and her eyes flew open. She couldn't see anything, it was too dark, but she knew his touch.

"Trace?" She whispered.

"Can't let go..." His fingers bit into her as he muttered those words.

Skye tried to shift toward him. They were in bed. It was the middle of the night and—

"Didn't want to...kill..."

His rasped words stole her breath.

"So...fucking sorry...have to do it..."

And his hands lifted—to her throat.

"Trace!" She screamed his name as real fear pulsed through her.

He stilled.

The only sound then was their breathing—both ragged. Panting.

"Skye?" Confusion thickened his voice.

His hands pulled away from her. *He* pulled away. Trace rolled to the side of the bed and flipped on the lamp. "Baby, what's wrong?" Trace demanded as his gaze swept over her. "Did you have another nightmare?"

She hadn't moved. She couldn't. His hands had been going for her throat as if—as if he would kill her.

Trace would never do that.

She licked her lips. Every single bit of moisture in her mouth seemed to have vanished. "You were the one having the bad dream."

Shadows were all around them. The lamp spilled a small pool of light onto the bed. Everything else — darkness.

"I was?" He raked a hand through his hair. "I don't remember it. I'm...sorry if I woke you."

Those words jerked Skye out of her stupor. She sat up, letting the sheet fall away. "I've woken you up nearly every night for the last month. Don't talk to me about sorry."

He stared at her.

"Something scared you. You said...you said you didn't want to kill, but you had to do it." Her stomach was in knots. "It's because of me. You killed to save me, and now the memory is there, tearing you apart —"

His laughter stopped her. Cold. Bitter laughter. "That particular memory has nothing to do with you." He leaned toward her, caging her with his body. "You think I regret what I did to Mitch Loxley?"

She tried to search his gaze. There wasn't enough light.

"Not for an instant. I'm glad he's dead. I just wish I'd made him suffer more before I sent him to hell."

She believed him. "Then what gives you nightmares?" Her question was a hoarse whisper.

He didn't speak.

"One secret." Skye grabbed his shoulders, desperate. "That's what we can start with. That's what I want from you, Trace. That's what I think I deserve." No, Skye actually thought that she deserved all of his secrets. And she'd get them. Sooner or later.

His hand came up to her throat. His fingers lightly caressed the flesh. This touch was so different from the one that had come before. "You were choking me," she said.

He flinched.

"No, no, *you* weren't." She'd screwed that up. In his dream, his memory, he'd been attacking someone else. "You went to touch my neck…you said you had to kill, and I called your name."

He turned away from her. Sat on the edge of the bed with his head hanging down. "I'm sorry. Scaring you is the last thing I ever wanted to do."

She leaned toward him and pressed a kiss to his broad back. He was so tense beneath her lips. So warm and hard and strong. "One secret at a time." Would that be so hard? They had to start somewhere. "I've told you about my nightmares. Tell me yours. Let me help you."

She needed to help him. Couldn't he see that?

His head lifted. He stared straight into the darkness. She didn't think he was going to speak at all, but then he finally said, "It was right after I left the military. I'd gone…independent with some friends. One of my teammates—the person wasn't who we all thought. A traitor. Leading us straight to hell. I had one chance to stop things. Kill or be killed." His voice was wooden.

"You killed."

"It turned out I was good at killing. Maybe too good."

She rose onto her knees and wrapped her arms around him, pulling his back against her breasts.

Trace's attention seemed to shift as he stared down at his hands. He'd taken off the bandages she'd applied so carefully before.

"I'd killed before, but that was in the line of duty. When I was following orders. This time, it was different. *It was my friend.* And I let my emotions get in the way." He drew in a ragged breath. "I have a lot of memories that won't let go of me. I went Black Ops six months after my enlistment. I did things…" His muscles were rock hard against her. "I wish I could forget them."

Because the memories haunted him. "You don't have to carry this alone." She pressed a kiss to his neck, just below his ear. "I'm here, Trace. I want to help you." She wanted *in*.

"You helped me back then."

She frowned, but knew he couldn't see her face.

"Every time I hunted, every time I killed, every time I thought I'd never taste anything but blood and death and the sand that got between my teeth or the snow that froze my bones...I'd see you."

Her arms tightened around him.

"I'd imagine you dancing, up on stage, with all the lights around you. I'd see you, and the hell around me would vanish for a few seconds. You were my dream, when I was in a nightmare."

Her lips feathered over his throat.

"I don't have nightmares about that time...at least, I haven't," he said, sounding angry now. "Not in years."

"But then Ben Sharpe came back."

He nodded. "Ben worked with me in Black Ops. I saved his ass a few times—that tends to make a man loyal."

But demons had started to chase Ben, even then.

"After I got out of the military, I brought Ben onto the independent team with me because I wanted to help him. He'd come to me, desperate, but working with me just made things worse."

Because of the traitor?

"Ben brought them back," Trace said. "But I'll forget them again. I'll shove the memories into the back of my head and lock the damn vault shut on them."

He hadn't looked at her while he'd spoken. Maybe it was easier for him not to see her when he saw the past.

"Thank you," Skye whispered.

"For what? Scaring you? That's not what I—"

"For giving me the first secret." A glimpse into his hell.

He turned then, caught her, and rolled so that Skye was beneath him in bed.

"Thank you," he told her, voice gruff.

"For what?"

"Without you, I would've been as lost as Ben."

"No, you—"

He kissed her. She wrapped her arms around his neck and kissed him back with all of her passion, all of her love. She wanted to show Trace that she was with him, through good and bad, and everything in the middle.

His tongue slid over her lips. His hands trailed over her body. He knew where to touch her. Where to stroke and caress so that she arched eagerly toward him. Wanting all that he had to give her.

But he didn't thrust into her.

Not even when she begged.

Instead, he put his mouth between her legs. He licked her. He tasted her. He drove her into a frenzy.

She came against his mouth. With her hands in the thickness of his hair. With her hips arching toward him.

Skye came that way, and she wanted more.

But Trace was the one in control. That fierce control that she wanted to smash into a million pieces.

He brought her to the brink of another release. Tears leaked down her cheeks. She cried out for him. Wanted *more*. "Trace, now, I need—"

He rolled away from her. Stood. His erect cock thrust out toward her, and Skye wanted it buried *in* her core.

She reached for him.

He backed away.

"T-Trace?"

His eyes squeezed closed. "Have you ever wanted something so much…so badly…but you were afraid you'd destroy that one thing if you actually took it?"

Her thighs quivered. Soft contractions still pulsed in her sex. "You won't destroy me."

His smile came then. Sad and cruel. "Oh, baby, you shouldn't be so sure. Tonight, I'm weak, and you don't want me without my control."

This was the moment that mattered.

Skye slid from the bed. Her knees sank onto the lush carpet. "I want you every way." Why couldn't he understand that?

She opened her mouth and tasted *him*. It was her turn to lick, to stroke, to enjoy the hot and hard length of his cock in —

He jerked her up. Spun her around. Pushed her onto the bed and lifted up her hips. Her stomach hit the mattress even as her hands fisted in the sheets. She heaved up and tried to glance over her shoulder at him.

Trace sank into her. A deep, hard thrust. There was no holding back then, he drove into her in a plunge that took her breath.

His hands were tight bands around her hips. He withdrew, thrust. Again and again. Each thrust was harder than the last.

She tried to arch back against him, but he was moving too fast, too fiercely.

The rhythm was wild and rough. Not like the controlled lovemaking that he'd shown her in the last few weeks. He was plunging so deeply — rubbing inside of her. She was slick and swollen from her release.

"Give to me," he gritted out. "Want...*everything*..."

Her heartbeat thundered in her ears.

"Mine..." His left hand freed her hip. Slid around her body. Closed around her breast. Stroked the nipple. Palmed her breast. "Every inch."

In and out...in and out...

His right hand moved then. Went around her hip and his fingers found her clit. He wasn't gentle. Rough, demanding —

And she exploded, bucking against him as the release slammed into her.

"Fuck, *yes*."

His mouth was on her shoulder. She felt the faint sting of his teeth.

And the hot surge of his release as he came inside of her.

He was around her, surrounding her, and she couldn't stop the waves of pleasure. They came and came. Hollowing her out and leaving Skye limp.

She sagged beneath him.

Trace without his control…

"I warned you." His voice was different. Stilted.

She found the strength to turn her head a few inches and look back at him. His face appeared leaner, harder.

"Next time…" Skye heard herself say, "fuck me harder."

His body tensed. "*Skye.*" And he started to fuck her again.

He wasn't treating her like a delicate doll or like a victim—and she wanted every single thing he had to give her.

A moan slipped from her.

Fuck me harder.

She was lost.

***

Trace stared down at Skye while she slept. The covers pooled around her, and Skye's hand was out, reaching toward his pillow.

As if she were reaching for him in her sleep.

After last night, she still wants me?

Talk about a miracle.

He'd given her a taste of the darkness that lived inside of him last night. She hadn't been afraid. Despite everything, Skye hadn't hesitated.

She'd given him pleasure. Demanded her own.

Fuck me harder.

His cock twitched just thinking about those words.

Was it any wonder that other women had left him cold? They'd never been enough for him, because they weren't Skye.

His fingers lifted and brushed lightly over her cheek. He wanted to let her sleep, but if he did, Trace knew Skye would be pissed.

She wanted to go to her studio. She wanted to start seeing her students.

And he wanted her happy.

He bent and brushed his lips over hers. "Wake up, baby."

Her eyes blinked open. For an instant, she seemed lost, then Skye focused her gaze on him. A soft smile curved her lips.

She was the sexiest thing he'd ever seen.

And he had to leave her.

He kissed her again. "I have to go in to the office today. Reese will to take you to the studio."

Her brow furrowed. "More guard duty? But I thought—"

"Humor me, just a little longer." Until he could get a better grasp on just what was happening in this town. Sharpe had spoken of a ghost and of the dead coming back. Trace had tried to tell him that the past was dead and buried but...

Was that past coming back?

She'll destroy you.

The hell she would.

"Tonight..." His fingers brushed down her arm. "I'm supposed to attend a charity auction and ball. It's something I agreed to attend months ago." Before Skye had walked back into his life. "I don't want to ditch because the money's going to the Children's Home and—"

"You have to attend," Skye said immediately.

He nodded. They'd both been through the foster system. Cast out. They knew what it was like to need a stable home.

"Do you want to go with me?" And, yes, he was actually holding his breath as he waited for Skye's reply. But he knew that she hadn't been to a big public event, not since before her car crash in New York. There would be plenty of reporters waiting outside of the hotel because so many of the city's elite would be attending, and Skye might not want to walk right into that feeding frenzy but—

"Of course, Trace, you know I'd go anywhere with you."

His heart ached at her words.

She pushed up, leaning toward him. "I'll always go where—"

Skye broke off when he caught her arms. Carefully, very carefully, he lowered her back onto the bed.

"Trace? What is it?"

He pushed the covers out of the way.

And hated himself.

He could see his fingerprints—dark smudges, brown bruises, on her waist. He'd held her hips so tightly last night that he'd hurt her.

He'd always known that he had to take care with Skye. She was too delicate. Too breakable for him. "I hurt you."

Her gaze followed his. She stared at the bruises on her flesh. Markings. *My mark.*

The ache in his chest grew worse. He'd never wanted to do this. Never—

Skye laughed. "That's nothing. Obviously, you didn't see the claw marks I left on your back."

His head snapped up at her words.

A smile lit her face. Made her eyes shine. She was more than just beautiful.

She was every hope and dream that he'd ever had.

She squirmed against him, and he let her. Skye immediately wrapped her arms around him and brought her mouth close to his. "In case you didn't notice, what with all the moaning and panting I was doing last night, I like things a little rough with you. I like it when you lose control."

She just didn't seem to realize that when he lost control, dangerous things happened.

"A few bruises aren't going to kill me," Skye told him, voice soft. "I didn't even feel you holding me that tightly last night. I was focused on, you know, *other* things." She licked his lower lip. "And I'm sure I'll be focused on those other things again soon."

Yes, she would be.

He kissed her. Not hard and wild. But deep. Using every bit of sensual skill that he had.

Did Skye want him as much as he wanted her? Did she crave him?

More than breath?

"Wear the diamonds tonight," he said against her mouth. "And if you need to buy a dress, use my card — *our* card — and get anything you want."

"I have what I want." Her eyelashes lifted to reveal the gorgeous green of her eyes. "See you tonight."

He should back away. And, slowly, Trace made himself do just that. It just took a huge effort.

But her words echoed in his ears. *I have what I want.*

He had exactly what he wanted, too. And no one would ever take her from him again.

***

Skye didn't buy a dress. She still had a few dresses left from her New York days.

Skye went with a black dress. *You can't go wrong with black, right?* The dress was a form fitting bit of silk that clung to her like a second skin. The front collar scooped around her breasts and the back — well, there wasn't a back. It plunged to the base of her spine, then the skirt fell, swirling around her feet.

She'd worn the dress once before, to a post-dance party after she performed as a particularly wicked witch. She'd thought the dress fit her character.

Daring. Dark.

Skye stared at her reflection in the mirror as she secured the diamonds. They were still cold against her skin.

Cold and glittering.

A fortune.

She didn't want to wear them.

But she did, for Trace.

The floor squeaked behind her. She turned at once, and her gaze caught his.

He was dressed in a black tux. One that made his shoulders look even wider. One that she knew had been cut just for him.

She stared at him and thought of sex. Temptation.

Because he looked good enough to eat.

"Have I ever told you..." Trace asked as his gaze glided over her. "That you're the most beautiful woman I've ever seen?"

He was lying. She knew she wasn't the most beautiful. She'd followed his exploits over the years. The man had kept company with supermodels. She was too thin, her breasts were too small. Her chin too pointed. She was—

He sighed. "Skye, what have I told you about leaving me?"

She blinked at him.

He was right in front of her. The guy sure moved fast.

"*Be* with me," he ordered.

"I am." Inches away.

"And believe me when I tell you...to me, you are the most beautiful woman I've ever seen."

Her breath slid out in a soft sigh. She believed him.

Skye smiled up at him. Fear had been trying to take root inside of her, but it vanished, drifting right away.

Trace reached for her hand. He lifted it up, and the diamond on her finger gleamed in the light. "Everyone will know you're mine."

"I've been yours since I was fifteen." The truth was there between them. They had no room for pretense. "I just had to wait for us to be together again."

She saw the flare of longing in his eyes. "You make me want to tell the rest of the world to screw off." He kissed her knuckles. Lightly licked the skin.

A hot spike of arousal fired her blood. "We have to go, but we don't have to stay there forever," she whispered back.

He smiled. Such a gorgeous, sexy smile. "I've been yours, too," he told her, voice rumbling. "Since the moment I first heard you call for me. You got to me, when no one else could." Then he eased back. His gaze swept her once more. "Every man in the room will want you."

She doubted that. "You're the only man I'll leave with."

"Always," he said.

Skye nodded.

Always.

***

A sea of reporters greeted them the instant the limo's doors opened. Reese hadn't driven them, not to this event. A posh limo escorted Skye and Trace toward Chicago's Magnificent Mile and deposited them right at the red carpet that led to the entrance of the illustrious Bartley Hotel, an icon that had been in the city since the early 1930s.

Trace exited first. She heard the reporters shout his name.

He ignored them and turned back toward her. Bending, he offered Skye his hand.

She put one high-heeled foot out. Then the other.

When she rose, there was a moment of silence. Perfect, complete silence.

Then the questions exploded.

"*Skye! Skye Sullivan!* Can you confirm the rumors that you and Trace Weston are planning to marry?"

She thought her ring confirmed that rumor.

"Ms. Sullivan! Is it true that you've been offered a spot as lead in Robert Wolfe's next ballet?"

That question made her falter. Robert had been her choreographer for years when she danced in New York. When it came to the top echelon of the New York ballet, Robert was the man in charge.

Skye found herself shaking her head. There was no return for her. Robert certainly hadn't come to ask—

"Is it true that you were in a mental facility for the last three weeks because you had a breakdown?"

Skye stiffened.

"Fuck," Trace growled in her ear. "Ignore them. Put on your killer smile and lift your head up, baby. Walk like they don't matter. *They don't.* You matter. Only you."

He was wrong.

Skye turned to the reporter. A curvy blonde with hard eyes.

"I didn't break down," Skye told her simply. "I survived."

And she walked away. With her head up. With a false smile on her lips. She took the steps past the swarm of reporters, and then she and Trace were heading into the Bartley.

Guards were stationed at the doors, and they made absolutely sure that the reporters didn't follow Skye and Trace inside.

Her heels tapped on the gleaming marble floor. From overhead, glittering chandeliers poured light down on her.

The other ball attendees headed forward, moving and laughing easily. They'd enjoyed their time in the limelight. Skye hadn't. She didn't care about photo opportunities or getting her name in the papers. If she had her way, she'd prefer to never see another paper or magazine with her face splashed on the cover.

Breakdown. Thanks, bitch.

Trace wrapped his hand around Skye's waist. "You're the strongest woman I've ever met."

She blinked. Glanced up at him.

"For a minute there, I was sure you were going to tell the blonde to fuck off."

Her lips twitched. The laughter escaped her, before she could even think to stop it. A light, quick bubble of sound.

Trace's face froze. "There it is," he rasped.

And he kissed her. A deep, sensual kiss that made her knees jiggle.

"Well, well…I guess this is how the mighty fall."

Skye pulled away from Trace with a little gasp, but he didn't let her go far. He kept a hold on her wrist as they both turned to face the man who'd closed in on them.

Tall, muscled, with wide shoulders that stretched the perfectly tailored tux he wore, the man stood just a few feet away. His hair was dark, nearly the same shade as Trace's, and his eyes were a burning, deep gold.

Those eyes were on Skye, assessing her with a fierce intensity. "The reporters could see the kiss, you know," the man murmured. There was a faint accent in his voice. Texas? "But maybe that was the point, right, Trace?" And his gaze trekked to Trace. "To stake the claim in front of them all. In case any of the blind fools missed the giant rock on her finger."

She expected Trace to fire an angry retort, instead, he laughed.

Laughed.

Skye glanced over at him in surprise.

"Noah," Trace murmured, "I'd heard you made a new acquisition in town." His eyebrows rose as he took in the hotel. "Nice. You've done well for yourself."

"As have you." That golden stare was back on Skye. Still too intense. "Very well," the man added as his voice deepened.

Trace wrapped his arm around Skye. "You said yourself, I've already staked a claim."

Skye licked her lips — and tasted Trace.

"Skye Sullivan, I want you to meet Noah York. Noah is…an old friend of mine."

The name clicked for Skye. *York Towers.* The guy had hotels all over the United States. Those Towers were usually in the biggest cities, but they were also found in some secluded, high-end getaway locations. Near pristine beaches. Cradled amid mountaintops.

Noah reached for her hand. He bent his head. "It's great to finally meet you."

Finally?

He released her and eased back. "I figured nothing would keep you away from this event, Trace." His shoulders straightened. "Not when we both know what it's like to *be* those kids."

Her gaze sharpened on Noah.

Then someone called his name. Noah sighed. "Business." He pointed at Trace and Skye. "But I'll be seeing you both later." Another nod, and then he was gone.

"We should go inside. The auction will be starting soon," Trace said.

She started walking automatically, but her fingers reached out to touch his arm. "Trace, what did he mean when he said it was *finally* good to meet me?"

His stride never faltered. "Noah and I go way back. Surely you realize that I've talked about you before?" He gave her a fast glance. "How could I not?"

His words were easy. The explanation was simple, but a knot had formed in Skye's stomach.

"Now, let's go bid a ton of money, baby. We're supposed to have fun tonight."

Yes, yes, they were.

They slipped into the ballroom. A stage had been set up for the auction. Business first, then Skye knew that the band would begin playing for the dancers.

This wasn't a night about fear.

This was about the future.

Starting fresh. Giving the children a future.

Once, Skye had been a lost teen. So scared. Alone. From beneath her lashes, she watched Trace. Then she'd found him, and everything had changed for her.

***

Noah had almost fucked up.

Trace kept his arms around Skye, moving fluidly with her as they danced across the ballroom. Her face was lit up, her eyes shining.

Skye loved dancing.

And she loves me.

Noah would have to be careful. Trace planned to catch the man alone at the earliest opportunity. Noah would understand—as many couldn't—just how important some secrets were.

He hadn't realized that Noah was already back in town. If he had, Trace would've talked with him sooner.

It was just a little slip. Skye believed what I told her.

Lying to Skye wasn't something that Trace enjoyed doing. She had so much faith in him. The lies he told her ate at his soul.

But he wanted her protected.

I have to make sure she doesn't find out.

The music ended. Because he knew that she liked it, Trace dipped Skye. Her cheeks flushed. More of that sweet, wonderful laughter slipped from her.

He eased her back to her feet, keeping a light grip on her. He hadn't noticed any weakness in her injured leg, but, when it came to Skye, Trace didn't want to take any chances.

The band announced that they'd be taking a short break.

Trace glanced over and saw Melanie Petrie, the organizer of the charity event, as she talked quietly with two of her staff members. "Can you excuse me for just a moment?" Trace asked Skye. "I need to speak with Melanie." Because he wanted to make a substantial donation, one that would be in Skye's name. He'd tell her later, when they were alone.

He couldn't wait to be alone with her again.

"Of course." She gave him an easy smile. "I wanted to step out on the balcony anyway. I've heard the fountains in the courtyard are quite incredible."

They were. Trace also knew that they were well guarded. The event had a ton of security in place. *And I have my own men here, too.*

"I'll join you there," he promised her.

Trace watched her walk away. He couldn't take his gaze off her back. All of that beautiful, silken skin.

"You're one lucky bastard."

He inclined his head at Noah's words.

"Is there a particular reason you were giving me a go-to-hell look earlier?" Noah asked him.

"You mean other than the fact that your eyes were looking at Skye far too damn much?" Trace turned toward him. His back teeth had clenched, and Trace had to force his jaw to relax. "She doesn't know about my past. I want it to stay that way."

Noah whistled. "You're marrying her, and she doesn't know?"

"How many women know about *your* past, Noah?"

Noah's brows climbed.

"The last thing I want is for her to fear me," Trace said. "Especially after everything that happened."

Noah nodded. "I'm sorry. I...I read the stories. Was it as bad as they said?"

For an instant, Trace remembered the basement. The darkness. The fear that had eaten at him.

She'd looked so beaten. Skye hadn't even believed that he was really there, not at first. She'd thought that she was seeing a ghost. He'd had to convince her...

I found you. You're going home with me. You're going to dance, and we're going to fuck and laugh and be happy. Do you understand?

Trace cleared his throat. "It was even worse."

Noah swore.

"Skye doesn't need any more fear," Trace told him, needing Noah to get the message.

His old friend nodded.

Noah started to walk away. Trace moved, blocking his path. "I want you to come to my office tomorrow. We have to talk."

"Look, I said—"

"Ben Sharpe was murdered."

Noah's lips parted in surprise. "The hell he was."

"He died right after he came to visit me, telling me that the past was coming back."

"The past is *dead*."

"Yes, that's what I said, too. Then Sharpe wound up butchered in an alley."

Noah backed up a step. "I'll be there, man."

Good. Because Noah had been in on the mission that went to hell. A mission that cost a teammate his life.

And taught them all the truth about just how deadly an innocent face could be.

CHAPTER SIX

The fountains were amazing. The water flew into the air, twisting and turning in a rhythm that perfectly matched the soft tunes that drifted from the outdoor speakers.

Lighting effects drifted over the water. Soft pink, light blue.

Beautiful.

"Miss?"

She turned and found a waiter at her elbow. The balcony was well lit, gleaming with candles. The waiter offered his tray of champagne. She took a glass, nodding her thanks.

Skye lifted the glass to her lips.

Then she stopped. Because she'd just caught sight of a man standing below. He had a hood over his head, and he was partially hidden by the shadows.

Her heartbeat kicked up. Her left hand pushed against the hard marble column of the balcony as she leaned forward, trying to get a better glimpse of the figure.

The glass tipped in her right hand and began to fall.

Long, masculine fingers caught the glass, and only a few drops of champagne dripped to the ground.

Skye looked into Noah's eyes.

"It's all right," he said softly, "I've got it."

"I-I—" Skye shook her head, unnerved by the intensity that seemed to cloak him. Trace carried that same, dark intensity, but she didn't fear the danger that clung to him.

Noah York was another matter.

"I saw someone," Skye finally said, pointing over the balcony. "Down there, in the shadows."

Noah followed her stare. "What was this person doing?"

"It was a man. I-I think. He was…staring up. Looking toward me."

Silence.

She squinted as she stared out at the fountains, but Skye couldn't see any sign of the watcher now. "He was *there*."

"I never said he wasn't." Noah put the champagne on the balcony and pulled out a phone. With his eyes on her, he said, "Dale, Jonah, do a perimeter sweep near the south-side fountains. Make sure that no uninvited guests slipped past security." He pushed the phone back into the inner pocket of his tux. "Some reporters can be very determined."

Reporters. Right. Her breath panted out too quickly. It had just been a reporter out there, waiting for a scoop. She had to stop looking at the shadows and seeing danger.

"Excuse me," Skye murmured, embarrassed now. "I'd better get back inside and—"

"Trace won't be much longer." Noah leaned back against the broad column and crossed his arms over his chest. "Why don't we take a few minutes to talk?"

Once more, she glanced back down toward the fountains. Now she saw two men—both wearing suits—heading toward the shadows.

"Those are two of my men," Noah said, not sounding particularly concerned. "If anyone else is down there, I'll know shortly."

There was just something about him that reminded her so much of Trace. Guessing, she said, "The two of you served together, in the military."

"I did a stint in the military, yes."

That was a vague answer.

Her eyes narrowed as she studied him.

"I'm very sorry for what you had to endure, Skye."

She swallowed to ease her suddenly dry throat. "Plenty of people endure worse all the time. I'm just lucky I survived."

Silence, then, "I don't think luck had much to do with it, but I agree, you *are* a survivor."

The candle light fell on his face, half revealing, half concealing. "How much do you know about me?" Skye asked him.

"I know that we share a similar past. You, Trace, and I— life wasn't always easy for us when we were younger, but we didn't let our pasts stop us. A past should never get in the way of your future."

"Your parents—"

"Unlike you and Trace, I never knew them. Not my real parents, anyway."

She stared back at him.

He laughed softly, but the sound held no humor. "This is the point where most women would say, 'I'm sorry' or 'Their loss.'"

Skye rolled her shoulders. "But like you said, we share a similar past."

His head inclined. "So you don't know if I deserve sympathy or envy."

"You're an unusual man, Noah."

"And you, Skye Sullivan, are not at all what I expected." He paused. "I wish that I'd had the pleasure of seeing you dance on stage. According to Trace, you're quite phenomenal."

"I was," Skye said. "Once upon a time…" She forced a smile. "But life is about change, isn't it? Moving forward." Always, forward.

He stepped away from the column. Stalked closer to her. "Do you love Trace?" Noah asked her.

"Of course." She didn't know how to not love him.

"Like I said, he's one lucky bastard."

She glanced toward the ballroom then, as a shiver of awareness slid down her spine. The band had started to play again—and Trace stood inside the open doorway.

How long had he been there? Listening? Watching?

She slipped around Noah and went to Trace's side. "I think I'm ready to leave." Seeing the reporter had rattled her, and she'd overdone at her studio earlier that day. Her legs were aching.

No, admit it — you just want to escape.

There were too many people in the ballroom. Too many eyes.

"Whatever you want," Trace told her. His arm wrapped around her shoulders.

"It was a pleasure to meet you, Skye," Noah called out to her.

She glanced back. "And it was very interesting to meet you."

He laughed. This time, there seemed to be real humor in that laughter.

"See you soon, Trace," Noah said. "Very soon."

They moved easily through the cluster of people in the ballroom. The dress that had felt so beautiful against Skye's skin suddenly seemed too revealing.

She looked to the left and found gazes on her.

To the right—she saw two women whispering and glancing her way.

Too exposed.

She didn't want all of the attention. She'd thought she could hold it together but—

Trace stopped. Right there, in the middle of the ballroom. He turned and pulled her into his arms. He stared down at her. "You are the most beautiful woman here. If eyes are on you, it's because no one can look away. If people are talking, then it's because they don't understand how an asshole like me got lucky enough to be with someone as perfect as you."

Her body trembled.

"There isn't anything to fear. You're safe."

Skye nodded. She had to stop jumping at shadows. Straightening her spine, she met his stare directly. "We're both safe."

He nodded.

They walked slowly from the ballroom. She kept her shoulders squared all the way. Kept her chin up. When they exited the hotel and the cameras flashed once again, she didn't flinch.

Skye just smiled.

Then she was in the back of the limo. They were cruising away from the hotel. Trace's arms were around her.

The fear leaked away.

***

Noah York watched the limo pull away.

Trace Weston...the man was in deep.

And they were all in danger.

He pulled out his phone. Dialed a number that he should have forgotten years ago. Even at the late hour, his call was answered on the second ring.

"We have a problem," Noah said. A deadly one. "And we need to act."

***

Trace brushed back Skye's hair. Her head was on his shoulder, and his arm was around her, holding her. Holding her was the most natural thing in the world for him.

She fit against his body. In bed. Out.

When he wasn't with her, he felt empty. Hell, he'd been lost all of those years that they'd been apart.

He wasn't planning to ever be lost again.

"The two of you were together during your time in the military."

Trace didn't let his body stiffen when he heard her soft words. "Is that what Noah told you?" He'd asked the man to stay quiet.

Trace hadn't worried when Skye had gone out on the balcony. He'd had a guard watching her. Actually, he had a guard *always* watching her...just as a precaution.

But when he'd seen Noah head toward her, he hadn't been able to get back to her soon enough.

Then he'd heard Noah ask Skye if she loved him.

"The two of you...you sort of remind me of each other," Skye said.

That response surprised him. "What do you mean?"

"I feel like you've both spent too much time staring into the darkness." Her left hand entwined with his.

The limo slowed. Trace figured they must be at a red light because they hadn't traveled far enough to be close to his penthouse, not yet. "I'm not looking at the dark any longer," he told her.

Her head turned. A soft light came from the back of the limo, giving him a perfect view of her face.

She started to smile.

The limo accelerated.

Trace bent his head toward hers.

The impact caught him off-guard. Metal screamed, glass shattered, and Trace felt his body flying forward. He grabbed for Skye, holding her as tightly as he could as the limo shuddered—and seemed to rip apart.

They hit the floor, and he did his best to shield her, but Trace still heard Skye cry out. Glass cut into him as the right side of the vehicle surged toward him.

Not Skye. Not Skye...

The scream of metal seemed to go on and on and—

Silence.

"Trace?" Soft hands feathered over his face. "Trace, are you okay?"

He heaved his body up. Glass rained off his back. Something wet dripped into his eye. Blood.

Rage built within him, but he kept a chain on the beast. He knew better than to let his fury out, especially with Skye so close. His hands slid over her, checking for injuries, making absolutely sure that she was safe and whole.

"*Trace!*" Her voice held definite bite now as she grabbed his hands. "Stop it and tell me—*are you okay?*"

Nothing that a few stitches wouldn't cure. "Yes, baby, I am." And so was she. He had to remember that.

"Mr. Weston!" The frantic shout reached him. "Mr. Weston! I'm coming to get you out!"

Trace lifted his head. He glanced over and saw that the right side of the vehicle was a tangled mess. The door was twisted. The windows shattered.

But a groan of sound heralded the opening of the door on the left-hand side of the vehicle.

The driver—a young guy named Matt Norris—peered in and, with a shaking voice, he asked, "Please, sir, please, tell me you're okay—"

"We're okay." It was Skye who responded.

Trace helped her to slide out, and he followed right behind her. As soon as they were clear of the wreckage, he grabbed Matt. His fingers fisted on the man's jacket. "What the *fuck* just happened?"

"Please, it's not my fault! I-I waited for the light to change, but the other car came out of n-nowhere!"

Trace's head turned to study the scene. They were in the middle of an intersection. It was close to midnight, and the dark road was eerily silent. Glass littered the ground. Chunks of metal from the crash were scattered across the street.

A blue BMW had smashed right into the side of the limo. The driver's side door hung open, swaying slightly.

"Where's the driver?" Skye asked.

"H-he ran off," Matt said. "I called out for him to stop, but he kept going."

A siren echoed in the distance. Trace shoved Matt away from him.

"He must've been drunk," Matt told them. "He ran cause…cause he knew the cops would realize it, right? They'd be able to tell that he'd been drinking."

Fury tightened Trace's body.

Another car braked near the scene. A man poked his head out. "Dear God, is everyone all right?"

Trace stared at the wreckage. A hit and run. A drunk driver?

"Trace…" Skye's hand wrapped around his shoulder. "You lied to me."

He flinched. "Skye, I—"

She wiped the blood from his face. "You are hurt. You need stitches."

"It could've been worse," he told her, and the words were true. So terrifyingly true. Because what if she'd been hurt?

The siren was coming closer. Someone, somewhere had called for help. Maybe one of the folks in the apartments down the road. Lights gleamed from those buildings.

Or maybe the call had even come from the SOB who'd hit them and fled.

His gaze tracked around the scene. Lifted. He stared at the red lights.

And at the cameras mounted near them.

A grim smile curved Trace's lips.

I'll find you, asshole.

Because no one hurt him and just walked away.

***

"What the hell happened to you?" Noah demanded as he stepped into Trace's office. Then his lips twisted. "Wait, let me guess, a fight with the little ballerina?"

Trace glared at him. He'd gotten the stitches only because Skye insisted. The cut was high on his forehead, deep and, yeah, he knew it would scar. He didn't care.

He rolled his shoulders, trying to push away the tension he felt, and said, "On the way home last night, some asshole drove right into the side of my limo."

That wiped the grin right off Noah's face. "You're not kidding."

When had he ever?

Trace motioned to the empty chair near his desk. "He left the scene, ran away on foot." But the guy wasn't escaping. Trace had already pulled some strings, and he'd be getting that video footage from the crash scene any minute. He'd see the man who'd walked — *ran* — away.

"You think it's related to Sharpe's death?" Now Noah's voice was cautious.

Exhaling slowly, Trace decided to put all of his cards on the table. "I don't know what the hell to think of Sharpe's case. I got the autopsy report." He nodded toward the manila file that sat on the corner of his desk. Getting a copy of that report had been easy enough. Just a matter of pulling more strings. "It wasn't a robbery. Sharpe was homeless. He had nothing to take."

Noah grabbed the file. His fingers flipped through the pages. "A knife thrust straight to the heart…and a slice right across his jugular."

Trace nodded. "There were no signs that Sharpe even had the chance to fight back." That worried him. "Sharpe was crazy, but he was a fighter. He wouldn't just stand there and let some SOB kill him." And, shit, he'd been the one to send Ben away from the penthouse — *without weapons.* Yet even without his knives, Ben knew a dozen ways to defend against an attack. Provided, of course, that he'd had the chance to use his skills.

Noah glanced up. "He didn't have the time to fight, that's what you're thinking."

"*You* could get the drop on someone like that," Trace pointed out. "You could get close enough to kill without making a sound. By the time the victim realized it, the knife would be in his heart." Because it was true. Noah might pretend to be the elegant businessman, but that façade was a lie.

It was the same lie that Trace presented to the world.

"And so could you," Noah retorted, voice hardening. "We had the same training. Same missions."

Trace tapped his fingers on the desk. "I didn't kill him."

Noah shrugged. "Neither did I. So we just need to figure out who the hell did."

"Sharpe said the past was coming back." This was the part that Trace needed to reveal. "That Skye was going to be my destruction."

Now Noah's face showed his concern. "A woman nearly destroyed us before."

An innocent face…to hide deadly intentions. "They both died."

They…

The woman who'd tried to betray his team. And her lover.

"It sure as hell seemed like they did," Noah agreed as he tossed the folder aside.

"Then why was Sharpe so afraid?"

Noah held his gaze. His lips tightened, then he said, "There's something I should tell you."

This wasn't going to be good. The man's tone told him that.

"Last night, right after you left, I called Drake."

Trace tensed.

"If the past is coming back, he needs to know, too," Noah snapped. "Look, the threat isn't just to you. If someone is striking at us—"

"Is Drake in the city?"

Noah nodded.

Great. Drake Archer wasn't exactly a safe fellow to have around.

And Drake and Trace hadn't ended their partnership on the best of terms. Mostly because Drake had been spiraling, and Trace hadn't been able to help him.

Drake didn't want help. He wanted to implode.

A knock sounded at Trace's door. He glanced over, frowning. "Come in..."

The door opened, and his assistant, Sara, poked her head inside. "The video footage should appear in your Inbox within the next five minutes."

Good. Grim satisfaction filled him. He might not have a handle on Sharpe's killer, not yet, but he *would* be taking down this asshole.

***

"So just how much longer are you going to be playing guard duty?" Skye asked Reese as she slanted a glance at him.

Reese gave her a smile. "Last night's crash put the boss on edge."

Right. Like she'd missed the frantic intensity that filled Trace.

But she was tired of being in his cage.

This morning, she'd started to feel as if she were suffocating.

"That was an accident," she said, shrugging. "Despite what Trace wants, he can't protect me from everything. The world is too unpredictable for that."

Reese reached for his coffee. Two PM, and she knew that he was hitting his fourth cup of the day. "You know Trace. Control matters to him."

It mattered to her, too. And she was *done* with the cage.

The nightmares had come back last night. She'd been trapped in that basement once more, and Skye had woken up gasping. Even the walls of the penthouse had seemed to close in on her.

She needed freedom.

Not a constant guard, even if that guard was her friend.

"My classes start tomorrow," she said. Excitement slipped through the words. She had full classes—every single one. Sure, some of those students might just be coming because they were curious about the prima ballerina who'd been splashed across all the papers.

But they'd see the truth soon enough. The classes weren't about sensationalism. Skye meant business. The studio was about the dance. About what she could teach her students.

And I'll teach them plenty.

She narrowed her eyes on Reese. "I don't want my students nervous, so the bodyguard bit is ending."

His brows lifted.

"Not that I don't love you, but I think your time can be better spent on activities that are a little more…dangerous." She used the word deliberately because Reese did enjoy his danger. "Now I'm going outside—*alone*—to get a few minutes of fresh air."

She'd taken four steps when Reese called out, "I love you, too, Skye…and that's why I'm playing guard duty. The last thing I want is for you to get hurt."

A lump rose in her throat, but she kept going. Reese had gotten underneath her skin. In the weeks that she'd known him, he'd become her friend. She didn't have a lot of friends.

He and Trace made her feel less alone in the world.

She grabbed her bag and then headed onto the sidewalk in front of her building. The air was warm, but not hot. Summer would be there soon enough.

Skye stared up at the sky. Blue, bright blue, like Trace's eyes.

A car horn honked in the distance. It was lunch time, so, of course, the street was busy.

Tomorrow, she'd open her dance studio. Her students would come.

Her gaze drifted around the street.

Tomorrow…

A man with a hood covering his head stood across the street. Half-hidden by the shadows as he stood under the awning of another office.

He lifted an object.

Snapped a picture.

Her breath sawed out. A reporter. Again.

She couldn't have the reporters bothering her students.

And I can't hide forever. Straightening her shoulders, Skye headed for the cross-walk.

***

Trace clicked the file and watched the image load onto his screen.

"The city needs to invest in some better quality equipment," Noah muttered as he leaned over Trace's shoulder. "Because that image is crap."

Yes, it was. Trace leaned forward. He hit the button to advance the footage.

The limo was there, waiting at the light.

And, just down the road, the BMW waited, too.

Waited.

When the limo accelerated, the BMW raced toward it.

"Shit, he's *aiming* for you," Noah said.

Yes, yes, he damn well was.

The phone on Trace's desk rang. He picked it up, still staring at the footage. "Weston."

"Mr. Weston, it's Joseph Hadden. I'm at the police station…"

There was a buzz of activity in the background. Joseph Hadden was one of Trace's agents. A guy on the rise who always got the job done. Trace had sent him down to the PD because he wanted to know exactly what was happening with the investigation.

Trace paused the video. The screen froze on the image of the BMW slamming into the side of the limo.

"They brought in the owner of the BMW," Joseph told him. "But that guy swears he hasn't driven the ride in months. He's claiming that someone must have stolen it. Says he didn't even notice it was gone until the cops started asking questions."

Eyes narrowing, Trace hit the button to advance the video. Glass shattered. Metal bent.

And the driver of the BMW jumped out. He didn't immediately run. He stopped. Stared at the wreckage.

It was too dark to see his face clearly, but Trace could see his body. Tall. Narrow.

"What does the owner look like?" Trace asked, fighting to keep all emotion from his voice.

"Alan Brenthouse is sixty-four, he uses a cane and—"

"And he's not the asshole who ran us down." Trace rewound the video. "Stay down there. Keep digging." He slammed down the phone.

Hit play once more.

The BMW waited.

The limo advanced when the light turned green.

The BMW raced forward.

The crash was brutal. Hard. Deliberate.

The driver got out. Stared at the limo.

"He tried to kill you," Noah said.

Yes, he had. "He should've tried harder." *Because now, bastard, I'm coming after you.*

***

The reporter spun on his heel. He yanked down his camera and hurried away from her.

Oh, no, he was not just going to run.

"Stop!" Skye called out as she hurried behind him.

He still had his hood up. Maybe it was the one who'd been there to catch her picture last time. Clyde. That had been his name. "Clyde!"

The reporter kept going. He turned, darting down an alley.

She pumped her legs, going faster—

Another man suddenly appeared before her. Tall, with wide shoulders, and dark blond hair. His green eyes glinted down at her. "I don't think you want to do that."

She stumbled to a stop. And, instantly, her hand dove into her bag. Skye had brought the bag along for a reason. She wrapped her fingers around her pepper spray that she kept in her bag. "You need to step away from me!" Who was he? Why would—

"It's been a while since I was on guard duty for you, Skye, but I doubt the rules have changed much." His lips hitched up into a faint smile as he gazed down at her. "Trace would never want you following some stranger into a dark alley."

It's been a while since I was on guard duty for you...

She backed up a step. The street was busy. Plenty of people were around. *I'm safe. I'm safe.* The mantra repeated through her mind.

The blond shrugged his broad shoulders. "Especially not if Sharpe was right...well, Trace sure as hell wouldn't want you following strange men."

"Look, buddy, I don't know who you are—"

"Drake Archer."

"—but I was following a reporter," she finished angrily.

"That wasn't a reporter. That was a man who seemed far, far too interested in you." His head tilted as his gaze swept over her. "He was so interested in you that I was able to get a good, up-close look at him."

In that instant, the sunlight that poured down on her seemed hotter.

Skye still had her grip on the pepper spray.

"Caucasian male, late twenties, a nose that looked like someone broke the hell out of it, blond hair—hair in need of a serious cut, and brown eyes. He was about six foot two, and as thin as he was long."

Her breath came a little faster. "Seems you did get plenty of time to study him."

"Plenty of time," he agreed. "Seeing as how he was outside of your place for the last hour."

Her gaze darted back across the street. "Just how long were *you* outside of my place?" Her stare returned to him.

He shrugged. "Long enough. Trace is slacking. He needs to be more careful."

She could only shake her head and back away. Her stomach had clenched with fear. "Look, Mister—"

"I told you, my name's Drake Archer."

"And that name means nothing to me, okay?"

Now he blinked. "Trace didn't mention me? And to think, the guy was once my friend. But I guess the friends you make in battle and blood don't always want to claim you later."

Skye stopped her retreat. "You served with Trace?"

"Trace. Noah. Ben." He gave a little salute. "Once we were unstoppable." He took a slow, gliding step toward her. "We were really damn good at killing. Too good. But from that little group of ours, I have to confess, your lover was the best. No one could be quite so efficient when it came to killing."

"*Skye!*"

Reese's voice thundered behind her.

"Ah, so there's the guard. A bit late, isn't he?" Drake shook his head. The sunlight gleamed off his hair. "I mean, if I'd wanted, I could've killed you by now."

This guy terrified her.

"Archer." Fury burned in Reese's voice. "You get away from her."

Drake tossed a smile Reese's way. "While you were sleeping on the job, I was keeping our girl safe. Just like the good old days, right?" He turned away.

Oh, hell, *no.*

Skye grabbed his arm. "Just which good old days are you talking about?" Ice had encased her skin, and she made herself say, "Back in New York?"

He nodded.

The ice grew thicker.

Reese swore.

"When I was dancing…" Skye continued. "You were sent to watch me then?"

Another slow nod. "You were important. Guess you could say that Trace has always had a bit of an obsession…"

No, no, *no.* This wasn't happening.

"We should go back," Reese said. He was trying to pull Skye away from Drake.

She wasn't in the mood to be pulled. "How long did you watch me?"

His eyes heated. "Until old Trace felt like I might be getting too attached."

This *wasn't* happening.

"I'm guessing he pulled off all the guards—that must've been when you were hurt in that crash. Bet that drives him crazy. If he'd just kept the crew in place—"

She spun away from him. "Taxi!" Skye yelled.

Reese tried to block her path. "Skye, just slow down. Listen—"

But she'd already heard plenty.

A taxi braked in front of her. She jumped in the back. "Take me to Weston Securities. Now." Because she had to see Trace.

And she had to stare into his eyes.

How long has he been lying to me?

The ice around her thickened.

The taxi roared away from the curb.

***

Trace's phone rang again. Only this time, it was his personal cell. Not the desk phone.

He picked it up. "Weston."

"Trouble, boss, big damn *trouble*." Reese's voice was shaking.

Trace surged to his feet. "Skye? Is she all right? Is she—"

"She's coming in hot, boss. Hot and *pissed*. Drake Archer was here. He got to her. Told her about his time in New York."

Trace squeezed his eyes closed. A frantic pounding began behind his temples.

"She *knows*."

"How long did they talk?" Trace gritted out the question.

"Just a few minutes."

Too long, but surely not long enough for Drake to reveal everything? "Where is he now?" The last thing he needed was for that guy to be loose in the city.

"He took off, jumped on a motorcycle and got the hell out of here."

But Trace would be seeing him again. He was sure of it. "Make sure her studio is secure, then cut out for the night. I'll take care of Skye." He hoped. Trace dropped the phone onto the desk.

"Problem?" Noah asked him.

"Yeah, I've got a problem." He was surprised that his voice came out sounding so calm. He stalked to the window and stared out at the city. "Your *friend* Drake just got to Skye. I don't know how much he told her—"

"Secrets have a way of coming out."

Trace whirled to face him. *"You don't get it!* Skye is my one thing — the only thing — that is any good in my world. Everything else is built on death and blood. *She* matters. She makes me feel like *I* matter."

Noah's eyes widened. "She's not just going to desert you, man. The woman loves you."

"Does she?" And this was the part that tore him up. That made him unable to sleep late at night. "Or does Skye love the guy that she remembers? The one who actually saved her when we were kids?"

He turned back to stare out at the city. Once, he'd been down in the streets. Penniless, desperate. His clothes had been torn, his pockets empty. He'd fought his way out of that poverty.

Now he had the world at his feet.

He put his hands on the cold glass.

And I could be about to lose everything.

CHAPTER SEVEN

No one got in her way. The suits at Weston Securities took one look at her, and they backed up.

She knew that Trace had probably told them she was coming. By the time the cab turned the corner, Reese would've been on the phone with Trace.

Alerting the boss.

"Uh, he's waiting for you, Ms. Sullivan," the man to her right said as he indicated the private elevator in the lobby. "You can go right on up."

Jaw locking, she did. With every floor that she ascended, her heart seemed to race faster.

She didn't want to believe that man—the stranger on the street. But Reese's reaction to the guy's claims had scared her.

I want Drake to be lying.

She wanted anyone to be lying. Anyone, but Trace.

The elevator gave a soft ding. The doors opened.

Noah stood before her.

Noah?

He winced when he saw her. "Maybe you can think about going easy on him?"

Was Noah insane? Were they all?

"Find out his reasons, okay?"

She stalked from the elevator. "Did you watch me, too?"

"Uh, I—"

"Did you watch me?" Her voice rose. "How many guards did I have? How many eyes have been on me?" For how long? She couldn't suck in a deep enough breath. She couldn't *breathe* at all—

"Skye." Trace's voice. Quiet. Calm.

He shouldn't be calm. Not when she felt as if she were about to explode.

"I'll, um, give you two some privacy." Noah backed away. "I'll see if I can find Drake." He edged away a few more steps then muttered, "Asshole that he is."

Skye focused on Trace. Sara, Trace's assistant, wasn't at her desk, and the woman was usually close. Maybe Trace had ordered her to clear out—the better for Sara not to catch the show that was coming.

Trace lifted a hand toward her. "Come into my office. We can talk."

She wanted to scream. Instead, Skye walked forward. When he tried to stroke her shoulder, she jerked away from him. An instinctive move. She just *couldn't* be touched right then. An explosion was too close to the surface for her.

She'd first walked into this office just weeks before. Back then, she'd been terrified. Desperate. Skye had known she was in danger, and Trace had been her only hope.

The door shut softly behind her, with the faintest of clicks. She stood in front of Trace's desk and braced her hands on the surface. Part of her didn't want to know the truth. Part of her wanted to pretend everything was okay.

But hiding does no good.

She straightened her shoulders and turned around to face him. "I met Drake Archer today."

Trace gazed back at her. His blue eyes were unreadable.

"He told me…he said that he'd been one of my guards, back when I was in New York." She shook her head. *"Tell* me he's wrong." Did it sound like she was begging? Skye was very afraid that it did.

Because she was begging, and it felt as if her heart was breaking.

But Trace didn't tell her anything. He just kept looking back at her.

"*Trace.*"

"For a time, Drake did watch you."

No, no, no. "Why?"

"Because I wanted to keep you safe." The words were said softly, but she saw his hands clench into fists.

"You didn't even talk to me for ten years! You left me, you joined the military. You vanished from my life, until I came looking for you—"

"That's not true. You already know I came to see you dance in New York." A muscle flexed in his jaw. "I could never stay away from you."

She whirled away. Her movements were jerky as she headed toward the massive window on the right side of his desk.

His desk. She looked down and saw the framed photograph there. The only photograph.

One of her. Smiling.

He'd taken that while they were in the Keys.

Pain rose and threatened to choke her. "How long did Drake Archer watch me?"

"Three months."

Her eyes closed. "Then you sent someone else, right? You kept sending someone, to watch—" Skye broke off. She started to laugh then, but the sound was brittle. "Oh, dear God, that's why you looked so shocked when I came to your office that first time." She forced herself to turn back and stare at him, even though looking into his glittering stare just seemed to hurt her more. "When I came to you and said, 'Someone's watching me,' your whole body stiffened." She hadn't put the pieces together then, how could she? "You thought that I'd found out about your guards, didn't you?"

"I didn't have guards on you then," he snapped out the words from behind clenched teeth. "Maybe if I had, then you would've been safe. That bastard doctor would never have gotten so close."

Her lips parted but she had no words. He hadn't just said that. He *couldn't* have.

"I have enemies." He took a step toward her. When she stiffened, he froze. "Dangerous enemies who would like nothing better than to hurt me. But you see, for some men, just hurting isn't enough. They like to destroy people. Wreck them completely."

She was as frozen as he was. The ice was back, thicker than ever.

"Do you know what would destroy me?" Trace asked her.

Skye wasn't sure if anything could.

"If someone hurt you, if someone *killed* you, that would fucking end me."

Tears stung her eyes. "So you put guards on me—"

"I've killed, Skye. For my country. For you." His shoulders rolled back, and he gestured to his plush office. "You think this place didn't come at a price? It's built on secrets. I learned plenty on a battlefield of blood and death. I learned to hunt my enemy, any place, any time. And I learned that, sometimes, you even have to be willing to fight the people who are closest to you…because those people can be the most dangerous."

"I'm sick of secrets." Her voice was thick with tears that she wouldn't shed. "You should've *told* me. It was my life. *Mine!*"

"And what did you want me to do? To take you off the stage, away from the lights you loved, and tell you that my enemies might be after you? That there could be a man out there who wanted to hurt you, torture you, because of something *I'd* done?"

"I never loved the lights." The words were a whispered confession.

He frowned, then Trace gave a hard, negative shake of his head. "I put protection on you until the threat was gone. I just wanted you *safe*."

He wasn't getting it. "You're talking about *my* life."

"I'm talking about the thing that matters most to me!" Trace leapt forward. His hands caught her shoulders. "I didn't want you afraid. Not of me, not of the men that could come after you. I made a mistake. A stupid mistake, and *I* put you on their radar."

"What mistake?"

His gaze held hers. "I took you with me. Fuck me, I took you."

That made no sense to her. It didn't—

"Your picture. I needed it, Skye. I needed you. But I should have left you behind, because by taking it, they knew my weakness. They knew that hurting you would break me."

"Who is 'they'?"

His fingers tightened on her.

"Stop it!" Skye yelled at him. "Stop keeping me in the dark and just tell me! Why do you think I can't handle this? I survived a freak who kept me locked in a basement without food for days. *I survived*."

His lashes lowered, concealing his eyes. "Some were traitors to our country. I worked Black Ops, Skye. It's off the books, things too classified for most people to ever know."

"I'm not most people. I'm the woman you kept in a cage, only I didn't even know it."

He flinched. She'd hurt him. In that moment, Skye actually thought...*good.* Now he felt some of the pain that was ripping her apart.

It didn't seem fair that she should be the only one who felt as if her heart were being torn out. "How many guards?"

"Does it matter?"

He *still* wasn't telling her.

"How long? Months? Years?"

His hands shoved into his pockets, but he didn't back away from her. "Only when I received intel to indicate that you might be in danger."

He'd taken her choice away. By not telling her... "Just what did they watch?" All of her personal moments? Her failures? Her successes? Her intimate time with friends...with lovers? Had eyes been on her then?

"They watched enough to make sure you weren't going to be hurt. When the threats were gone, they pulled back."

Fury seemed to choke her. "You should have *told* me."

"I wanted you to have a normal life! I didn't want you to be afraid all of the time — *like you are now!*"

Her breath sucked in. The pain hit her, even sharper than before.

"No, Skye." Now he did back up, frantically, and his blue eyes widened with an expression of horror. "That's not what I meant."

"My nightmares," Skye whispered.

His right hand raked through his hair. "I didn't mean—"

"And I was afraid last night at the party. You were constantly keeping me close, weren't you?" Her brows lowered as she thought about the ball. "Even when I was on the balcony, you had a guard on me. That's why Noah was there."

"Noah wasn't the guard, but..." His chin notched up as he gave a grim nod. "Yes, I had protection on you."

Every breath she took was cold. Ice coated her body and froze her lungs. Trace didn't think that he was doing anything wrong. To him, *she* was the wrong one. The one who was afraid. The one who always needed protection.

Sharpe had said that Skye was Trace's weakness.

Because I am weak?

Because she couldn't survive in the dangerous world that Trace lived in?

"It doesn't change anything," Trace told her. His voice had softened. "So I had protection on you a few times. I was looking after you, the way I always have. My feelings for you are the same. And your feelings—"

A knock sounded at the door, cutting through his words.

Trace snarled, "Not fucking now!"

But a voice—Noah's voice?—called back, "Oh, I think you're gonna want this fucking now." A pause. "Drake's here, and you need to listen to what he has to say."

"I need to smash his damn face in…" Trace whirled and headed for the door.

Wait, he just—he went for the door. *What. The. Hell?*

"Stop!" Skye yelled at him.

He stopped.

"In case you didn't notice, we're in the middle of something that is pretty important here."

And he was—what? Choosing to go and talk with Drake while she stood there and felt as if her world were splintering?

"It's about Skye!" Noah shouted. What, was the guy eavesdropping through the door? "Drake says you need to know who's been following her."

"Who hasn't been?" Skye snapped.

Trace opened the door.

Both Noah and Drake stood there. Noah was glowering. Drake was smiling. And Sara was behind them, watching nervously.

"Uh, Trace?" Sara called, her voice hesitant. She craned her head around Noah and Drake. The light glinted off her blonde hair, and her blue eyes showed more than a hint of nervousness. "I know you said Mr. York was clear, but, um—"

"It's all right, Sara," he said. "I can handle them."

"Right." Sara nodded quickly. "Then I'll just leave you to all of…that."

"Old buddy," Drake murmured as soon as Sara had slipped away, "it's been too long." His lips twitched.

Trace threw a hard swinging punch that caught Drake in the jaw and sent him stumbling back. "Not long enough."

Drake fell into the hallway.

Sara gasped.

Trace followed Drake out and drew back his fist to punch again. *"You went to Skye."*

Skye leapt forward, racing across the room.

"I knew this would happen." Noah sounded disgusted.

"You told her —" Trace continued.

Skye grabbed his arm. "Don't! Just — *stop!*" His muscles were tight beneath her grip.

"You heard the lady," Drake rasped. "Stop."

Her gaze flew to him. Trace had busted Drake's lower lip, and blood dripped down onto his chin, heading for the faint cleft there.

"We all need to calm down," Noah said.

"Th-that sounds like a plan," Sara echoed. She'd jumped behind her desk.

Trace turned his head and his gaze met Skye's. "You already look at me differently."

Because she wasn't sure that she knew him at all.

"I'm not the only guy from the past tracking your Skye," Drake said. "Has she already told you about her near-miss today?"

Trace's eyes sharpened on her. "What near miss?"

This wasn't important. "A reporter —" Skye began.

"A white male in his late twenties. Broken nose. Shaggy blond hair." Drake seemed to be ticking off the description one point at a time. "About six foot one, lean, wearing a hoodie, and focusing only on your lady there."

Trace dropped his fist.

Drake slowly rose to his feet. He swiped his hand over his bleeding lip. "Still got that killer hook, huh, Trace?"

"And you still have a death wish," Trace threw right back at him.

"Guess some things never change," Noah added. "Look, can we cut through the bull and get down to business?" He marched past them and headed back into Trace's office. "Before we give Sara there a heart attack, let's bring the party back inside."

Skye didn't want them inside. She needed to finish talking to Trace. He couldn't just blow her off.

But Drake had sauntered inside too.

Trace stood there, staring at her.

And Sara's gaze was filled with fear.

Right. Skye gave the other woman a little nod and marched back into Trace's office. He followed on her heels and secured the door.

"Now, isn't that better?" Noah asked. "We can tear each other apart in private...or, if we're feeling sane, we can actually talk."

Trace folded his arms over his chest and focused on Drake. "Tell me more about the guy at Skye's place."

Drake swiped away more blood. "I saw the same guy, yesterday, just hanging near her studio." Drake's words were musing. "Only then, he drove off in a blue BMW. There was no sign of that ride today."

Trace's whole body stiffened.

"Trace..." Skye whispered.

"Broken nose," Trace repeated. "Blond hair...six foot one...*Sonofabitch*."

Drake glanced at him with a raised brow. "So you know the jerkoff in question?"

"A blue BMW crashed into Trace and Skye's limo last night." Noah was somber now. "From your description, it sounds like our guy..."

Trace grabbed his jacket. Actually started rushing back toward the door.

She put herself right in his path. "Where are you going?" He *couldn't* be leaving.

Trace's body vibrated with fury. "Don't you get who did this to us? Who tried to kill us both last night? The broken nose, Skye. The blond hair. The build—don't you see who this is pointing to?"

She didn't want to see. "That was a long time ago. Do you really think a man would hold a grudge for that many years?"

"I think a man can want revenge forever."

"Uh, who are we talking about here?" Noah wanted to know.

"A jerkoff named Parker Jacobs," Trace's voice was clipped. His gaze didn't leave Skye's face as he said, "I knew I should've done more than just beat the shit out of him back then."

"You don't know that it was Parker," Skye said. This was crazy.

"I'll know," Drake offered, sounding all helpful. *She* wanted to punch him. "Show me a picture of this Parker Jacobs, and I'll tell you in an instant if it's the man I saw at her studio."

Skye hadn't seen Parker in years. She hadn't wanted to see him.

He'd nearly raped her when she'd been fifteen years old. If Trace hadn't been there…

Her hero.

And he'd almost killed Parker that night.

Trace headed back to his desk with slow, measured steps. He bent over his computer. Tapped quickly on the keys, and then straightened. "Is that the man?"

Drake leaned in close to stare at the screen. "Yeah, yeah, that's the guy I saw jump into the BMW yesterday—*and* he's the one who was watching Skye today."

She had to stop this. "We need to call the cops. If Parker did hit us last night, then let's get them to handle it. Let's call Alex. Detective Griffin can—"

"All I'm going to do right now is pay our old foster brother a visit. Ask him a few questions." All of the emotion had vanished from his face and voice. "I'm not going to hurt him. Just talk to the bastard."

She didn't believe him. Skye shook her head. "Call the cops," she said again. "Drake can tell them what he saw. I don't want you anywhere around Parker, do you understand me?" Because she was scared, so very scared, about what Trace might do.

She didn't want him to just be a killer.

And Skye was already afraid there might be too much blood on his hands.

Everyone waited in that room. *Waited.*

The tension thickened.

Then Trace reached for his phone. "Get me Detective Alex Griffin."

Her shoulders slumped.

"For you, Skye," Trace said as his gaze lifted to meet hers. "Only for you."

***

The office door closed softly behind Skye.

"Seriously? You're just turning that guy over to the cops, knowing that he might have tried to *kill* you last night?" Drake demanded. His voice was thick with disgust. "Who the hell are you and when did you become so whipped?"

Trace offered him a grim smile. "I put in a call to the detective. I left the information that I had with the desk sergeant. Now, if the powers that be at the Chicago PD can actually find Alex Griffin and relay that information *before* I get to my dear ex-foster brother, then good damn deal for them."

Noah whistled. "You're still going after him."

"I never said I wouldn't." Skye was gone. Before she'd left, Skye had promised that they'd talk at home.

Where Noah and Drake weren't watching.

"I told Skye I would call the authorities. I did. But that doesn't mean I don't have my own share of questions for Parker."

"So just what did you do to this guy?" Drake asked. "Did you work your usual charm? Did that piss him off enough to make the fellow want to take you out?"

Drake was still *his* charming asshole self. "I caught him trying to rape Skye, and I beat the shit out of him."

Noah rocked back on his heels. "That would do it…"

"Now, if you will both excuse me, I need to make sure that Parker stays the hell out of my life."

He strode to the door.

"By any means necessary?"

Drake's question didn't stop Trace.

"That is your way, isn't it? *Our* way," Drake added.

When it came to Parker Jacobs, it was the only way.

Don't think of Skye. Don't think of the pain in her eyes. Don't focus on that now. His fingers tightened around the doorknob. He owed Drake for what he'd done with his shit-for-timing revelations to Skye, but now wasn't the time to repay that debt. He had to handle one SOB at a time.

When Skye had walked out of that elevator, all Trace had wanted to do was take her into his arms. To try and make her understand.

But Trace wasn't sure there was any understanding. He'd put guards on her. Kept secrets.

I'm still keeping them.

"Skye isn't going to like this," Noah said quietly as he came toward the door. "Not when she finds out."

"If Parker is trying to hurt her, I have to stop him." They didn't get it. Noah and Drake had never cared about anyone the way he did for Skye. They didn't have the connection. The need.

The vulnerability.

They fucked their women, and then they walked away. No emotions. No weaknesses.

He couldn't live that way.

"Now, gentlemen, get the hell out of my office." *Because I have an old enemy to hunt down.*

***

There was no sign of any cops at Parker's apartment. Good. Trace lifted his hand and slammed his fist into the door.

He heard a muffled curse from inside. The shuffle of footsteps headed toward him, then the door opened, just a few inches. "What the hell—" Parker's muddy brown eyes widened. "*You!*" He tried to shove the door closed.

Trace shoved right back. Wood splintered and Parker stumbled away.

"Y-you can't be here!" Parker yelled at him. "Get out of my place!"

"Ah, I see you remember me." Trace said as he straightened his coat. "And I definitely remember you, Parker."

Parker gulped. His Adam's apple bobbed. "Wh-what do you want?"

"To know why you tried to kill me last night."

Parker shook his head, a frantic gesture. "I didn't! I swear!"

"Now, you see..." Trace stepped toward him. "I don't exactly believe that. You and the truth don't have the best history together."

Parker spun away and grabbed a baseball bat that had been propped up against the wall. He swung it at Trace.

Trace ducked, then he drove his fist right into Parker's ribs. All of the breath left Parker with a *whoosh* of sound. The bat dropped from his limp fingers.

Trace punched him again. Again.

Parker fell to the floor. "Y-you're gonna get my blood on your fancy suit..."

"Like I give a damn," Trace muttered. He grabbed Parker's shirt and hefted the guy up. "You've been watching Skye."

Parker spat at him.

Wrong move.

Trace drove his fist into the man's face. Parker howled at the impact.

"Right, I can break that nose again. I can do it in an instant. So start talking. *Why were you following Skye?*"

"Because he-he made me realize how much the two of you had messed up my life!"

"He?" Trace caught immediately on that point.

"He made me realize…it's all screwed because of you. You and your rich ass!" Parker smiled at him. "But I'll get mine, and I'm about to get it right now…"

"You're not going to get any damned thing," Trace promised him. "Nothing, do you hear—"

"Weston! Let him go, *now!*"

Parker's smile widened.

The authoritative shout had come from behind Trace. It was a voice that Trace easily recognized. Detective Alex Griffin's voice.

Hell. I left the door open. He'd shoved his way inside and had left the door ajar behind him. He'd been busy with other things, like getting the truth from Parker, and he'd made an amateur mistake.

But it will be my only mistake.

"Trace," a softer cry sounded then. Feminine. "*What are you doing?*"

Skye.

No, she *couldn't* be there.

"Help!" Parker cried suddenly. "This man just broke into my apartment, he attacked me! Help!"

Sonofabitch. But did Parker really think he wasn't prepared for this situation? He'd known it was possible that the message he'd left actually *would* get to Alex.

I just didn't count on Skye being here.

Trace stepped back. His control was in place. Holding
steady. "I came here to talk with Parker. H-he jumped me
right after I knocked at his door." Trace rolled his shoulders,
wincing a bit as if he were in pain. "I had no choice but to
defend myself."

"No!" Parker screamed. *"That's not what fuckin' happened!"*

"Of course," Trace murmured, "Now that you're here,
Alex, I'll step back."

"He attacked me!" Then Parker leapt at Trace.

Trace took the punch. Because he knew the game.

"Stop! Step back!" Alex's cry.

Then the cop was between them, shoving Parker away.

Alex had his weapon out and it was locked right on
Parker. *Go ahead. Pull that trigger, Alex. Do us all a favor.*

But Alex was showing no signs that he'd be ending
Parker's life.

Unfortunately.

Skye wrapped her arms around Trace and pulled him
back beside her. "You said you'd let the authorities deal with
him."

Why was she here?

"And you said you were going home," Trace told her, his
voice grim. "I suppose that means we both lied."

She dropped her hold.

"Why the hell are you all here?" Parker demanded.
"Griffin, get them out! Wait, *arrest him* for assault!"

"Parker..." Alex sighed his name. "Do you know
anything about the hit-and-run on Mayer Boulevard last
night?"

Parker shook his head, but his eyelids flickered.

"Are you sure? Because the driver of a blue BMW got cut
at the scene of that accident. His blood is in the car. That
means we have his DNA."

Parker blanched.

"It was you," Skye said. *"You* came after us."

"Because you kept sending the cops after me!" This time, Parker lunged for her.

The hell he did.

Trace drew back his fist, more than ready to break Parker's nose again and do a whole lot more.

But Alex caught Parker in a steely grip. He spun the guy around. Slammed him into a wall, and cuffed him.

"Parker Jacobs," Alex stated, voice biting, "you're under arrest. You have the right to remain silent..."

"*No!*" Parker howled. "It should be him! Not me! Trace attacked me!"

Alex kept right on going, reading the struggling Parker his rights even as Parker shouted.

Then Alex hefted Parker around and marched him toward the door. "It's not over," Parker growled as his gaze darted from Trace to Skye. "Not even close."

Trace leaned toward him. "For you, it's over." His words were a promise.

But Parker laughed. "You won't see him coming. I told him. Told him *everything.* And you won't be able to stop him!"

"*Move,*" Alex barked.

"He'll take what you value most—and then he'll destroy you!" Parker was still laughing.

Skye shivered and followed Alex into the hallway.

Trace glanced around Parker's apartment. The place was a mess. It was—

A glinting object caught his eye.

Trace bent over the couch, and snatched up the object.

Small, rectangular.

A military issued dog-tag.

His fingers smoothed over the ID.

His ID.

"Weston, get out of there!" Alex called.

Trace pocketed the dog-tag. The last time he'd seen that dog-tag, he'd been fighting for his life.

He'd survived the battle.

His best friend hadn't.
Or at least that was what I thought.

CHAPTER EIGHT

The penthouse was silent when Trace opened the door.

Skye was there, he knew she waited inside, but no sound alerted him to her presence.

He dropped his briefcase to the floor. "Skye?" He was ready for the fireworks that he was sure would be coming.

"I'm here."

His gaze slid toward the floor to ceiling window on the right. She stood in front of the glass, staring back at him. She was dressed in jeans and a tight t-shirt. Her hair was swept back, accentuating the high cut of her cheekbones. Her face was scrubbed free of makeup, and she looked so incredibly lovely.

But sad.

I did that. I hurt her.

Jaw clenching, he headed toward her. "I hate you found out this way —"

"As opposed to what?" Skye asked as she slowly advanced to meet him. "Continuing to not know? Letting you keep your secrets?" When she was close enough, Skye paused and tipped her head back to gaze up at him. "Is that the way you wanted things to be? You controlling everything while I wandered around in the dark?"

"Hell, no, Skye, I just —" He broke off, yanking his temper back in check. She deserved her fury. He just had to find a way to get her calm again.

"I can see it, you know."

His brows lifted.

"Right now, you're trying to figure out how to handle me. I'm a problem, and you want me fixed."

Trace shook his head. "No, no, you're not a problem."

"Then maybe you are." And she pushed by him.

That was when Trace noticed the little bag that rested at the end of the couch. A small, overnight bag.

His heart stopped. "You're leaving." No, no, she *couldn't* leave.

"I need some space. This place…" Skye waved her hands. "I see you everywhere. I feel you everywhere."

He didn't move toward her. If he did, Trace was afraid that he'd grab her and hold on tight.

"I need to think, and I can't do that when I feel like you're surrounding me."

Right then, he could barely think. Just breathing was a monumental effort.

"I didn't want to leave before you got back, because I knew you'd just worry about me."

He forced his back teeth to unclench. "Where will you go?"

"The studio. I have the apartment upstairs there, and I've been working on it for the last few days, getting it set up."

What? "You *knew* you'd leave me?"

"No." A sharp shake of her head. "I just wanted to have a place set up, just for me. We all need our refuges."

But she wasn't supposed to need a refuge when it came to him. He wanted to *be* her refuge.

"I don't want you to leave me." The words felt torn from him. Because they were.

She glanced down at the bag. "And I don't want to leave." Her laughter was soft. Even sadder than her eyes. "You know what I really want to do? I want to act as if nothing has happened. As if you didn't keep guards on me for years. As if you didn't lie to me. I want to sweep it all under the rug and just be with you."

Hell, yes. He closed in on her. "Then do that. Nothing has changed. Not the way I feel about you. Not the way you feel about me."

"I love you." Her whisper sank into his skin. "Loving you is as natural as breathing for me, and I'm afraid. So afraid."

He didn't want her to fear him.

That was why she still didn't know his darkest secrets.

"I'm afraid that if I don't watch myself, I'd forgive you for anything." Her lashes lifted. Her eyes held his. "I don't want to lose myself in you."

He didn't have a response for that. His gaze fell on her left hand, on the ring that still gleamed there. She hadn't taken it off.

She's just asking for a night.

He swallowed the lump in his throat. "I'll have a car take you to the studio."

"And you'll have a guard watch me all night?"

His lips thinned.

"No guards. I need to live the way everyone else does. I want to be on my own. I want to be able to face the darkness and not always need—"

"Me," he finished gruffly.

Skye stared back at him, but then she nodded. She bent and her fingers curled around the handle of her bag. Then she was walking toward the door with her usual, graceful stride.

Was she just going to leave without looking back?

She paused. Stared straight ahead. "There are more secrets, right?"

Yes, there were.

"I don't want secrets between us. I want all of you. Good and bad. And when you don't tell me everything…" Her shoulders hunched. "That says that you think I'm weak. That I can't handle you as you really are."

No, it wasn't like that.

"I don't want secrets. And if you only give me part of yourself…" She drew in a deep, shuddering breath, "That's not going to be enough for me." Tears thickened her voice.

He stood, rooted to the spot, as she left him.

The door closed softly behind her.

***

He didn't run after her. Skye had never expected Trace to do that. He wasn't the running sort.

She managed to keep her tears back until she was in the elevator. Then they slid down her face.

The overnight bag dropped from her hand.

Leaving him felt so wrong.

I need a night. Just a night to think.

Because if she stayed, Skye had no doubt that they'd wind up in bed together. The need and lust always seemed to burn between them, surging strongly no matter what else was happening.

How many lies has he told me?

The elevator doors opened. She wasn't particularly surprised to find Reese standing on the other side of those doors. Without a word, he bent and scooped up her bag.

She swiped away her tears and crossed the lobby.

They rode in silence to her studio.

Reese parked, then came to open her door.

When she rose, his fingers slid around her wrist. "You know he's not an easy man. He just…he just wanted to keep you safe."

This was the part that Trace didn't seem to understand, either. "For ten years, I thought he'd forgotten me. Just left me. I ached for him, and he was gone." *His choice.* "Now I learn that for the whole time, he had guards on me. He sent them, but he never said a word to me." Inside, she felt a seething mix of pain and betrayal. She looked up, but the darkness concealed Reese's expression. "You know more of his secrets than I do."

"Don't *you* know he's afraid?" Reese asked. "He doesn't want to lose you."

"So I'm supposed to forgive everything? Live with his secrets?" She shook her head. "I *can't*." Skye took her bag from Reese and went into her studio.

***

"She's safe and sound, boss."

Trace stared down at the bed. Without Skye there, it seemed too big and too damn empty. "Thanks, Reese." Her sweet vanilla scent drifted in the air.

"You want me to stay here? Keep an eye on the place tonight?"

Skye wanted her solitude. And she wanted her guards gone. *I'm the woman you kept in a cage, only I didn't even know it.*

"No." His voice was hoarse. "If she's in the studio, then you're done." The place was wired with a top of the line security system. *His* system. She'd be safe.

"All right...but...are you okay?"

"Of course," Trace said as he stared at the bed. He ended the call.

And he threw the phone across the room. "*Never. Fucking. Better.*"

***

The little ballerina had left Trace Weston.

The move was unexpected.

Infuriating.

She wasn't supposed to leave him. She was supposed to stay with Trace. To make him weak.

Did she leave you? Or did you tell her to leave? It was so hard to be certain. Trace was good at driving people away from him.

Nothing would work if Trace wasn't tied to the woman. He couldn't suffer if he didn't love.

And he'd been so convinced that Trace loved her.

Lights glowed from the second floor of the converted studio.

All alone.

He could get to Skye Sullivan right then. He could kill her easily, but if Trace was severing ties with her, what would be the point?

Wait…wait and see…

This game was all about Trace Weston. About him paying for the crimes he'd committed and the lives that he'd stolen.

And it's about me getting what I deserve.

The lights flashed off.

Sleep well, ballerina. I'll join you soon enough.

***

"What the fuck do you mean…Parker made bail?"

Trace glanced up from the pile of papers on his desk. He'd been at the office since 4 a.m. Sleep hadn't exactly been happening at home, not without Skye there, so he'd escaped to the office.

Alex Griffin shifted uneasily before him. "The judge granted bail. Fifty thousand dollars."

Trace surged to his feet. "And where did Parker get that kind of money?"

"Hell if I know."

Parker was out. On the streets. "Have you told Skye?" Trace demanded.

"I called her." Alex inclined his head. "I wasn't overly worried that she'd go out and beat the crap out of the guy, though. I figured that was more your department."

Right. "And that's why I warranted the private visit."

Alex's gaze dipped to Trace's hands. "I can't help but notice that nice bruising you got on your knuckles. You know, Parker never stopped spinning the story about *you* breaking into his place and assaulting him."

Trace forced himself to take slow, easy breaths. "You think I'm going after the guy again?"

"I think you needed a warning. Watch yourself, Weston. A jerk like Parker isn't worth the trouble you can find heading your way." Then Alex gave him a little salute and turned for the door.

But Trace wasn't done. "Why did you bring Skye to Parker's place yesterday?"

Alex glanced back at him. "Because she called me. She wanted to confront Parker, and she wanted me at her side."

Trace's heart raced faster.

"She was afraid of what might happen if you got to him before the cops did." One brow crooked up. "Seems she knows you pretty well."

She knew I was lying to her.

"Have you learned anything else about Ben Sharpe's death?" Trace asked the cop.

"Ah, you mean since I'm actually a *homicide* detective now?" Alex gave him a grim smile. "It wasn't a robbery gone wrong. The killer worked fast, and he worked efficiently. Obviously, it wasn't his first kill. First kills are sloppy, unorganized."

Trace waited.

"This kill was planned and deliberate. Someone wanted Sharpe out of the way." A low sigh. "At least Sharpe didn't suffer long."

"You're wrong," Trace said, glancing over at the photograph on his desk. "He suffered for years, but his pain is gone now."

He kept staring at that photograph, long after Alex left.

Alex had been watching him with a too-careful stare. *You think I might have killed Ben Sharpe?*

Did Alex realize that his alibi was bull?

Maybe…

His hand pushed into his pocket and he pulled out the dog tag. There should've been two tags. There always were.

He'd found one.

Where was the other?

Time to find out just where Parker had gotten this one.

***

Parker glanced over his shoulder as he hurried down the street. Were the cops still following him? He hoped that he'd given them the slip.

Bail. Freaking-A. He couldn't believe that someone had actually ponied up the money for him.

He rounded the corner, and saw his benefactor waiting on him. Parker smiled. "Sure am glad to be seein' you again."

"You told me that Trace Weston would never give up his dancer."

Parker blinked. The guy sounded angry. He took a quick step toward him. "Weston's been obsessed with her for years. No way will he ever walk out on her—"

"You tried to kill them the other night."

Parker's lips snapped closed.

"That wasn't part of the plan."

"I got pissed, okay? Seeing them on the TV, all the freakin' time. Why does he get so much attention?" While Parker had nothing. "Trace is trash. He should be the one in the gutter." Instead, Parker had to fight for every single thing that he had.

Life hadn't been easy. No damn way. After Trace's attack, it had been so tempting to just pop those little pills that would take his pain away. Again and again, he'd taken them.

Then he'd taken other things.

Trace Weston had risen, and Parker had fallen.

"You want him to lose everything, don't you?"

Parker nodded.

"And you'd do *anything* to see him fail?"

"Anything..." Parker immediately swore.

"Good."

His partner—because they were partners, right? Partners in the destruction of Trace Weston—stepped away from the wall. The sounds of the city were muted there, barely trickling past the thick brick walls of the alley.

Parker smiled at him. "What's our next step? What do we need to—"

A blade shoved into his chest.

A gurgle slipped from Parker's mouth.

"You need to die, and the world needs to start seeing Weston for the monster that he truly is."

Parker felt his blood spurt from his chest when the knife jerked back. "Y-you…"

The knife slashed toward his neck. Parker tried to lift up his hands, but it was too late.

He fell to the ground, unable to scream, as the blood poured from him.

"You should die happy, you know. *You* will help to destroy Weston."

Then he dropped something onto Parker. But Parker didn't feel the object connect with him. He didn't feel much of anything then.

***

The dancers collected their gear. They were soaked with sweat as they filed out of the studio.

Skye watched them go, smiling and waving even as the sweat dried on her skin. That had been an incredible class. Phenomenal.

I'm going to make it.

The smile wouldn't leave her face. She needed to call Trace and tell—

Her spine straightened. She would be calling Trace, but not yet.

"Looks like your students are happy."

She glanced toward the front door. Noah stood there, watching her carefully.

She'd had the door open, and unlocked, all morning.

She wasn't going to live her life under lock and key, not anymore. The studio had to be open during the day so that her students could come and go as they pleased.

"They are happy." She flashed her smile once again. "Even though I just worked their asses off." And her own. Her tights and her leotard clung tightly to her skin.

Noah's lips stretched in a half-grin. She saw a dimple flash in his left cheek. "Why do I get the feeling you could be a drill sergeant?"

"Because I can be." When it came to dance, that was her domain. She walked toward him, aware of a faint pull in her lower left calf. The leg had been doing so well lately, but she'd sure pushed hard during the morning class.

Don't limp.

The old mantra slipped through her mind.

His gaze slid over her body. Lingered a little too long on the expanse of her legs. She shook her head at him. "You know, I am engaged to Trace."

"Are you? I wasn't sure, not after that scene yesterday."

Her lips pursed. "I can be pissed and still love him."

He edged closer to her. "I envy him."

"I'm surprised you envy anyone." Were billionaire bad boys supposed to envy other people?

"He's always had you, hasn't he?" Noah glanced away from her. "Do you ever wonder what he'd be like if you weren't there?"

"He *hasn't* always had me." She picked up a towel. Swiped it over the sweat on the back of her neck. "We were together when we were teens, then apart for a decade. I don't think that counts as always." She looked up and found his gaze back on her.

His head was tilted to the right as he studied her. "My mistake."

Yes, it had been. She sucked in a deep breath. She was furious with Trace, but not with this guy. "I'm sorry, you've been nothing but kind to me, and you don't deserve for me to be snapping at you."

Surprise flickered over his face.

"What?" She forced a laugh. "I promise, I'm not usually a mega-bitch."

"I never thought you were."

Skye wondered just what he *had* thought. He opened his mouth as if he'd ask her a question, but then his lips clamped together.

Her hands tightened around the towel. "What is it?"

"You knew your parents, right? You didn't join the system until you were much older."

She nodded. *The system.* The trail of foster homes that she'd visited over the years.

Skye pulled on a loose sweatshirt and a pair of jogging shorts. She felt too…exposed talking to Noah in just her leotard and tights.

"I never knew my birth parents." Anger slipped through his voice. Pain. "I always wondered…where did I come from? Who the hell am I, really?"

Skye tossed aside the towel. She slid off her ballerina slippers and put on her tennis shoes. "When I was a little girl, my mother was amazing. She was the center of my life. We baked cookies. Read stories together at bedtime. Played hide and seek for hours." The memories were there, warming her heart as they always did. Skye tied her shoe laces and then straightened. "But then she…got sick."

"I'm sorry."

"Her mind wasn't right." Such simple words to describe the psychotic episodes that had started to plague her mother. "She killed my father one night. They were driving home. People saw them. She was at the wheel. He was trying to grab it, to take control, but she drove them straight to their deaths."

And they left me alone.

"Christ, I didn't—"

"I know my past. I know where I came from, and each day, I wonder…is that where I'm going? Will I wind up like her?"

He swore.

"Sometimes, not knowing isn't so bad." She said this with a certainty that came from her soul. "When you don't know, then you can think the best." She gazed into his eyes. "You were given up because your family wanted you to have a good life. They wanted you to thrive."

He looked down at his hands. "I did. For the first thirteen years, my adoptive parents were my world."

The first thirteen… "What happened?"

"They loved to sail." His breath blew out slowly. "Their boat sank when a storm came up. The winds were so strong. I tried to save them, but I just wasn't strong enough."

Her stomach clenched. *He'd watched them die.*

"I kept my mother up the longest. I told her that I wouldn't let go, no matter what happened." Pain darkened his eyes. "And I was still holding her, when the rescue teams finally came in. They pulled her from my arms, and I realized then that she'd been dead for hours."

She couldn't just stand there. Not with that much pain in his voice and his eyes. Skye stepped forward and wrapped her arms around him.

At first, Noah didn't move. He seemed stunned.

"I know, I probably stink to high heaven," she said, trying to lighten that pain, "but sometimes, we just need a touch." *To say that we're not alone.*

His arms lifted and closed around her. "I envy him," he said again. His voice rumbled against her. Then he let her go, and he headed for the door.

When Noah was gone, Skye glanced around her studio.

Noah was lost. She'd been that way once. So scared and alone. Then she'd found Trace.

Or had he found her?

Rolling her shoulders, she turned away from the wall of mirrors. Another class would be there in a few hours. She needed to get ready to go for them.

And she needed to figure out what she was going to say to Trace when she saw him again.

She hadn't slept the night before. Just been in the dark, in that narrow bed, thinking about him.

Her phone rang then, the soft tone instantly alerting her because it was *his* ring tone.

Skye hurried over to the desk she'd set up. She grabbed the phone. "Trace—"

"He needs you."

The voice was low and raspy. Definitely male. But…it didn't sound like Trace. "Who is this?"

"Don't you want to help him?"

Despite the sweat still drying on her, Skye felt chilled.

"The alley is just a few blocks away from you. Hurry. Go fast. Maybe you'll save him."

She didn't move. "Is this some kind of joke?"

"Look for the art. He had a killer view."

The call ended.

Skye pulled the phone from her ear. This was crazy. She immediately tried to call Trace back.

She just got his voice mail.

So she dialed his office. A direct line that should've connected her to him.

Voicemail.

What was going on?

Maybe you'll save him.

Skye grabbed for her bag. Her pepper spray waited inside.

She rushed from the studio. Glanced to the left, then the right.

There was an art shop just four blocks away. She took off running. Maybe this was just some ridiculous prank.

Or maybe Trace needed her.

Her feet pounded over the cement. She dodged some pedestrians, barely paused at the stop lights, then, finally, she could see the sign for the art shop.

And, just beyond the shop, she glimpsed the little alley on its right.

Her hand dove into her bag. Her fingers closed around the pepper spray. Armed, Skye crept into the alley.

The scent hit her. Old garbage. Rotten food. And—something else. Something that sent an instinctive shudder through her.

"Trace?" Skye called. "Trace, are you there?"

Her phone rang then, vibrating—and peeling *his* ring tone.

She jerked and her left hand drew the phone out of her pocket. All the while, she kept a steady hold on her pepper spray. Her fingers swiped across the phone's screen. "Listen," she snapped. "I'm here and—"

"What?" Trace voice. Distinct. "Skye, where are you?"

"The alley." Her words were quiet. She took another step forward.

She saw the foot then. A sneaker clad foot on the ground.

"What alley? Why are you there?" Trace demanded. Then, almost instantly, "*Skye, get out of there, now.*"

But it was too late.

Because she'd seen the foot, and she could also see the blood.

Bile rose in Skye's throat as she stared down at Parker. His shirt was soaked a dark red, and his neck bulged open, a gaping smile of red where his throat should've been.

He was dead. She knew he was dead, but Skye still found herself dropping to her knees beside him. "Parker?"

"*What?*" Trace's roar.

She dropped the phone. Skye leaned toward Parker. His eyes were closed. His face was ashen. And that terrible smell…

Gulping, she tried again, saying, "Parker?"

Then she saw that…*something*…was on his chest. Something small. Metal. Silver?

Right in the middle of all that blood.

Her eyes narrowed on the object.

It looked like a military dog tag. She inched closer and noticed the outline of the letters.

W-E-S-T-O-N.

"Skye?"

The shout came from the entrance of the alley.

Her hand swiped out. She grabbed the dog tag and shoved it into her pocket.

Footsteps thundered toward her.

She glanced up and met Alex's shocked stare. Two uniformed officers stood behind him.

Those officers had their guns drawn and pointed straight at her.

Skye lifted her hands, holding her palms up. "I found him like this."

Alex's gaze was on the dead man. "That's Parker Jacobs."

"I didn't kill him."

His eyes lifted to study her hands. Crap. Had she gotten blood on her fingers when she snatched up that dog tag? "I-I saw him and tried to help."

"There's no helping the dead."

No, there wasn't.

Maybe he isn't the one I was sent to help.

Skye rose, slowly. "I'm not a threat."

Alex frowned.

"Th-the guns," she said.

He looked back. Swore. "Drop the weapons!" Alex ordered, his voice snapping with command. "And call the ME. We're gonna need the wagon for this one."

He advanced toward her. Skye realized that she'd dropped her bag and her phone. They were still on the ground near the body.

And, of course, her phone would begin to vibrate and ring right at that exact moment.

An image of Trace filled the phone's screen.

CHAPTER NINE

Police cruisers blocked the mouth of the alley. Trace jumped from his vehicle and rushed forward, but a uniformed cop held up a hand, blocking his way. "Sorry, sir, but you need to step back."

What he needed was to find out what the hell was happening.

As if on cue, a dark van pulled up behind him. The side of the van held two simple words written in garish yellow: *County Coroner.*

Then he saw her. Trace caught a glimpse of Skye's dark hair as she bent near the side of a patrol car. She was climbing into the back seat of that cruiser.

Being arrested?

He lunged toward her. "Skye!"

Her head turned at his call, and the man next to her straightened. Trace wasn't particularly surprised to see Alex Griffin there.

"What happened?" Trace demanded. He wanted to reach for Skye and pull her into his arms, but after the scene last night, he didn't know how she'd react to his touch. To him.

"I found Parker's body." Her voice was low.

His heart wouldn't slow down.

"He'd been stabbed. And his throat was slit."

And she'd seen that.

He glanced away from her too pale face and found Alex watching him. The suspicion was obvious in the man's gaze.

"I just got here," Trace growled at him. "Go talk to your uniforms. They *saw* me arrive."

Because he'd raced like hell across town. When Skye's phone had cut out, and she hadn't answered his calls back, Trace had panicked.

"Oh, don't worry, I'll definitely be talking to the uniforms." Alex focused his attention back on Skye. "I still don't understand why you were in that alley."

She licked her lips. Cut her gaze away from Alex. Looked at Trace. Then back to the cop.

A sign she's lying.

"I was taking a break between my classes. I-I wanted some air so I went for a walk," Skye said.

"Into an alley?" The detective was obviously doubting her answer. *He knows that she's lying, too.*

"I was looking at the art in the window." She pointed to the shop on the corner. "Then I — I thought I heard someone calling for help in the alley, so I went-"

"Men who've had their throats slit don't usually call for help," Alex pointed out, voice flat.

She jerked, but her gaze kept meeting the cop's. "Then I guess I imagined the voice."

"I guess you did," Alex muttered.

No way. Screw this. Trace stepped forward. He caught Skye's hand. Threaded his fingers through hers. Together, they faced the cop.

"A slit throat. A knife wound directly to the heart. This sure does seem familiar." Alex's brows furrowed. "Is it seeming familiar to you, too, Weston?"

Sharpe's murder. "Yeah, it's familiar." So why bullshit when they could cut right to the chase? "Two similar kills in the same city. Looks like you've got someone hunting here, Detective."

"Yes, I do."

Trace shifted his gaze to Skye. "But it's not her, and you know it."

"You're so sure?"

Yes, he was. "Wounds like you're describing…I know what they can do." Too well. "When Parker's throat was cut, there would have been spray. The blood would have gone straight toward the attacker. Gotten on the skin. The clothes." He tightened his hold on Skye. "She doesn't have a drop of blood on her."

"She did…Skye had a few drops on her fingers."

"Because I tried to help him!" Skye said. "I *told* you that already!"

"You knew he was dead from the first glance, Skye." Alex fired back at her. "Doesn't make sense to save the dead."

"It does if you're desperate."

Alex slapped his hand against the top of patrol car. "You *hated* the man. You think I don't know that? After what he did? Look, when I found out, I wanted to beat his ass, too. But you know what you *don't* do? You don't try to save the man who nearly raped you. The man tried to run you down and kill you. No one does that shit so *stop lying to me*."

"That's enough," Trace told the detective, his voice hard and grim. "You don't talk to her like that. No one does." And sure as hell not in front of him. "Skye's answered your questions. You can see clearly that there is no arterial blood spray on her—"

Alex's brows shot up.

"*She didn't kill him.* Now you can back off. Any other questions can be handled through my attorney, Craig Guthrie."

"I never thought she'd killed him," Alex snapped back. "The guy's head was nearly severed, and she sure doesn't look like she has the strength to do that. But you…" Now his stare swept over Trace. "I think it would be easy for you to do something like that. Especially if rage was pumping through you. Making you crazy."

"We should leave," Skye said. She shifted from her right foot to her left.

"You killed for her once before, right, Weston?" Alex was still pushing. *Pushing.* "Did you do it again? You were furious when I told you that Parker had made bail—"

Hell, yes, he had been. "Because he could've come after Skye again!"

"*Trace.*" Skye's voice was urgent.

"And you had to stop him, right? Had to make sure that he never had the chance to get at her again."

Trace lifted his hands, and Skye's hand rose with him because he wasn't loosening his hold on her. "Do you see blood on me?"

"Maybe you were out changing. *That's* why I didn't find you at the crime scene."

"Good luck proving that."

The body was loaded into the back of the coroner's van. Covered in a black bag, zipped up, then shoved in the rear of the vehicle.

Probably not the ending that Parker had expected.

"How'd you know to come down to this alley?" Alex demanded. Suspicion filled his gaze. "If you're such an innocent guy, Weston."

"I was looking for Skye. When I got to the street, it was rather damn hard to miss the flashing lights."

Alex advanced until he and Trace nearly stood nose to nose. "You think I don't know what you are?" Alex whispered.

"I think you have no clue." The noise around Trace dimmed. "And believe me, you don't want to push me."

"I can see right through the veneer you wear. You're a killer. Through and through."

Trace smiled.

"*Enough!*" Skye demanded. "Just...*stop!*" Then she shoved between them. "If you want me to come down to the station and answer more questions, Alex, I will—"

"*With* our attorney," Trace threw in.

"He's not our attorney. He's yours. And I don't have anything to hide." Her breath heaved out. "Neither does Trace. He wasn't even here."

"So where was he?" Alex queried. "I mean, I'm sure he has an alibi. Just like last time, right?"

Not exactly. "I was in my office. Working."

"And someone can verify that?"

"I'm sure my assistant, Sara, can." Like she'd ever go against anything he said. Sara owed him.

"Right. Your assistant." Alex's lips twisted.

"I-I have a class to teach." Skye suddenly blurted. "I have to go. It starts at two."

Now that seemed to surprise Alex. "Skye, you can't—"

"I'm not just going to leave my students." She was adamant. "It's four blocks away. If you need me, you know where to find me." Then she marched away from the detective, and she kept her grip on Trace, pulling him with her.

Alex's glare followed them.

A crowd had gathered to watch the scene. Curious folks who were whispering about the murder that had happened so close to them. There were a lot of murders in that city each year—too many—but when the crime was fresh, the fear struck everyone the strongest.

Skye was silent as they walked down the street. Trace noticed that she had her left hand shoved into the pocket of her sweatshirt. Her right hand held his. But, after a few more feet, she pulled away from him.

"Skye," he began.

"Not here."

Trace had to strain to hear her words.

"Not yet," Skye added.

He frowned at that response.

Then they were back at her studio. A few dancers were waiting outside, their gear bags at their feet. Skye pasted on a smile for them, welcoming each person.

She unlocked the door. Waved them inside.

When the dancers slipped in to begin their stretches, Skye turned back to him. She seemed to brace herself in the doorway. Her eyes searched his. "You're glad he's dead."

He saw no point in lying about that. "I'm sorry you found him. I wish you'd never seen him that way."

A laugh—no, a sob?—trembled from her lips. "That's not what you're supposed to say. He was butchered in that alley and thrown away."

He braced his hand up on the door frame. "Tell me the truth, baby. Aren't *you* glad he's dead?"

The little bit of color in her cheeks bleached away.

Trace tensed. "Skye…"

"I-I have to take care of my class."

"I'll wait for you." Because she looked so fragile.

"No." Her immediate denial. "I-I'll come to you when I finish today. We need to talk."

"You found a dead body. Do you really think I'm just going to walk away and leave you on your own?" When it looked like she could shatter any minute?

"I want you to walk away now, Trace. I'll come to you."

Something was off. "Why were you in that alley?"

She glanced over his shoulder. He didn't even need to turn his head in order to see the uniform who waited on the other side of the street. Trace had been aware of the guy following them from the crime scene. No doubt, on Alex's orders. "I went for a walk," she said, her voice wooden.

Lie.

"I'll come to you." Then she left him as she went inside her studio.

Trace turned around slowly. His eyes locked with the cop's.

First, Sharpe had been killed.

Now Parker.

Who would be next?

I won't risk her. With his eyes on the cop, Trace pulled out his phone. Two seconds later, Reese was on the line. "I need you to guard Skye."

She'd be furious when she found out what he'd done, but she'd be *alive.*

***

Skye had made it through the day. Her muscles ached, her stomach was tied in knots, and she was limping.

For the first time in ages, that damn limp couldn't be controlled.

She pulled on her sweatshirt and shorts. Grabbed her bag. And when she went outside, Skye wasn't even mildly surprised to find Reese waiting on her. After what had happened, she'd known Trace would be back to his old routine.

Reese focused on her face. "Not gonna yell at me for doing my job, are you?"

"Too tired to yell. Well, at you, anyway."

His lips hitched up into a half-smile.

"Take me to him," Skye said as she climbed into the back of the car.

Reese nodded and closed the door behind her.

When the car eased down the street, her gaze found the alley and the line of bright, yellow police tape that sealed it off. She couldn't get the sight of Parker's body out of her mind. His neck…*I will never forget that image.* She could still smell the blood, too. Blood and garbage and death.

She'd hated Parker.

But had the man deserved to die like that? Did anyone?

Her hands tightened on her bag. Life wasn't supposed to be like this. She wasn't supposed to be so afraid.

And she sure wasn't supposed to fear the man she loved.

All too soon, they were pulling up to the curb. She didn't wait for Reese to come back to her. Skye jumped out of the car. Henry was waiting at the door. He frowned at her. "Ms. Sullivan, are you all right?"

She was far from that. "I'm fine." She didn't slow down because she didn't want Henry looking too closely at her.

When the private elevator doors closed behind her, Skye exhaled in relief. Goosebumps covered her whole body.

Parker's head had nearly been severed from his body.

Was that what it had been like for Sharpe, too? Had that poor man been attacked so viciously?

Only a monster would kill like that.

The elevator stopped its ascent. Skye crept out and made her way inside the penthouse.

The door squeaked open.

Trace sat on the couch, waiting. He was leaning forward, his hands between his knees.

His eyes locked on her.

For an instant, she thought about turning and running.

"Skye?"

She shut the door behind her.

He didn't move, but he watched her with the gaze of a predator. Part of her wondered if he was about to pounce.

"I realized today…" She took a step toward him. "I would do anything for you."

"You *know* I would do—"

"You would never hurt me. I'm certain of that. Not physically, anyway."

He jerked as if she'd struck him.

"But there are other ways to hurt," she whispered. Another step brought her closer to him. Her fingers were tight on the straps of her bag.

"It's the guards," he said, swallowing. She heard the faint click of his throat. His hair was tousled, as if he'd plunged his fingers through it over and over again. "I've told you about my enemies…"

He hadn't told her enough. "Sharpe was here. He threatened me."

She remembered that instant so clearly. She couldn't forget how Trace had reacted. *Are you threatening her?* She glanced to the left. Trace had put his forearm under the man's throat. Right there. In that exact spot.

She wet her lips. "And Parker tried to kill us both." Her gaze turned back to him. "Both of those men…they threatened me, and they wound up dead."

His eyes widened. "You think I killed them?"

"I think you killed to protect me before." But this…*this wasn't the same.* "But Sharpe—he never so much as touched me. He needed help, Trace. He needed—"

Trace shot to his feet. "Why haven't you asked me if I killed them?"

Her fingers shook, fumbled, and dove into the bag. She found what she needed and she lifted the object, her hand a fist around it. "I found this on top of Parker's body."

She dropped the dog tag onto the end table.

"Your name, Trace. Your tag."

"*Fuck.*"

She felt the same way.

He lifted his hands, as if he'd touch her, but then he hesitated. "They're not my kills."

She studied his eyes, searching desperately. She'd been able to see his lie before, but this time, Sky just wasn't sure. *He's too good at hiding from everyone, even me.* "I can't tell when you're lying or when you're telling the truth. There should be some sign, right? I should know?"

"*They're not.*"

"You lied about your alibi at the time of Sharpe's murder."

"I told you, I was back here. You were sleeping."

"And…I tried to call you before I found Parker's body, but you didn't answer me. Not on your cell, not on your office's private line."

His jaw hardened.

"You weren't in your office, Trace." That had been another lie.

"I wasn't in the alley killing Parker!"

Her gaze fell to the dog tag. "I didn't hesitate. When I saw that on him, right in the middle of all that blood, I took it." Her arms wrapped around her stomach. "What does that make me?"

The violent image was there again, rising fast in her mind. Parker's head, sagging back against the dirty ground. The blood thick around him. A twisted smile where his neck should have been.

And I touched him. I took the tag from the hole above his heart.

She squeezed her eyes shut, but the image wouldn't fade. Nausea built, and she tried to fight it. Again and again and again.

She couldn't.

Skye ran for the bathroom. Trace called her name, but she slammed the door shut behind her.

***

Trace stood in front of the bathroom door. "Skye?" He jiggled the knob. She'd locked it. "Baby, let me help you."

"Go away." Her voice was soft.

"I want to help you." Trace felt as if he were tearing apart.

"Don't, Trace. *Don't.*"

He backed away. Forced his gaze off the door.

The damn dog tag waited. Trace grabbed it, smoothing his fingers over the letters of his name. This tag should've been in an icy grave.

Maybe I should've been in that grave with it.

The tag wasn't buried, and neither was his past.

He heard the rush of running water. His shoulders tensed. Skye would be coming back.

I have to tell her.

His fingers were trembling. That wasn't supposed to happen. He was always rock-steady. Never hesitating.

He'd been dead-on in battle. In the boardroom.

His business was secrets. Protecting them. Exploiting them.

He'd kept his own secrets so well over the years. But Trace knew with utter certainty that if he didn't tell Skye everything, he would lose her.

The dog tag was a message.

The bathroom door opened. Light spilled behind Skye. "I wash and I wash my hands," she said, sounding a little lost. Not at all like Skye. "But I just can't seem to get all the blood off."

He dropped the tag. Went straight to her. He caught her soft hands in his. "There's no blood on you, baby."

Her head tilted back. Her hair had come loose from the knot at the base of her neck. "If it's on yours, then it's on mine. What touches you..." Her smile broke his heart. "It touches me, too."

I realized today...I would do anything for you.

The smile didn't reach her eyes. "I thought you'd killed Parker, and do you know what my first instinct was? To protect you."

"I *didn't* kill him."

"What does that say about me? If I'd steal evidence from a dead man's body, then what else would I do for you?"

Everything.

The answer was there, stark and chilling between them.

"I can't live like this." Grim finality had entered her voice. "You were right. I-I should've seen someone after the attack. My mind's jumbled. The nightmares won't stop, and I'm not even sure who I am anymore."

"I know who you are." The only woman he'd ever loved.

She pulled away from him. "I can't do this."

No, no, she *had* to do this. But she was walking away from him.

"I'm very good at killing, Skye." Those weren't the words he'd meant to say. They sure as hell weren't words that were going to reassure her. "The military taught me how to be good. How to get close to the enemy. How to take out my prey swiftly and silently. My main job was infiltration. Infiltration and hostage rescue."

Rescue of military personnel who'd been taken by the enemy. Rescue of dignitaries. Of rich corporate CEOs who'd been taken because they'd been at the wrong place. Because they'd trusted the wrong men.

Some of those rescued men had been grateful. They'd remembered him when he left the military. They'd jumped at the chance to use Weston Securities for their corporations.

He'd kept their secrets.

But he was spilling his own.

"I saved lives, but I took lives, too. The lives of the enemy, the captors who'd taken the hostages." *Tell her.* "And the lives of-of those on my team who turned against us."

Very slowly, she faced him again.

He hated the strain on her face. His past had done this to her. "I thought it was better if you didn't know." He looked at his hands. "I still have the blood here, and you know the *only* time I ever feel clean? It's when I'm touching you. You make me feel like I can be someone else." And not just the lie that he presented to the world.

"You're telling me this *now?*"

"You need to know."

She shook her head, hard, and the last of her hair broke free from the knot, tumbling around her shoulders. "First I get that crazy phone call. I-I thought it had to be Reese, wanting me to help you, and then—"

He zeroed right in on that. "What phone call?"

"I race to that alley. I find him—"

"*What phone call?*" Trace snarled.

She stumbled back a step.

"Skye." He tried to soften the harshness of his tone. He failed. "Please. What phone call?"

"Your number. It was your ring. Your number on the caller ID. But the voice didn't sound like you."

Fear was a living monster inside of Trace.

"He told me to go to that alley. That you needed me. That I had to help."

"And you went?" Claws ripped at his insides.

"I tried to call you back first. But I couldn't get you, and I was so afraid something had happened. I knew Parker was out—"

I knew I'd do anything for you.

"So I ran to the alley." A sad shrug of her shoulders. "And I stole evidence."

"Give me your phone."

She blinked at him.

Trace didn't wait for her to comply. He rushed to her discarded bag. He searched fast and yanked out the phone.

He scanned through her received calls list. Saw his name. His number. "I didn't call you then."

"Reese—"

"Reese was visiting his girlfriend earlier today. They have a standing lunch date each week."

She blinked. "I didn't—"

"He hacked into my account." Smart SOB. "And he called you." She could have walked straight into a slaughter. *Her own.* Trace wouldn't have been able to do damn thing to save her.

"Who?" Skye was beside him now. "Who did this?"

Tell her everything.

There would be no going back now. "After a while, after we'd served our tours, the team knew we were good at what we did. Very damn good. We started our own rescue service. That's what Weston Securities was, in the beginning." And it still was, when the situation demanded it. "I tried to get Reese to join me back then, because he'd served with us, but he wanted to come home. He'd said that he'd had his fill of blood and death."

Smart bastard. Reese hadn't joined them, but later Trace had told his friend all about the nightmare that had destroyed the team.

Trace continued, because there was no stopping now. "So when the team started, there were five of us. Noah, Drake, Ben, Tucker, and me."

Her shoulder brushed against his. "Tucker?"

"Tucker Hawk." Tucker had always seemed to be the most easy-going of the group. The one who'd laughed the easiest. Loved the easiest. "Tucker had a girl. Anna Jean. She'd just finished a tour with the Air Force, and she wanted to join our team. She could fly like a dream, so I knew she'd be useful." Back then, he'd always thought in terms of usefulness. "But Anna had other plans. On our last run together, she decided she could get more money by playing both sides. She set us up, telling the enemy our extraction plans. Telling them our weaknesses. Telling them *everything*."

"But you made it out. You survived."

"Ben was hit hard. Drake...Drake was captured. Tortured. I carried Ben out and left him at the chopper with Noah. Then Tucker and I fought like hell to get Drake out." The gunfire had blasted. A continuous thunder that shook his world.

"We killed every man between us and Drake." He couldn't look at her as he revealed this. "Blood soaked me, and I just wanted to get out of there. I wanted to get home again." His eyes closed. "I wanted you."

She twined her fingers with him.

"We got to Drake. Pulled him out. We were almost home free, then Anna Jean appeared. She'd slipped up behind Drake, and she was about to shoot him." There'd been a knife in Drake's hands. His only weapon.

"Drake spun to attack. He stabbed her, and she fell back." But they just hadn't counted on one thing... "You can know some people are evil. You can know that they've betrayed you, but if you love them, if you really fucking love them beyond reason, then, sometimes, I don't think you care about what they've done. You only see them. Nothing else."

That was the way it had been for Tucker.

"He screamed," Trace recalled. "When Drake's knife went into her chest, Tucker cried out her name. He blasted two bullets into Drake, and Tucker ran for Anna Jean." That anguished scream had frozen them all.

Tucker had known than Anna Jean betrayed them.

He hadn't cared.

She'd been what mattered most to him, and when he lost her... "He broke right before my eyes," Trace said. Tucker had fought, shot, attacked — and gotten to Anna Jean on that snow covered field.

They'd been in Russia. So far from home. Cold. *Frozen.* The white snow had been stained red.

Skye watched him with her big, solemn stare. He didn't want to see himself reflected in that stare. Because the part that was coming...

Man up and tell her everything. "Drake needed medical attention. We had to get out of there, but Tucker wasn't just going to let him walk away, not after what he'd done to Anna Jean."

"But he was protecting himself—"

"It didn't matter. Anna Jean died in Tucker's arms, and the man he'd been before vanished. He attacked Drake. Tucker shattered Drake's wrist and took Drake's knife. Then Tucker went in for the kill."

Trace had shouted then. Yelled for Tucker to stop. "I could've taken a shot at them, but they were so close. Tucker and Drake were fighting, rolling around in the snow. So I ran forward. I grabbed Tucker, and I pulled him off Drake."

Her gaze seemed to see straight into Trace's soul. *You won't like the darkness there, baby.* "Tucker had his knife. I had my gun. I *told* him to stand down. To get his control back."

Even as he'd said the words, Trace had known that wouldn't happen. *If I'd lost Skye, I would've reacted the same way.* "She was everything to him, and Anna Jean was dead at his feet." The blood had spread beneath her in that snow, looking like bloody angel wings.

She hadn't been an angel.

Tucker hadn't cared.

"He said Drake had to die. Tucker lunged at me. He *wouldn't* stop." *Fuck, fuck, fuck.*

The memories were so sharp.

Tucker, stand the hell down! We're your friends!

But Tucker had stared him straight in the eyes. *You're dead men. Every single one of you. You did this — you could've brought her in alive. You. Did. This!*

"The last time he came at me, I fired." Close-range, one shot right to the chest. "He grabbed my dog tags, and when he fell back, they were still in his hands."

"Trace…"

"We didn't even get to bring his body home. Anna Jean's reinforcements arrived. Blasting from the east. I could've carried Tucker — he was still alive then — or I could've gotten Drake out of there. *I* made the choice."

Her fingers curled around his. "Would Tucker have been able to survive his wounds?"

That was the same damn thing he'd asked himself that day. And every day that followed. "I thought I'd hit his heart." He *should* have hit it. That close… "But there wasn't exactly time to stand there and do an exam. I grabbed Drake. Threw him over my shoulder, and I dodged fire as I ran. Noah brought the chopper in because without an aerial extraction, we were dead." He stared down at their hands. His looked big, rough.

Hers were so delicate.

"Heavy snow started falling. In that part of Russia, the snow can drop from the sky for days. It can bury everything and everyone in its path. I thought…I thought the snow became their graves." After Ben and Drake had been secured and patched up, he'd gone back to try and retrieve the bodies, but it had been hopeless. He'd searched, nearly getting hypothermia, but there had been nothing to find.

"Why didn't you tell me this sooner?"

Trace knew his laughter held a bitter edge. "Why didn't I tell you that I shot my best friend and left him to die in the middle of a snowstorm? Maybe because I didn't want you thinking I was a cold-blooded killer."

She flinched. Her hands pulled from his.

Oh, right. "But then, you do think that now, don't you? So confessing to my kill in the past hardly matters at this point."

Trace turned away from her and paced toward the window. The glittering lights of the city stared back at him. At least it wasn't snowing. He hated the snow. Every time he saw it, he thought of blood.

"Tucker is the one who attacked," Skye said, voice soft. She hadn't followed him to the window. "You were protecting yourself. Your other teammates."

The lights were so bright. "I understood, that's the worst part. I knew exactly how he felt. He loved her so much that nothing else mattered, and without her, there was no control for him. He was desperate, hurting, *and I left him there*."

Only the ghosts from his past had come back to wreck his life. "Tucker liked the up-close attacks. They were his specialty." His...and Trace's. "He could get close to anyone without his prey ever knowing. Slip right up and slip his knife into his enemy's heart."

He heard her sharply indrawn breath.

"A-a knife to the heart?" Skye asked. "Just like—"

"Like Sharpe and Parker? Yes." And there was more. "Slicing the throat is a personal way to kill. We saw attacks like that during our time together. When you wanted to send a message, when you wanted to be sure that your prey—and their family—didn't talk, the killers slit their victims' throats."

In the glass, he saw her reflection. Skye walked—very tentatively—toward him. "What are you saying?"

"I'm saying that my dog tags should've still been in a grave outside of Siberia. But I found one in Parker's apartment, and you found the other on his dead body. When it comes to messages, I think that's pretty clear." He faced her. "Maybe I didn't leave a dead man out there after all. Maybe Tucker survived, and now he's come back to make sure that I suffer for what I did to him."

"You think...you believe he's going to kill you?"

His hand lifted, and he stroked her cheek. Such smooth, silken skin. "I told you that I understood how he felt."

She nodded.

"Killing me would be too easy. Death won't be quick for me. He'll want me to suffer." He and Tucker had been too alike, in many ways. "At the end, he made me a promise."

"What sort of promise?"

"He said, 'You'll know...you'll lose...all.'" And Trace knew exactly what Tucker meant. Tucker had wanted Trace to feel the same agony that he experienced.

"H-how will he do that?"

Trace stared back at her, and he forced himself to tell her the terrifying truth, "By hurting you."

CHAPTER TEN

Alex Griffin shone his flashlight to the left. Then to the right. He was in another alley. One that reeked of piss and garbage.

He had a small team of uniforms with him. Grumbling rookies who weren't happy to be on the backstreets of Chicago searching through dumpsters.

Like he gave a damn if they were happy or not.

Trace Weston hadn't needed to carry on about the arterial spray from Parker Jacobs. Alex had seen the splash of blood before at crime scenes. He knew how death worked. His job gave him an up-close and personal look at death each day.

Even before Weston had spoken, Alex knew that Parker's killer would've been hit by the spray of blood.

And I also knew that the killer would need to ditch his clothes.

Because when you walked around, covered in blood, peopled tended to notice.

"He wouldn't have gone back to the main street, not right after the kill," Alex said.

The uniform closest to him, Sean Coleman, gave a quick nod. "So he ran away through the alleys."

"I don't think it was a panicked run." Alex stopped next to another big, green dumpster. "I think he planned to kill Parker all along, and I think he had back-up clothes waiting." The better to blend in with everyone else.

Sean raised his brows and glanced at the dumpster. "Hell, another one."

"Up and in," Alex told him, shining the light.

Sean hefted himself into the dumpster. "It's like finding a microscopic needle in a—" Sean broke off.

Alex grabbed the side of the dumpster. "What is it?"

Sean rose. His gloved hands held a shirt, and when Alex's light hit that shirt—*blood.* "I've got you," Alex whispered. That shirt was his key. The techs could scan it for DNA, for evidence...*this was it.*

He was going to stop the killer. No more victims would fall on Alex's watch.

***

The shower water thundered down on Skye. After Trace's confession, she hadn't exactly been sure what to say.

She'd survived the attack of one maniac before. Now she was supposed to just wait, knowing that some other crazy jerk wanted to come after her?

Sometimes, life could just be a hard kick in the face.

You think you're happy. You think you have a chance...

And then the chance is ripped right from your hands.

She leaned forward, putting her face under the spray. All of the blood was gone now. It should be. She'd scrubbed herself until her skin felt raw.

Tendrils of steam floated in the air around her. The glass that surrounded the walk-in shower had completely fogged over.

She put her hand on the glass. It was hard. Cool.

The water pounded down.

Her fingers swiped over the glass. She cleared a small section so that she could see—and, through that glass, Skye saw Trace.

Standing on the other side. Watching her.

She opened the door. The shower had been so loud that she hadn't heard him come inside the bathroom.

He was still dressed. In his too expensive designer pants and the shirt that she knew must've been cut just for him.

The faint lines on his face were deeper. The shadows under his eyes were darker.

"Why were you just standing there?" Skye asked him. She didn't try to cover her nudity.

"I wasn't sure you wanted me with you."

Ah, that was the part he just didn't seem to get. "I always want you." That was the problem. She lifted her hand to him, inviting him closer.

He took a fast step forward, then stilled. "I don't want any more secrets. If you stay with me, I'll tell you everything."

"Don't make a promise you can't keep."

"I'll keep it. I swear."

She kept her hand up. "Tell me that you didn't kill Parker." Skye hadn't asked for the words before because she'd been afraid of his answer. But now...

"I didn't kill Parker."

Her lips trembled, then curved. "I need you."

Skye thought he would strip before he joined her. The clothes had to be worth a small fortune but—

Trace didn't strip.

He came straight into the shower, the water—pumping from two shower heads—poured down on them. His mouth took hers. The kiss was deep and hard. Consuming.

Exactly what she wanted.

Her hands closed around his shoulders. The water soaked his shirt, making the fabric cling to him. Her bare breasts pressed against his shirt-front, her nipples pebbling.

Trace.

Only Trace.

He was the one man who'd always been able to get past her defenses. The one man who could make her want and need more than anyone else.

His fingers slid down to her waist and he lifted her up against the marble wall of the shower. His mouth didn't leave hers. His tongue thrust past her lips, and Skye arched toward him. In that moment, she was greedy and desperate for all that he'd give to her.

He was aroused. Trace's thick cock pushed against the front of his pants, and she felt the ridge against her. She wanted that ridge *in* her.

Her hands shoved between them. She unhooked his belt. Fumbled enough to get the button and zipper undone, and then that thick, strong cock spilled out.

Two seconds later, his cock was just where she wanted it to be. Driving deep inside of her.

She cried out when he filled her because it felt so good. He thrust deep, as far as he could go. His hips pinned her, her legs clasped his hips, and his hands caught hers.

He pushed her hands back against the marble. Lifted them up high and held her prisoner while he thrust.

The pleasure built. She clamped down her inner muscles, holding him as tightly as she could. Faster, faster, harder, deeper…she was chanting and she didn't care.

Trace was fucking her, and this moment — *this* — was what she needed to banish the hell around them.

She came with a fury, exploding hard and fast as the orgasm rocketed through her. It took her breath. Made the world grow dim for an instant, and she reveled in it.

He came right after her. Another hard thrust, then he was pumping within her. He kissed her while he came, and Skye was sure that she could taste his pleasure.

There was no room for doubt. It was just her. Just him.

Slowly, her feet slid from his hips and she —

Laughter escaped Skye. The water was still just as warm. Jetting down just as powerfully. And… "You left your shoes on."

He smiled down at her. One of his real, rare smiles. The kind that made the dark, cold places inside of her feel a little bit warmer.

"I was afraid that if I stopped to take them off, you'd change your mind."

His words, so gruff, had her pressing a fast kiss to his lips.

"You didn't run when I confessed. You believed in me," Trace rasped the words against her lips. "I had to have you."

And she'd needed him the same way.

He turned off the spray of water. Tossed away his soaked clothes. Ditched the Italian shoes.

He'd been wearing his shoes!

Then he wrapped her in a towel. So carefully. They went into his bedroom. *Their* bedroom. The darkness surrounded them as they slid into the bed. She put her fingers over his heart, reassured by the steady beat. Then her fingers trailed to the right, just a few inches. To the thick, red scar that marked his chest.

Trace had been shot by the bastard who'd abducted her. Skye tried not to think about what could have happened if Mitch Loxley had been a better shot.

I can't think about that. She bent and put her head over his heart, needing to hear that strong beat.

His fingers brushed back her wet hair. "You are the most important person in my life." His words rumbled beneath her. "I will do anything it takes in order to keep you safe."

She squeezed her eyes shut because that *anything* – it was what she feared most.

***

Skye was in the basement once again. Handcuffed to the pole that wouldn't move. She'd screamed and she'd screamed, but no one had come to save her.

She knew that she was going to die in that pit.

"Trace!" His name was a desperate cry from her. He would be the last person that she thought of. The last man that she—

"Why do you call for him?" The voice drifted from the darkness. "He's the reason you're here."

She shook her head and yanked harder on the cuffs.

"You're hurting, you're *dying* for him."

"Let me go!" Skye begged. "Just let me—"

Then she saw the glinting flash of a blade. The knife slashed down toward her chest.

Skye screamed.

***

"It's okay," Trace said, his arms strong and warm around her. "I've got you."

Her breath expelled in heaving pants. Her gaze flew around the room. Sunlight slipped through the curtains.

"The dreams will stop," he said, as his fingers stroked reassuringly down her arm. "One day, the memories will fade."

Only this hadn't been her usual bad dream. A new, terrifying twist had slipped into her nightmare.

"Your memories haven't faded any," she told him, too aware of the drying tears on her cheeks. "How long has it been since you watched Anna Jean die?"

"Five years."

She had *that* to look forward to? Years of nightmares and memories that haunted her? Great.

But at least I'm alive.

Yet that time period also gave her pause. She turned in his arms and stared up at him. "If Tucker really survived, then don't you think he would've come after you by now?"

A dark growth of stubble lined his hard job. "Sharpe was right when he said that you were my weakness. The whole world knows how I feel about you." He brought her hand to his lips. Lightly kissed her ring finger.

"Because you killed to keep me alive," she whispered.

"I kept your picture with me back then, just like I told you. Tucker saw it. All of my teammates did. So did my enemies." His fingers kept stroking her. "Once I fell behind enemy lines on a retrieval mission that went south, and I was tortured for hours."

She *hated* the thought of him in such pain.

"They were good, I'll give them that. Never left a sign on me. But then, that's what water boarding is all about, right? Destruction on the inside."

She'd never realized he was in such danger. He'd been in the military, she'd worried for him but—*I never knew this*.

Maybe she hadn't let herself think the worst.

"I made a mistake by having your picture with me. My captors took it. Taunted me. Told me that they'd find you. Rape you. Kill you." His voice was so wooden that he chilled her. "But they were the ones to die. Most of 'em, anyway. A few slipped away. I got out, thanks to Noah and Tucker. And when I was free, Tucker gave your photo back to me." His eyes blazed down at her. "He knew, even then, how much you meant."

She hadn't known.

"But when I came back to the U.S., I didn't go to you."

"You just sent guards instead."

He nodded. "They'd threatened to hurt you. They knew what type of missions I'd completed. I'd attacked their allies before. The men who escaped could've come after you. They could've told others...I just couldn't risk anything happening to you."

Except he'd missed one huge basic step. She lifted her hand and cupped his jaw. She loved the slightly rough feel of his stubble against her palm. "Next time, tell me. We're partners, so that means you can't leave me in the dark."

He nodded. "If I'd...if I'd come to you then, what would you have done?" But then he shook his head, as if he regretted the question. "You were with the choreographer then, so you wouldn't—"

The choreographer. Her jaw dropped. "You knew exactly when I was sleeping with Robert?"

"Yeah, I knew about the Brit." Anger hummed in his voice and his face had tightened.

Well, hell. Back when they'd been trying to figure out who might have been stalking her, Trace had demanded a list of her lovers. "Why did you want me to tell you about my lovers if you already knew them all?"

"Because I *didn't* know them all." Ah, definite anger vibrated in his voice. "And it wasn't like I wanted to hear you talk about those assholes. I'd rather never hear about them again if I had the choice."

"There's no need to hear about them." She pressed an open-mouthed kiss to that delectable stubble. "Because I certainly don't want to hear about any of your ex's." Quickly, Skye rolled away from him and hopped from the bed. "Now come on, we need to—"

"I told you before, they were all you." He was looking straight at her. "In the dark, that's all they were. And come dawn, I couldn't stand to be with them any longer because the light showed that *they weren't you.*" His lips twisted. "I was seventeen, and you destroyed me for everyone else."

She'd felt that way before...destroyed. Skye grabbed for her robe and belted it quickly. "I'm starving. Let's go get some breakfast together."

"I'll call the chef," Trace said at once. "I'll have him prepare anything you want."

There he was — being too eager. When she'd been held captive, Skye had been starved for days. Trace was still overcompensating for that, seeming to be there, every instant when she so much as suggested hunger. They both needed to get past that. "I thought we'd try baking breakfast together. You know, the way most couples do."

For an instant, an expression of absolute horror slipped over his face. "You want me to cook?"

"Don't worry, I'm sure we'll burn the eggs together just fine." She had to laugh because the horrified expression on his face was just so *not Trace*. Then Skye hurried from the room, her heart feeling lighter. In that moment, she had hope for them.

She didn't necessarily have hope for the eggs.

Her feet thudded as she hurried down the hallway, and in moments, she was in Trace's crazy, glorious kitchen. Normally, his chef Collins would come up and work his magic.

Today wasn't about working magic. It was just about the two of them.

She grabbed for pans. Got the butter. Hmmm…they could use cheese, too. She cracked the eggs and was starting to scramble them when Trace's arms wrapped around her. He nuzzled her neck. Licked her.

"Trace!" His name came out as a yelp. "You're going to make me destroy breakfast before I even really get started."

His mouth rose to her ear. His lips pressed against the delicate shell. "Fuck the breakfast," he growled.

Oh, he tempted. Carefully, she turned in his arms. "I'd rather fuck you."

Skye pressed up onto her tip-toes. The better to get into kissing position.

There was a sharp, hard pounding at the penthouse's front door.

Skye put her hands on his shoulders. "Are you expecting company?" *At barely 7 a.m.?*

Trace shook his head. "Unexpected company doesn't happen here."

Not with the security he had in check. The staff downstairs would never let anyone access his private elevator. Not unless...

Trace rushed from the kitchen. She turned off the burners and followed quickly behind him. Trace glanced through the peephole on the main door.

When he shot her a fast glance, she caught the worry in his stare. His body was tense. He'd donned a pair of black pajama pants, but his muscled chest was bare. She could see the tautness in his broad shoulders.

"Who is it?" Skye asked, frozen five feet from him.

Trace opened the door.

Alex waited on the other side. He had his badge clipped to his waist. Two uniformed officers were behind him.

No, most people wouldn't have been able to get past security and get up to the penthouse. But a detective wasn't most people.

"I-I'm sorry, sir!" A voice called out, and she saw John Ford, the building manager, as he peered around the cops. "I had no choice but to bring them up because they have—"

"A warrant," Alex finished. He pulled out a folded piece of white paper. "I've got a search warrant for your penthouse. So, Weston, step outside and let us do our job."

***

It wasn't going to be good. Trace knew the truth, even before the uniforms called for back-up and more techs swarmed his penthouse.

They were tearing his life apart, one piece at a time.

"It's all right," Skye said. Alex had given her a chance to dress. A fast few minutes in the bedroom. Trace still wore his pajama pants—*is that supposed to bother me, Alex? Cause it doesn't.* Trace didn't give a damn what he wore or didn't wear.

Skye was a different matter. If the cops hadn't given her time to dress, Trace would've had every single one of them pulling traffic duty by the end of the day.

But Alex hadn't hesitated with Skye. She now wore a pair of form fitting yoga pants and a loose top. Her hair was pinned up. She looked beautiful and worried and *too good for me.*

He didn't want to lie to her anymore. He *wouldn't.* "You know he found something to tie me to Parker's death already, or else no judge would've given him a warrant." The judges in this town should have been too afraid to issue those warrants under any circumstances.

Milligan. Vermont Milligan. He'd been the judge to issue this warrant, and Trace's lawyer was out earning his retainer right then as he attempted to figure out just what the hell was happening.

What did Alex find that led him back to me?

But then two of the techs spilled out of the penthouse. They were carrying several clear, plastic bags. Trace saw a few of his shirts in those bags.

Alex exited behind them.

Trace lifted a brow. "Looking for some new apparel, Detective?"

"Actually, I found some recently." Alex sauntered toward him.

The building manager was huddled in the corner, watching nervously.

Skye was still at Trace's side.

"I went dumpster diving earlier. Not my favorite sport. Well, technically..." Alex looked over his shoulder. One of the uniformed cops had just come to join them. "It was Officer Coleman here who had the honor of that first retrieval."

Skye stepped in front of Trace. "Just what are you talking about?"

"We found a shirt—a shirt very similar to the others that Weston owns—thrown in a dumpster a few blocks away from the Parker Jacobs crime scene."

Sonofabitch.

"The shirt was covered in blood." Alex's eyes looked over Skye's head, at Trace. "Arterial spray will do that, you know. Cover an attacker in his victim's blood."

"I didn't kill Parker," Trace snapped. "I told you that already."

"Actually, you *told* us that you were at your office, working, but your assistant spun a different story. When I interviewed her, Sara Kramer told me that she came into your office, wanting to talk with you, but you weren't there."

Trace kept his expression blank.

"She didn't like turning on her boss, but when I showed her the crime scene photos, when I let her know just what type of man she was dealing with, Sara was fast to tell the truth." Alex's gaze flickered down to Skye. "Some women can see the monsters in front of them. Others stay blind."

Skye reached back and took Trace's hand. "Trace told you he didn't kill Parker."

"And is that what he told you, Skye? Or, when you were alone, did he tell you the truth? Did he tell you a story about how he worried for you? How he just couldn't keep on knowing that Parker was out there, that he might hurt you?"

Parker would've hurt her, but Trace hadn't killed the bastard. He'd had other plans for Parker. Plans that involved a jail cell.

"Trace didn't tell me any story about that. He just said that he didn't do it. I believe him."

"I don't." Flat. "He has no alibi, and I'm betting the bloody shirt we recovered—hell, I could tell it was one of those fancy-ass, too expensive shirts like Weston wears from the first glance."

"Good for you and your fashion eye," Trace muttered.

Alex glared at him. "I bet it's yours. I bet you left your DNA on it. A strand of hair. A drop of *your* blood that you don't even remember losing when you were slashing out with that knife. Something will tie back to you." Alex's glare gave way to a shark's smile. "And then you're done, man. You won't be on the streets anymore."

He was supposed to be afraid. Only this cop didn't scare Trace, not after all he'd seen and done. "I get that you're trying to do your job, and I even understand why."

John Ford had crept closer. No doubt, the better to overhear. Trace figured that the building manager's eyes couldn't get much bigger before they exploded from his head.

The uniform, Coleman, also leaned toward them.

"I know what happened to your sister," Trace said.

Alex's gaze cut to Skye.

"She didn't tell me. I have a damn security company. I can learn anyone's secrets, just with the press of a few buttons."

Fury blazed in Alex's eyes.

"I'm sorry you couldn't save her," Trace said and he meant those words. "But I'm not the bastard who hurt your sister. And no matter how many times you try to put me away, it won't bring her back."

Alex stumbled back a step.

"Here's something else for you to think about," Trace added, voice low and rumbling. "If I'd wanted Parker Jacobs dead, I could've just made the man disappear. No evidence would have ever been left behind. He would've vanished in an instant." Trace snapped his fingers. "Just like that because *that* is the kind of power I have. A sloppy kill wouldn't be my style."

"But you *did* get sloppy," Alex snapped. "You screwed up!"

"No." Skye's certain voice captured everyone's immediate attention. "Someone is trying to set him up, don't you see that?"

A furrow appeared between Alex's brows. "Why the hell would anyone want to do that? We're talking about murder here. Two murders."

"Because he has enemies," Skye said. "And some men will go to anything in order to get their vengeance."

The other uniform appeared then. It looked as if the guy had collected every single knife that Trace owned. Seriously? Did Alex truly think he could be such an amateur that he'd kill with his own knives? And Trace had already taken the liberty of ditching the knives he'd taken from Ben.

"I don't believe you would've sent a flunky after Parker," Alex said, giving a sharp nod to the uniforms. The two men— and the techs—headed for the elevator. John rushed forward to use his keycard for them. "I think, for a job this personal, you wouldn't mind getting your hands dirty." Alex's eyes were narrow slits of suspicion. "That dirt is gonna come back and bite you in the ass. Our lab techs are going to scan all the evidence we've got..."

He followed the others.

Skye laced her fingers with Trace. "You've got nothing," she called out.

She sounded so confident.

The elevator doors closed and their uninvited guests were gone.

"Nothing," Skye whispered as she pushed her hand into the loose pocket on her top. When her fingers came back out, she was holding the dog tags.

And one of those tags would have definitely tested positive for Parker's blood.

"I took a minute to pick these up as soon as I saw who our guests were."

Protecting him. Covering for him.

He took the tags from her. It was time he made them vanish. Then Trace cupped her chin in his hands and leaned toward her. "I'll make this end."

"No." Skye was adamant. "*We* will. We're in this together, Trace."

Together.

Because death wasn't about to part them.

***

When she heard the knock, Sara Kramer hurriedly opened her apartment door. Her lover waited in the hallway, and Sara threw her body against his. "I'm so glad you're here." Because she'd been afraid, for hours.

Trace would know that she'd talked to the cops. What would he do?

Fire her, no doubt. But what else? He'd helped her before, when she'd been desperate, and turning on him now seemed so wrong.

"Shh. Easy, my love." His hands were so gentle on her. He was always gentle. "I told you that I'd take care of you."

She pressed her face against the front of his shirt. "I don't think I should've talked. I-I don't know Trace did this and—"

His hand slid between them. He tipped back her chin, forcing her to look up at him. "You did the right thing."

Her heart finally stopped racing. Sara pulled back from him. "Come inside." She wanted him to stay with her. No, after everything that had happened, she *needed* him.

He shut the door. Locked it.

Sara dropped her robe. She wasn't wearing anything beneath it. The robe pooled at her feet. She gave him a smile. "Why don't you try to make me forget why I was so afraid?"

He'd been the one to convince her that she couldn't protect her boss. Trace had lied. A man was dead.

She didn't know Parker Jacobs. She'd never seen him in her life, not until Detective Griffin had shown her photos of the dead man.

The photos had brought back too many dark memories for Sara.

So much blood.

She'd been afraid. If Trace was a killer, if he'd done that...*then I didn't have a choice.*

She took a step toward her lover. She'd kept on her heels, for him. He liked her in heels and nothing else. "Please make me forget," she said, and Sara hated that a pleading note had entered her voice. She'd meant to sound seductive.

He bent toward his boots. Lifted up the left leg of his pants.

Sara frowned. What was he—

A knife was strapped to his ankle.

"Don't worry," he said as he rose, that knife gripped easily in his hand. "Soon you won't need to forget anything."

No, no. This was *not* happening.

"Y-you can't be serious." Her voice shook. Her whole body shook. "Is this some kind of game? Because I don't like it." Not with her past.

"I'm very serious." The blade gleamed. He stepped toward her. "You've worked with Trace for several years now. You've been his confidant."

She grabbed the robe. Yanked it over her shoulders. Her gaze flew around the room. She had to find a weapon. Had to *run.*

"So I think you should be the one to call Trace. Who knows...maybe he'll even get here in time to save you."

She was crying. The tears had leaked from her eyes and fallen down her cheeks. That terrible image of the dead man— his slashed throat, his bloody chest—flashed through her mind once more. "It was you." *Why?*

"Sometimes you think you know someone." He looked down at the knife. "But you only know what that person shows you. The deepest, darkest parts of ourselves are always hidden."

She spun to run.

Sara made it two feet when he grabbed her. He yanked her head back, gripping her hair tightly, and he put the knife to her throat.

Sara whimpered.

"Listen carefully," he whispered into her ear. "Because I need you to relay a very specific message for me."

***

The cops had tossed his place, and they sure appeared to have enjoyed the job.

Someone's ass is going to get burned because of this.

"Are they supposed to leave it wrecked like this?" Skye asked as she bent to grab some fallen couch pillows.

"No," Trace growled. "They're not." Alex was playing out of his league, and the detective was about to get slapped back into his normal game position. He reached for his phone.

It rang, vibrating as it gave a quick peal of sound. Trace glanced at the flat surface of the phone's screen and saw Sara Kramer's face. Frowning, he answered, "Sara? What's going on?"

At first, he only heard silence. Then...

A gasp?

"Sara?"

Skye glanced up at the sharp bite in his voice.

"You n-need to know..." Sara said quietly.

"What is it? Sara, are you okay?"

"You n-need to know what it feels like..." Sara was whispering. And crying?

"Sara, are you alone?" Because he was afraid that she wasn't.

A sob. Choked off. Then, "You'll know what it-it feels like to...lose it all..."

His blood chilled.

"Take care of my sister," Sara gasped out. "Please!" Then she cried, "*My apartment—*"

The line went dead.

Trace tried to call her back. The phone just rang. Trace ditched his pajama pants and dressed in an instant. Then he ran for the door. Skye rushed after him, but he spun, throwing up his arms and blocking the elevator before she could come with him.

"I think it's him," he said, the words too quiet.

Skye's eyes were wide. "What's happening? I thought you were talking to Sara."

"He has her." That message had been too deliberate. "If I don't get to her, she'll be dead." Hell, it might already be too late. Trace pushed the button on his phone that would connect him to Reese. "Stay here," he told Skye as he backed into the elevator. "I've got to help her."

Skye watched him with troubled eyes. The elevator doors began to close.

Reese answered on the second ring. "Yeah, boss, what's up?"

Skye jumped into the elevator.

She wasn't supposed to do that! "Get to Sara's place," Trace told Reese. "As fast as you can. I'm sending a full team behind you." He glared at Skye.

She punched the button for the lobby.

"I think...I think the killer's after Sara. Get there. *Get there.* I'm on my way." He ended the call. "What the hell are you doing?" Trace asked, trying to choke back his fear and fury. "You can't come. It's too—"

"Dangerous? Yes, it sounds that way. Dangerous for Sara and for you, and there is no way on earth that I'm just going to sit in the penthouse while you rush off to face whatever is happening at her place." She gave a firm nod. "Team, remember? That's what we are. Now call more of your men and tell them to get their asses over there."

The elevator doors opened.

Trace got more of his men on the line.

He and Skye rushed through the lobby. Henry hurried to open the door for them. The bright light hit them outside and—

"What's the rush?" Alex demanded, hands on his hips as he whirled toward them. "Not making a run for it, are you, Weston?"

Before Trace could do more than snarl at the man, Skye told the cop, "His assistant just called. Trace thinks that she's in danger."

"Sara?"

Trace ended the call. Tried Sara's line again. It just kept ringing. "The killer is at her apartment. I *know* he is. My men are on their way to her place and—"

Alex pointed to his car. "Get your asses in there, and let's go."

He didn't have time to waste, and Trace knew a cop would get them there hell fast.

They got their asses in.

***

"I-I did what you wanted…" Sara's whole body shook. "Please…let me go."

Instead, he spun her around to face him. "What the hell was that about your sister?"

Claire. Claire would be alone if anything happened to her. Sara had been desperate when she'd made that plea. She'd promised her parents that she'd always look after her sister…

Trace will take care of Claire.

"I'm sorry," she whispered.

"Don't worry, I won't hold that against you." He smiled. "Weston is coming. We have to give him something to find, don't we?"

No, they didn't. "Let me go. I won't tell anyone. I swear, I won't ever tell them who you are."

His gaze searched hers. "You know, I think I believe you." He pulled the knife away from her throat. "I didn't originally intend to bring you into this, but you were so close to Weston. And I promise, it's not personal."

Fucking her hadn't been personal?

Beneath Sara's fear, anger boiled. The lamp on the end table was just four feet away. She could lunge for it. Throw it at him. Maybe gain enough time to make it to the bathroom. Then she could lock the door and stay barricaded inside until help came.

She knew Trace would get to her as fast as he could.

"I like you," he told her, "and you were so useful."

Her breath heaved out as she understood. She'd been useful because of her access to Trace — and Trace's office. She was the only person at Weston Securities who had free access to Trace's inner domain. She'd let him in just days before, when Trace had been out. She'd thought nothing of the encounter until now.

"Passwords, files..." He shrugged. "You gave me everything I needed. Thank you."

He still had the knife. Sara knew, with utter certainty, *he's not going to let me go.*

So she could die easily or she could fight.

Sara dove for the right, surging toward that lamp. Her fingers stretched. She almost had it. Almost —

His body collided with hers, and she fell to the floor. They hit the end table on their way down, and the impact sent the lamp crashing down with them.

"Goodbye, sweet Sara," he whispered to her.

She opened her mouth to scream.

His left hand clamped over her lips and his right — his right drove the blade of the knife into her heart.

CHAPTER ELEVEN

They arrived on the scene silently. No siren. No screeching brakes. Skye knew that they were trying not to alert the killer who could be waiting with Sara.

Alex and Trace jumped from the car. Skye hurried right after them. Two more vehicles pulled up behind Alex's car, braking to a quick stop. Black SUVs. Three men and two women in suits climbed from those vehicles and immediately headed toward Trace.

Trace's agents.

"Cover the back stairs," he said, pointing toward half of that new group. "Then you guys cover the front."

The remaining agents nodded.

Trace glanced at Alex. "And I'm guessing you're going to want to lead the charge inside."

"With you right behind me, huh, Weston?"

"No," a sharp voice called out. Skye turned to see Reese rushing toward them. "With *us* right behind you."

Alex pulled out his gun. He nodded and took off.

Skye hesitated. What was—

Trace caught her fingers in his. "You came here, and I'm damn well not leaving you alone for a second. That SOB could be watching us right now, waiting for another attack."

They hurried inside the complex. An old converted warehouse, the place was now full of high-end condos. Trace got them immediate access to that building. He had Sara's key code, and that code opened the entrance gate in seconds.

They hurried up the stairs. Stopped on the second floor.

"She's number two-oh-six," Trace said.

Alex stopped in front of the indicated door. That door was ajar, open just a few inches.

Alex and Trace shared a hard look, then the detective rushed inside. "Sara Kramer!"

There was no answer. There was only thick silence, then, Alex snarled, "*Dammit, no!*"

Trace leapt inside. Skye and Reese were with him, and they only had to take a few steps before they saw Alex. He was bent on the floor, crouched over the prone body of Sara Kramer.

Skye's hand flew up to cover her mouth, an instinctive reaction. Blood soaked Sara's robe. And there was a big, gaping wound where her throat should have been.

Just like Parker.

Sara's throat had been slit open, a wound that stretched from ear to ear.

Alex yanked out his phone. As he surged to his feet, she heard him say, "This is Detective Alex Griffin, badge number four—one—one—eight. . I'm at a murder scene. Brighton Condominiums, number two-oh-six."

A soft knock sounded at the door behind them.

Skye whirled around.

The unlocked door swung open. A woman stood there. A woman with hair the same light blonde shade as Sara's. Her eyes were like Sara's, too—a deep blue.

The woman hesitated as she stood there. "I, um, I'm looking for my sister—"

No, dear God, *no.* Skye rushed toward her, trying to grab the woman before she could see the body on the floor.

"Her name's Sara Kramer," the blonde continued, stepping forward, "and she's—"

Skye shoved the woman back toward the door. A hard shove that sent the other lady stumbling with a yelp. "No!" Skye snapped. "You can't—"

"Who are you?" The blonde demanded. "What's happening? Where is Sara?"

She's dead on the floor. And you don't need to see her that way. You don't. "I'm sorry," Skye said, dropping her voice. "Something has happened."

The blonde grabbed Skye's hands. "To Sara?"

Trace came to stand behind Skye. "You're Claire. Sara told me that you were coming to town."

Claire frowned at him, then her eyes widened with recognition. "You...you're Mr. Weston, Sara's boss, right?" Claire appeared to be about twenty-five or twenty-six. She was slender, her skin a soft gold, and her expression was slowly becoming terrified. "Please tell me what's happening."

Sirens screamed from outside.

"I'm sorry," Skye whispered. Claire was still holding her hands in a tight grip. Claire's gaze was now full of fear and desperation. *Tell her.* "Your sister is dead."

Claire shook her head. "No."

"A detective is in there now. More police are coming."

"*No!*"

"We need to go downstairs," Skye said. "The apartment...it's a...crime scene."

Claire tried to lunge past Skye, but Trace caught her, stopping her before she could burst back into Sara's place. "You don't want to see her like that," he told her, voice soft, sad. "You *don't.*"

"Sara!" Claire screamed.

Then the tears broke from her.

***

Trace stood in his office, his gaze on the city that spread out before him. Noah and Drake were seated behind him. After Sara's death, he'd had to call them both in.

"He used Sara," Trace said, his shoulders stiff. "In order to get close to me. He gained access to my personal phone line." He turned toward them. "The SOB hijacked the line to make a call to Skye. He could've lured her any place."

Noah swiped a hand over his face. "And you think he might be using people at my organization, too? Doing the same damn thing to me?"

It was a definite possibility. "The guy sure as hell seems focused on me right now, but the two of you needed to be warned. If he hasn't already gone after you, he will."

Drake gave a grim nod.

"I think he stole my shirt right out of the office." The back-up clothing that he normally kept at the office was gone, so there really wasn't any *thinking* about it. Now he knew how his shirt had wound up at Parker's crime scene. *You wore it while you killed him, didn't you, bastard?* "I'm sure he used Sara to get access to the clothing."

Poor Sara. She'd been caught in a battle for nothing. Used. Thrown away.

"Your security footage got his face, right?" Noah said as he leaned forward. "I mean, this is Weston Freaking Securities that we're talking about. This place is wired from the floor to the ceiling."

It was, but… "Sara Kramer had access to all the security information here. She was my right hand." Grief was there, painful, twisting grief that clawed inside of him. Sara had been a friend. "I trusted her, and it looks like, a few days ago, she took the security offline for fifteen minutes. The whole building went dark."

Drake swore.

Yes, that was just how Trace felt. He'd been distracted — the security breach had happened right after the car crash. He'd learned that his team had reported the problem right away, only they'd reported to Sara, not him because he'd been getting stitched up at the hospital.

"So we're saying a dead man is doing this?" Noah surged up from his chair. "Because I don't believe that crap. No way. I don't—"

"You were flying the chopper that got us out of there," Trace told him. Because that had been Noah's job that day. Trace had barely made it to the rendezvous point. "The snow was coming down hard, and you could barely get the bird back in the sky."

Noah glanced over at Drake. "I was convinced he'd die before we got him to a doctor."

Drake's gaze strayed to the window. "Do you two ever think...maybe I should've been the one to die? Maybe Trace made the wrong choice out there. He grabbed the wrong friend."

Noah's eyes narrowed to chips of golden fire. "Stop being a dick, Drake. You both told me what went down out there. Tucker turned on you. He would've killed you both in an instant."

"Instead, I thought that I killed him." Trace flattened his hands on the desk. "But if he's dead, then how'd my dog tags wind up in Chicago? How'd Parker get them? They should've been frozen in Siberia, with Tucker."

"And with Anna Jean," Drake said, his voice tight.

Trace frowned at him. There had been a different note in Drake's voice then. Pain.

Anger?

Well, the guy was entitled to his anger at Anna Jean. She'd tried to kill him. She'd screwed them all.

"You're the best shot I've ever seen," Noah said, as he braced his legs apart and studied Trace. "From what you told me all these years, it was a point blank shot."

Trace inclined his head.

"So how would you miss?" Noah demanded. "You hit his heart. You *know* he was dead."

"Someone found the body," Drake said as he straightened. "The snow melted. Someone was digging—the damn bodies were found, and with them, the dog tags."

Trace's lips curved in a mirthless smile. "You think I didn't consider that? If that were the case, I figure that I would've gotten a blackmail threat. Not this...the kills are personal." They all had to see that.

"Personal," Noah agreed. "For you. Sharpe came to you, tried to warn you, and he died."

"Parker Jacobs wasn't interested in warning me about anything. He was more interested in destroying me," Trace said.

"So that's why he was used." Noah was speaking faster now. "Sara was used, too. Both of them were pawns in the game."

Drake's hands clenched on the leather arm-rests of his chair. "So this is all just a game?"

"To someone, yeah, it is," Noah agreed. "We just have to figure out who that someone is, because I'd bet my life that it *isn't* Tucker. He's dead and gone."

"What do we know about Tucker's family?" Drake asked as a furrow appeared between his brows. "Maybe one of them found out what happened. Maybe one of them—"

"Tucker was an only child. His mother died before he enlisted, and his father is still living down in Texas."

"Then he could—"

"Quint Hawk is disabled, living on a fixed income, and the man sure doesn't have the physical strength needed to commit these crimes." Trace's breath whispered out. "And as soon as this mess started, I had an agent head down there and verify that Quint was still at his old ranch."

Trace hadn't seen Quint in person, not since the day of Tucker's funeral service. He and Quint had been the only two there that day, standing in the rain, mourning the life that was gone.

A life I took.

"Then what about Anna Jean?" Noah said, giving a quick jerk of his head.

Because Trace was watching Drake so closely, he saw the other man flinch at Noah's question. Taking his time, Trace slid around the edge of his desk and closed in on Drake. Considering now, Trace said, "When we came back, we all dealt with the past differently. Noah there...he slept with every woman he could find, and he made sure that he never saw the same woman twice. I figured he was trying to make sure he never fell into the same trap that Tucker did. He didn't want to latch on to one woman and become—"

"Weak," Noah said. But his voice was hesitant.

"You...you Drake, at first, you seemed solid. You were the one who nearly died. You and Ben. Ben wasn't the same, though, we all could see that. The demons chased and chased him, but *you*..." Trace exhaled. "You seemed stronger."

"Strong enough that you sent me to New York to keep an eye on the woman you loved." Drake pushed from his chair. "And then I walked away."

"*Why?*" Drake was holding back on him. He knew it.

Trace had kept tabs on the man over the years. Drake had returned to his home in the south, right along a strip of Mississippi Beach. He'd opened three casinos down there. He'd started two more in Vegas. Drake seemed to spend his days and nights surrounded by power players.

But Trace knew just how deceptive appearances could be.

"You shouldn't have trusted me," Drake said. "If you knew...you'd never have sent me after her." Drake spun and marched toward the door. "If Tucker really is back from the dead, he'll kill me long before he takes his knife to you."

"Uh, what the hell are you talking about?" Noah snapped.

Drake paused at the door. He glanced back with a sardonic smile on his lips. "After all, I'm the one who fucked Tucker's girl. I screwed Anna Jean, and the blind fool never even realized it. None of you did." He yanked open the door and stormed out.

Well, well...

"Huh." Now Noah sounded musing. Trace glanced at him. Noah shrugged. "I guess that explains why Anna Jean tried so hard to kill him. She didn't want to take any chances on Tucker finding out that she'd been screwing around with his friend." Noah exhaled heavily. "Talk about twisted shit."

Yes, it was.

Noah crossed to Trace and slapped him on the shoulder. "But, look at it this way, if the guy wasn't just BS'ing right then, you have some extra time. Because, hell, yeah, Tucker would go after the man who screwed Anna Jean. He'd *destroy* the guy."

"Drake didn't exactly look scared to me."

"Well, that's because I'm pretty sure the guy is insane. He doesn't have the sense to be scared."

No, Trace didn't think that was the case at all. "He's got a death wish."

Surprise flashed on Noah's face.

"He wants to be punished. He's wanted that for years." But the problem was that if you wished for death too long...

Death would come for you.

Noah's lips thinned. "You know, you never did answer my question about Anna Jean's family. They could be looking for some payback, too, you know."

"Anna Jean's parents are dead. She had one half-sister, Piper. A school teacher in Atlanta." He'd checked on her after he'd come back from Russia. Made sure that Piper's college was covered. Then he'd stayed the hell out of her life. "She doesn't seem to have her sister's killer instinct."

"Yeah, well, if you ask me, that's a good thing." Noah shoved his hands into his pockets. "But it sure seems to me that someone out there *has* got that instinct, and that person is closing in."

***

"I don't have any place to stay." Claire sat on the couch in the penthouse, her fingers twisted in front of her. Discarded tissues formed a pile around her. "I was supposed to be moving in with Sara. I-I just got into town a few hours early. She was going to help me find a job here." A silent tear tracked down her cheek. "She can't do that anymore." Her voice was hoarse. "Sara can't do anything now."

"You can stay here tonight," Skye said immediately. "There is plenty of room in this place."

But Claire glanced around the penthouse, fear flashing in her gaze. "I can't." Whispered. "I just...*can't.*"

Skye frowned at her. "We have an extra bedroom." Four of them. "You'll be safe here."

Claire shook her head. "I don't really...I've heard stories about Mr. Weston—"

"Trace?"

"He scares me. I used to ask Sara if he scared her." Her lips twisted into a sad smile. "She said, 'Every day. But that's half the fun.'" Claire laughed then, and the sound was heavy with tears. "But Sara was lying to me, you see. I don't think she was ever really afraid of anything. She isn't like me." Claire's shoulders hunched.

Skye gazed at her, her heart aching. There was something about Claire that reminded her...

Of me.

"I'll get a hotel. It'll be fine." Claire stood up. Squared her shoulders. "I don't need—"

"There's an apartment over my dance studio," Skye said, rising with her. "You can stay there. No one will bother you."

Claire's lips trembled. "Th-thank you." Then she paused. "I...know about what happened to you."

At this point, Skye was sure most of the world did. She lifted her chin. "I didn't—"

"Surviving is hard, isn't it? But at least you know he's not out there anymore, watching you." Claire licked her lips. "That part is the scariest."

Skye felt her heartbeat race. *She's speaking from experience.*

"Never knowing…it's the hardest." Claire's eyes squeezed shut, then she whispered, "It's my fault that Sara is dead."

"What?" Skye shook her head and then realized that Claire couldn't see the move. "No, no, it isn't."

Claire's body trembled. "He killed my parents, and he killed her, too."

"*Claire.*" Skye snapped out her name. "What are you talking about?"

"My lover," she said as her eyes opened. "My one and only. He said I was his forever, and he's made sure that I am."

Goosebumps rose on Skye's arms.

I see me in her. The same fear. The terror that lurked in Claire's eyes.

"I thought I'd escaped, just like you had. But I didn't." More tears slid down Claire's cheeks. "And Sara is dead."

"It *wasn't* because of you." Skye wanted to shake the other woman. So she did. Hard.

Claire blinked at her.

"I don't know what happened to your parents or what happened to you, but Sara's death *isn't* on you." Skye sucked in a sharp breath. "Someone is killing in this city. This is his third attack. The crimes are all the same. The victims are all —" Skye broke off, not wanting to reveal the gory details to Claire.

"Th-third attack?"

"Two men were killed before Sara."

"You're sure it's the same killer?"

"Yes." Because the killer was from Trace's past.

"*Why?* Why would he go after my sister?"

"We think…" It was so hard to say this as she stared into those tear-filled eyes. "We think the killer was using her in order to get at Trace. And after he'd gotten what he needed from Sara…"

"He killed my sister." Hollow words. Words that matched the look in Claire's eyes.

Skye nodded. Claire deserved the truth, and she was determined to give it to her.

One survivor to another.

"I need to see her," Claire said. "Please..."

The body had been transferred down to the coroner's office hours before. Skye knew the ME wouldn't be finished with the exam, not yet.

"*I need to do it.* I'm all that Sara has."

"I'll call Alex." The detective might be able to arrange something for them.

At least Claire wouldn't be seeing her sister's body, soaked in blood. They could get the ME to only show her face to Claire. They could do *something*.

Because if they didn't, Skye was worried that Claire might just break apart.

***

When his phone rang, Trace snatched it up immediately. "Reese? What's happening?" Reese had orders to stick close to Skye. She was *not* going to end up like Sara.

"Uh, boss, they're heading to the ME's office. Skye and Sara's sister."

The ME's office.

"Just thought you should know."

"I'm on my way." He stood. "Noah, start checking your personnel. I've already got a team backtracking through the last few weeks of Sara's life. Someone saw the guy. Somewhere, sometime." They just had to talk to the right person. The one who remembered the SOB.

Noah nodded and walked to the door with him. "Where are you going?"

"To see the dead."

***

"I should come in with you," Reese said as they stood in front of the police station. "I can help."

Claire wouldn't look straight at Reese. Skye had noticed that Claire also stiffened her body whenever Reese got too close to her.

"Alex is waiting for us inside." Skye gave Reese a wan smile. "But thank you."

He nodded. His gaze drifted to Claire. "I'm sorry about your sister. Sara was a good woman. She didn't deserve an end like that."

Claire pulled in a rough breath. "Thank you."

They hurried inside. The steps they climbed seemed huge, but then they were past the swinging glass doors and in the lobby of the Chicago PD. The Medical Examiner's office was located just behind the PD, but in order to gain access, they had to make sure they had Alex with them.

Skye signed in, then asked to be directed to Detective Alex Griffin's desk.

"I'm right here," Alex said.

Skye looked up. Alex marched toward them, the lines near his mouth making him look grim. Tired.

Alex's gaze slid from her to Claire. "Ms. Kramer."

"I want to see my sister." Claire's hands had fisted.

"The ME isn't…ah, the autopsy hasn't been completed."

Based on what she'd seen, Skye was pretty sure what the cause of death would be.

"I have to see her." Desperation filled Claire's words.

"Soon," Alex promised. "First, we need to talk." His hand lifted and his fingers pressed into Claire's shoulders.

Claire flinched and pulled away from him. "I don't…I don't like being touched." Flat. Hard.

But Claire hadn't objected at all when Skye touched her.

Skye saw the flash of understanding in Alex's eyes. After the things he'd experienced in his own life and the darkness he saw each day, Skye realized that he understood Claire perfectly. "Of course. My apologies," Alex said as he dropped his hand.

Claire's shoulders sagged. "I'm not interested in talking. I *have* to see my sister."

The glass doors swung open again. Skye glanced back and saw Trace striding determinedly toward them.

Of course, he walked as if he owned the place.

He didn't. Yet.

"Now it's a party," Alex muttered.

"Damn right," Trace said, obviously catching the detective's comment. "I think you were about to escort us to the ME's office."

Alex leaned toward Trace. "It's better, but she's not...she's not exactly show ready yet."

"I can handle it," Claire said. "But I have to know for myself. I have to see...*that it wasn't him.*"

Trace's head jerked up. Alex's gaze snapped to instant attention. "Him?" Alex repeated.

Trace stepped toward Claire. Unlike Alex, he didn't make the mistake of touching the other woman. "Claire," Trace's voice was low, soothing. "Ethan Harrison is still locked up. He had nothing to do with your sister's death."

Trace knows about her past.

And he also knew to treat Claire very carefully. He glanced over at Alex. "She just needs to see Sara's face. Give her that."

Alex nodded, but then he said, "You tell me what the hell is going on."

"Of course," Trace murmured.

Alex waved toward Skye and Claire. "You two wait in the conference room, and we'll get things ready."

***

The conference room door closed with a faint click. Skye sat down at the narrow table. Claire didn't. Claire wrapped her arms around her stomach and stood near the right wall.

Skye reached for the coffee pot that someone had conveniently set up for them. "Let me get you a cup of coffee. It might make you feel a little better." Right. Like coffee would fix what was wrong with Claire.

"You're not asking about Ethan." The words were sharp, accusing.

Skye shook her head.

"Is it because you already know? Did Trace tell you? Do you know all about my breakdown?"

At that, Skye flinched. "No," she said softly and she put the coffee aside. *Definitely won't help.* "I don't, Claire."

"You must think I'm so weak." Claire swiped at her tears. "You survived. I read your story — he had you for days. You made it out."

"We each have our own hell." Skye was coming to realize that statement was true more and more each day.

Claire rocked back on her heels. "Yes, we do."

***

"I should've known you'd be showing up, Weston," Alex muttered. "Where Skye goes, you follow."

They'd just left the main PD building and were taking the stairs that led to the ME's office.

"I need to see the other bodies," Trace said.

Alex glanced back at him. "And I'm just going to give you access to them because—"

"Because after what happened to Sara, you have to know that I'm not the killer. She was still *warm* when we got there." Trace had touched her skin. He'd hoped that maybe—

Too much blood.

"You didn't kill her, but that doesn't mean you didn't take out the others. And maybe you just sent someone else to kill Sara. After all, she blew your alibi to hell and back and you—"

"Showing me the bodies won't make me any less or more guilty. But maybe… maybe I'll be able to see something," Trace said, his words rolling over Alex's.

"Something?" Alex parroted as he squared off with Trace. "That's what we have an ME for. To find that 'something' left behind by the killer."

He wanted to grab the detective and toss him against the nearest wall. "*Listen*. The killer is playing a game with me. You've got to see that. He might've left a message for me *in the damn kills themselves*. Just let me see the bodies, okay? I won't touch anything. You can stand there the whole time and watch me."

Alex's jaw tightened. "One condition."

"What?" Trace snapped.

"Save me some time. I can go and dig into Claire's past and find out who this Ethan Harrison is, or you can tell me now."

Trace raised a brow. "So I'm doing your detective work for you."

"You are such a dick. You already did the work, tell me — and we both know I'm going to research later to make sure you're not just blowing smoke up my ass."

Fine. "Ethan Harrison is Claire's ex-boyfriend. She met him when she was a junior in high school..."

So young to meet such evil.

***

"I didn't have a lot of money growing up." Claire's blue gaze seemed focused on the past. "But that never seemed to matter. So my clothes weren't new. So I didn't go on big vacations. My family was happy. *I* was happy, and then I-I met him."

"Ethan?"

"He was the most handsome boy I'd ever seen. The first time he smiled at me, I swear, I felt that smile go straight through me."

Skye knew exactly what Claire meant. She felt that way when she got Trace's rare smiles.

"I worked at a diner in town, and he came in there one day. Everyone was whispering about him. His dad was a senator, and Ethan...he drove this cherry-red convertible. All the other girls wanted to ride with him." Her voice dropped. "They wanted to do everything with him, but Ethan seemed to only want me."

Hearing the pain in the other woman's voice, Skye hurt for her.

Claire's lashes lowered as she stared at the floor. "I hadn't dated before Ethan. I was nervous and scared, but he seemed so patient with me. He sent me flowers. Waited for me after work. He seemed so perfect." She glanced up. "It didn't take me long to realize that perfect was just a lie."

***

"A few months after Sara came to work for me, she told me about her sister." Trace remembered the way Sara had approached him. She'd been so hesitant. So protective.

"Claire had a boyfriend when she was a teen. He was charming to Claire and her family, at first, but the deeper the relationship went, the more his real side started to show."

Alex cursed. "Let me guess, that real side was ugly."

"If Claire was late for a date, he thought she was cheating on him. He started by yelling at her, threatening her, and then...he hit her."

"Bastard." Trace heard the fury humming in the one snarled word.

Trace nodded. Yes, Ethan Harrison was one sick bastard. "Claire was scared. She broke things off with him. Her parents sent her out of town because they wanted her away from the guy." Trace's lips twisted. "He had connections, you see. To an Alabama senator. That was his old man, and the punk was used to getting authorities to look the other way whenever he got a little rough with his girlfriends."

Red stained Alex's cheeks.

"But something was different this time. Ethan didn't want to take no for an answer. Not when it came to Claire. He went to see Claire's parents, and when they wouldn't tell him where she was…"

***

"He killed them," Claire whispered. "One shot to the head each. First my mother. Then my father. Th-the police said that based on the blood…they were probably kneeling. He made them kneel, right in front of him, then he shot them."

Skye jumped from her chair and hurried to Claire. She opened her arms, then stopped.

I don't like to be touched.

"He found me," Claire said, still staring into her past. "Right after that. I think he must have searched the house until he found a note that I'd sent to them. He came looking for me at the cabin. He had the gun with him."

"I'm so sorry," Skye whispered.

"I didn't know they were dead when he arrived. I'd been trying to reach them, but no one answered my calls. He was walking toward me on the dock." She gave a sad shake of her head. "It was an old, rickety dock at my grandfather's fishing cabin. Ethan's convertible stood out there like a sore thumb. But he didn't care who saw him. He didn't care what anyone said. He was coming for me."

"He didn't get you," Skye said, her voice hard. "You're safe."

Claire blinked. She seemed to *see* Skye once more. "He did get me that day. He found me on the dock. He put the gun to my head. He made me get on my knees."

Dear God.

"And he pulled the trigger. He laughed when I screamed and he told me that he'd already used those bullets."

On Claire's parents.

"He told me that I could be his or I could be dead."

***

"The senator couldn't cover up two dead bodies. The cops started a manhunt, and they found Ethan two days later—he was in the woods with Claire."

Trace could still see Sara in his mind. She'd stood in front of his desk, her voice soft, emotionless, as she'd told him this tale.

"A sniper shot Ethan in the leg. The cops got Claire away from him."

"The leg?" Alex's eyes turned to slits. "He should've aimed higher."

Yes, he should have. But the senator had been standing behind the sniper, and it had been *his* call.

"They took Ethan in and that's when the SOB got real creative. His daddy got him the best lawyers he could, and they claimed that Claire was the mastermind. That she was the one who'd seduced Ethan and pressured him into killing her parents. He was just an innocent boy who'd been led astray."

"Tell me the jury didn't buy that bull."

"Claire tried to kill herself during the trial."

Alex tensed.

"She was admitted to a psychiatric ward, and she stayed there for five months."

"Sonofa—"

"The jury didn't buy his story. They found Ethan Harrison guilty of both murders."

"I hope they scheduled him an appointment with the needle or shoved his ass in the electric chair."

"The judge gave him two concurrent life sentences."

"So what—the asshole could be out in fifteen years, provided he has good behavior?"

"He was almost out three years ago," Trace said. Sara's image was crisp in his mind. *I know I don't have the right to ask, but I need help. And I swear, I'll work off the money. I will.* "His daddy was still throwing his money around, and he hired new lawyers. An appeal was going up before the court."

"I'm guessin' this is where you come in…"

"Sara thought it was a matter of money. Convincing the right people that Ethan Harrison needed to stay in jail. But, of course, bribery is against the law. You know that well, *Detective.*"

Alex held his gaze. "Sometimes, it's not about money. It's about power. And we both know you have too damn much of that."

***

"People believed him when Ethan said I told him to kill my parents. I could see it…people who'd known me for my entire life were suddenly doubting me. Strangers called me a whore. Men on the street shouted that I should die. So…I thought maybe I should." Claire glanced down at her wrist. Skye saw the faint, white line there. "I'd almost bled out by the time Sara found me."

I'm so glad Claire didn't see Sara covered in all of that blood.

"I got better," Claire said with grim pride. Then she whispered, "But the nightmares never stopped."

They were about two feet apart. Claire was a few inches taller than Skye. A little younger. But, on the inside, Skye felt as if they were the same.

"I have nightmares, too." Skye said. "Sometimes, they're memories. Other times, they twist. They become something else."

"*Yes.*"

"But when I wake up each day, those nightmares fade away." That was the way it had been when her parents died, and that was the way it happened for her now. "Because nightmares can't hurt us. We're alive. We're getting through this world, one step at a time, and it doesn't matter what anyone else says or what anyone else calls us." Skye willed Claire to believe what she was saying. "All that matters is that we know…we're survivors."

Claire rubbed at her eyes, obviously trying to stop the tears. "He almost got out a few years back. On some kind of-of technicality." Her chin lifted. "But Sara fixed that for me. She had connections, see. She used them. They sent him back. She told me that Ethan would never hurt me again."

"She was protecting you. Sara sounds like one incredible sister."

"She was. I just-I wish I could've protected *her*."

***

"What the hell is your deal, Weston?" Alex demanded. He jabbed his index finger into Trace's chest. "You know I want to hate you."

"Yeah," Trace replied, "I got that clue."

"You're twisted. I can feel it in you. I know because—"

"Because when you look at me, you see the same darkness that stares back at you from the mirror each day?"

Alex clamped his lips together and yanked his hand back. He stomped down the hallway.

"*Dammit to hell.*" Alex's growl.

Trace lifted a brow that the detective couldn't see.

"Fine," Alex snapped. "You can see the other two bodies, but you so much as touch them, and I'll have you in a cage." He threw a glare over his shoulder. "Understand me?"

"You're welcome," Trace told him.

More red heated Alex's cheeks.

"And that 'you're welcome'—it was actually for me not going straight to the DA and demanding that your ass get yanked to traffic duty after that little stunt you pulled with the search warrant." As if Trace had forgotten about that incident. He took his time heading down the hall. "You were right when you said I had plenty of power. Remember that the next time you feel the urge to get...overzealous with me."

"The door..." Alex huffed out the words, "is to the damn left."

Trace inclined his head. Then he opened the door. Inside, the temperature was a good five degrees cooler, and the room smelled of bleach.

And death.

A tall, curvy redhead appeared. She pushed her glasses higher on her nose and frowned at Trace. "Can I help you—"

"Dr. Dulane," Alex said as he followed Trace inside, "we need to see the three stabbing victims."

Dr. Dulane shook her head. "But I was just finishing some work on the female—"

"Sara," Trace forced the name out. "Her name is Sara Kramer."

Sympathy flashed over Dr. Dulane's face. "Are you family?"

"Close," Trace said.

Alex added, "Her family's outside. Her sister needs to see the body. Get her...presentable, would you, doc? Face only. The woman out there needs some closure."

Dr. Dulane pulled on a pair of latex gloves. "Seeing the dead here never gives them closure." She inclined her head. "But I'll do what I can." Her gaze flashed back to Trace. "Come with me, and I'll show you the others."

She led them into the back.

When Trace saw Sara, he stumbled to a stop. Her body was drained of color now. Her hair spread behind her. The blood had been washed away. She looked—

Broken.

I'm so sorry, Sara. I will find him. I will make him pay for what he did.

Trace jerked his gaze off her, and he found Alex staring straight at him. "Watching my reaction?" Trace growled at him.

"Your reactions are always off, unless Skye is close. That's the only time you ever seem even half-way normal."

Well, when he was with her, those were the only times he *felt* normal, too. Alive. Instead of feeling as if he were just going through the motions. Mimicking everyone else around him.

"Her attacker drove a blade into her heart," Dr. Dulane said. "Based on the size of her injury, I think it was the same type of blade used on the other two victims. But this time…there were defensive wounds."

She pulled back the sheet and pointed to Sara's wrists. "The bruising is coming through. It looks like he had to restrain her."

Take care of my sister. "Sara had something to fight for."

"Did she get the perp's DNA?" Alex asked. "Tell me you found it under her fingernails."

Dr. Dulane shook her head.

"There were no signs of forced entry at Ms. Kramer's house," Alex said. "And she was…dressed provocatively."

"She was sleeping with the man who killed her." Trace had already figured that part out himself.

"She didn't sleep with him the day she died. There was no sperm," Dr. Dulane said with a shake of her head. "No sign of any sexual penetration."

So the guy hadn't fucked her before he killed her. Was that supposed to be some kind of mercy act?

Trace wanted to destroy the bastard.

"Show us the other bodies," Alex directed.

Dr. Dulane headed toward a wall of vaults. She bent. Swung open one door, and pulled out a slab. A black body bag filled the space. The hiss of the zipper seemed too loud as Dr. Dulane revealed the body.

Sharpe's body was ghost-white. His eyes were closed. His muscles tight and frozen in death.

"A two-sided blade went into his chest here," Dr. Dulane said, tapping her gloved fingers near the wound. "The assailant knew exactly what he was doing. The attack was dead-on."

Trace had already reviewed the report, so he knew about the type of blade used.

Tucker had always carried a two sided weapon. Always. "There were no signs of struggle?" Trace asked. There had to be something there. If the killer had left Trace's dog tags with Parker, then some sort of message had been left with Sharpe.

Trace just had to find the message.

"None. The fact that Mr. Sharpe didn't have time to struggle is a good thing. It meant he probably didn't have long to suffer."

"He would've wanted to fight." Dying easily hadn't been Ben Sharpe's style.

"*I'll be damned.* You have an idea who the killer is, don't you?" Alex suddenly demanded.

Trace looked over his shoulder at the detective. "Not yet."

Alex's gaze called Trace a liar.

"Nothing else was found with the body?" Trace asked. He had to be missing something.

But then his gaze fell on Sharpe's throat. On the wound there. "That's wrong."

Alex pressed closer. "Yeah, getting your throat sliced open is wrong and—"

"No, I mean the wound looks wrong." His stare flashed to Dr. Dulane. "I need to see Parker's body. *Now.*"

She opened the next vault. A burst of cold air drifted out, rising as the body bag appeared.

The zipper hissed down. Trace leaned forward, studying the knife wound at Parker's throat. Parker's throat had been sliced clean, from ear to ear.

But with Sharpe...

"The wound stopped half-way across." He could see the jagged V where the knife had lifted out of Ben Sharpe's throat for an instant. "Then the killer finished the job."

Not a defensive wound.

A hesitation?

Why? The kill had already been complete by that point.

Then, understanding came. *You didn't want to cut his throat.*

He whirled around and rushed back to Sara's body. He stared at her throat and saw that same V notch on the skin. Just a jagged tear, but Trace *knew* exactly what he was staring at. *You didn't want to cut her throat, either. But you did.*

"The killer hesitated with her, too," Trace said.

"I-I made note of the injury pattern in the file," Dr. Dulane said, sounding a bit offended. "I measured the wound and included that—"

"You didn't say the killer hesitated," Alex snapped.

"Because you can't know that for sure! Maybe the blade slipped. Maybe—"

"Why didn't he hesitate with Parker?" Alex asked, focusing on Trace.

Trace knew the answer, and that made this dangerous game even more complicated. "Because he thought Parker deserved to die."

And if that were truly the case, then it meant that the killer had been watching him—and Skye—very closely.

For a long time.

You know about our pasts. And you're using them against us.

***

Claire edged carefully into the morgue. Skye was at her side. Skye had only been in a morgue once before. When she'd gone to identify the bodies of her parents.

The smell was the same. The cold chill—one that reminded her of death—it was the same, too.

A redhead in a white lab coat stood near the door. "Ms. Kramer?"

Claire nodded.

Alex appeared beside the redhead. "This way."

Claire shuffled forward. Skye hesitated. This was private. She shouldn't go in.

But Claire turned toward her. "Come with me?"

Skye nodded. She entered the viewing room with her chin up.

Sara was on the table. Her body was covered with a sheet, all the way up to the top of her neck. Only her face was visible. Her face was perfect. No wounds. No pain.

"It wasn't him," Claire whispered. "H-he always shoots in the head. *It wasn't him.*"

Then Claire grabbed Skye and held onto her tightly.

Skye stared over Claire's shoulder. Her gaze locked with Trace's. He'd been there, watching them all along. His eyes glinted.

No, a monster from Claire's past hadn't committed this crime.

Sara had just gotten caught in someone else's battle.

Who else did the killer plan to hurt?

***

Drake Archer drained the whiskey and slammed the glass on the bar. The liquid barely burned as it slid down his throat.

Once, he'd turned to drinks too much. To try and shut up the ghosts in his head. But then he'd realized that the booze didn't stop the voices.

The alcohol just made them louder.

"Another?" The bartender asked.

Drake shook his head and tossed some cash onto the bar. He rose, aware of the looks that were tossed his way. He'd come to the darkest, roughest bar he could find. He liked places like this dive. Places that often let him fight and push out some of the wildness that lived within him. Places that reminded him of exactly where he'd come from.

But there were no fights to be found tonight. The others eased away from him as he headed toward the door.

Darkness waited outside for him. Drake rolled back his shoulders and stalked down the street.

He'd been in a thousand towns. Walking. Fighting. Fucking. They all blurred together during the night, and when dawn came...

I'm always alone.

He turned off the main strip. The sounds were muted now. The horns distant. The growl of car engines barely discernible.

He'd rented a place close by. Coming to the city had been a mistake. But when Noah had called him...

Noah and Trace were the only friends I ever had.

Friends, enemies. Same damn thing some days.

He halted and heard the faint rustle of a footstep behind him.

Such a soft sound. One that he could've imagined but —

In instant, he'd yanked out the knife that he kept tucked in his boot. Ben Sharpe had been the one to get him hooked on that particular habit.

Drake whirled around. *"Who in the hell is there?* Show yourself!"

But only an empty street stared back at him. An empty street, and the ghosts in his head.

CHAPTER TWELVE

"I want you to come with me," Trace said, his voice and eyes tense as he gazed down at Skye.

They'd just dropped Claire off at the studio. Skye had made sure that Claire was settled in the upstairs apartment. She'd hated to leave Claire, but she'd realized that the other woman needed time alone.

Sometimes, you needed to grieve in private.

"Where are you going?" Skye asked him.

"Texas."

She blinked at that terse response. "Why?"

"Because that's where Tucker grew up. I need to take another look at that town, at the people there. I could send some more agents but...*it's personal.*"

"I-I have my studio. Classes will—"

"Tomorrow's Sunday. You don't have any classes scheduled then, and we'll be back Sunday night." His voice dropped. "Please, Skye. I don't want to leave you here while I'm gone. I need you with me."

"What about Claire?"

"Reese will keep watch on her. Hell, I'll call Noah, too. They'll make sure she's safe."

Skye nodded. "Okay."

His breath expelled in a fast rush. "Thank you, baby." His fingers slid up to cup her chin. "I need you close right now. I think about what happened to Sara—that *can't* happen to you."

She pressed a quick kiss to his lips. "And it *won't* happen to you." Her vow.

***

The plane rose higher and higher into the air. Trace kept his gaze locked on Skye as they ascended.

Her eyes were currently squeezed tightly closed. Skye hated flying.

The light flashed indicating that he could unbuckle his seatbelt. He did, then slid forward and pressed a quick kiss to her lips.

Skye's eyes flew open. "Trace—"

He kissed her again. Her lips had parted, and he was able to easily slide his tongue right into her mouth. "Do you remember the first time we made love on this plane?"

She gave a little gasp at that question, and he drank it up greedily.

Then his mouth moved down to her neck. He knew she liked it when he licked her there. "You surprised the hell out of me then. And I've been wanting to return the favor."

"Trace?"

Lucky for him, she was wearing a skirt. He pulled up the loose fabric of her skirt, edging higher and higher. And her thigh highs. *Fuck, yes.* His fingers slid up her thighs and found the silk of her panties. "This time, it's my turn," he said.

She arched against him.

"I get to give you pleasure," he told her, "and I get to make you forget all about your fear." His fingers slid under the edge of her panties. He found her sweet flesh—warm and wet. He stroked her, loving the way her breath caught in her throat, and she tipped her hips toward him.

Skye's response always made him hot.

Made him want to take her endlessly.

He pulled her panties down. Thrust his index finger into her.

"Trace..."

"I don't want you to be afraid. I don't want you to feel anything but pleasure." Because he hated it when her green eyes shone with fear.

He pushed a second finger into her. Her teeth sank into her lower lip. His thumb began to massage her clit, rotating in slow circles.

He licked her throat again. Bit her lightly.

Withdrew his fingers. Thrust. Again.

Worked her clit.

"Trace!"

Her body was tight against him. So damn tight. He loved it. He wanted nothing more than to drive into her as deeply as he could go.

And that was why he didn't.

This is just for Skye. She needed to know that he could put her first.

She came with a gasp. Her inner muscles clenched around his fingers as she rode out her orgasm. So beautiful.

So perfect.

His Skye.

He held her while she shuddered. Then he slowly withdrew his fingers. Positioned her skirt once more.

Kissed her soft lips again.

Her hand grabbed his forearm. "Trace, you didn't—"

"I'm a selfish bastard most days. Hell, we both know that."

"No," she said quietly, with certainty, "you're not."

But Trace knew the truth. "I am with you. I see you, and all I want to do is take." His heart raced in his chest. "So this time, this once, just let me give." He had to look away from her because while he was talking a good game…

I want in her.

"Do you want to know how I see you?"

Trace nodded.

"I see a man who is sexy as sin. He's strong and he's powerful, and sometimes, he drives me absolutely crazy because he tries to control everything."

Trace winced.

"But he's the man who's saved me — twice — in my life. He was the first man to give me flowers. The only man to ask me to marry him. He's the man right there beside me when my nightmares come to haunt me."

She was the only woman he'd ever dreamed about.

"So don't talk about him as if he's a selfish SOB. *I* can do that," Skye said, her voice rough. "But no one else gets to say a word about him, got it? No one, not even you."

His lips curved. His gaze came back to her. The lust was still there, always there, but so was something else. "I love you, Skye."

She smiled at him. "I know."

***

Weston was out hunting. The guy thought he was such a security expert. That he could catch any criminal. That he could save the day.

Too late.

There wasn't going to be anything left for him to save this time.

Weston's empire would crumble. So would he.

One loss, for another.

The killer gazed across the street and up at the lights that burned on the second level of Skye Sullivan's dance studio.

Sara Kramer's sister was there. He knew that.

Just as he knew everything.

Did the sister know about him? Sara and Claire had been so close, and they'd talked frequently. When the grief eased, would Claire remember some half-forgotten conversation?

Will she remember me?

It was a chance he couldn't take. Claire shouldn't have come to town. Sara hadn't told him about her sister's arrival.

If she had, he would've planned his attack better.
Too late for regrets.
Claire was in the game now.
Until death.

***

The plane touched down on the runway. A small, narrow patch of concrete in the middle of Piedmont, Texas.

The town was a dot on the map. Tucker had talked often of the place. He'd said that it let him breathe. That he could see for miles and miles there.

That the place made him feel free.

Trace walked away from the plane, his hand locked with Skye's. He'd come to this town because he needed to see one person. A phone call wouldn't have done the job.

The light of dawn rose on the horizon. Trace climbed into the rental vehicle that waited. Arranging for the SUV had been easy enough.

The meeting that was coming?

Not so damn easy.

"I know you have a plan," Skye said.

He did.

"Want to share it with me?"

He drove away from the little landing strip. He'd been in Piedmont twice before. Once with Tucker.

Once when he'd come to bury Tucker. Only…Tucker hadn't been in that empty grave. It had just been a ceremony. A headstone with no casket in the ground.

"Tucker's father still lives in the area. I have some more questions for him." Because if Tucker truly had somehow made it out of that frozen hell, he would've come home. Tucker had been so close to his father.

"Did you tell his father you were coming?"

Trace shook his head. "He doesn't exactly like me, Skye. The man blames me for his son's death." His fingers tightened around the wheel. "With damn good reason." But Quint Hawk just thought Trace hadn't done a good enough job of covering Tucker's ass on the mission.

He didn't realize that Trace had been the one to fire the shot that ended Tucker's life.

They rode in silence. The miles drifted past. They turned off the pavement and fish-tailed down a long, dusty dirt road. The road ended in front of a ranch house. Two dogs ran out to meet them, barking excitedly.

Trace killed the engine. Stared at that house. Tucker had grown up there. Laughed and lived.

The front door opened. Quint appeared, holding tight to his cane.

Trace climbed from the SUV. He hurried around to Skye's side, but she'd already slipped out.

"Who the hell are you?" Quint demanded. "And what are you doin' on my property so damn early?"

Bracing his shoulders, Trace advanced. "It's me, Mr. Hawk." He took a few more steps. The dogs bounced around him, their tongues hanging out as they panted. "Trace Weston."

Quint shuffled forward. *Tap. Tap.* His cane hit the wooden floor of the porch. "What are you doin' back here?" His eyes narrowed as he glanced over Trace's shoulder. "And who's she?"

"That's my fiancé," Trace said. "And I'm here because I need to ask you a few more questions about Tucker."

"We don't got nothin' to say." Quint pointed a bony finger at Trace. "Now load up your pretty girl and get the hell off my property."

Right. That was the reception he'd expected and why he hadn't just called. "I can't leave. No, I *won't* leave." Trace strode toward the house. "Not until we talk. I know you blame me for Tucker's death. And you're—"

"He had a fiancé, too," Quint suddenly said, cocking his head. "I got his last letter to me. A week after I buried him, I got that letter."

Trace tensed. He looked over his shoulder and saw that Skye had come closer to him. Then he focused on Quint. "Do you have that letter, sir?"

"It's all I have left of him." Quint's hold on his cane tightened. "When I got it, I thought—them bastards were wrong. My boy's alive." He stared down at the porch. "Then I realized…he'd just sent it to me before he died. Mail is so slow…so slow…but for a moment there. A moment…I had my boy back."

"Sir, I'd really like to see that letter." *A fiancé?* Tucker had never said that he and Anna Jean were getting married.

"He did some bad things." Now Quint's shoulders stooped. "I know that now." His gaze found Trace's. "That's what killed him, isn't it?"

Trace shook his head. "Tucker was a good man."

"Once, he was." His knuckles whitened around the cane. "If I let you see the letter, I never want you comin' back, understand? You…" His voice thickened. "You remind me too much of what I lost."

Trace nodded. "You'll never see me again." Beside him, Skye was silent.

Quint disappeared into the house. *Tap. Tap.*

Trace didn't follow him.

"Did you know about his engagement?" Skye asked softly.

"No."

"Do you…do you think there were some other things that you didn't know?"

Tap. Tap.

Quint pushed open the door. Crept onto the porch. His fingers were shaking as he handed Trace an envelope. "Take it, then burn it."

Trace frowned. "But—"

"I was better off not gettin' that note." Quint leveled a hard stare at Trace. "And, son, you're better off not readin' it."

No, he wasn't.

Quint turned away. Stopped. His back was to Trace as he said, "My debt is paid to you, son."

"You never owed me a debt." Trace carefully held that envelope.

"I was losin' this place. The bank was gonna take it from me. Then...one day...I come out here to see the deed in my mail box. Paid in full." *Tap.* "I know what you had to do to my son. But you don't owe me anymore. And I don't owe you. We're done."

The door closed behind him.

"Trace?"

He knows.

Trace jerked his head toward the SUV. The dogs were still barking like crazy. "Let's get back inside."

After Trace shut the passenger-side door behind Skye, he walked back around the vehicle. He paused in front of the SUV. The sun was rising. He glanced at the old, wooden fence on the right. For an instant, he could imagine Tucker there. Laughing.

Then the image of Tucker was gone.

Trace climbed back into the SUV and slammed the door behind him. He stared down at the old envelope. The handwriting had faded some but he still easily recognized it as Tucker's writing. The stamp had torn, but he could make out the post date—a week before Tucker had died.

He opened the envelope. Pulled out the paper. He could feel Skye's eyes on him, but she didn't speak.

Trace unfolded the paper.

Dad,

I know I don't write enough, and I'm sorry about that. I think about you. About mom. I still miss her so much.

I'm in love. I always wanted to find someone to love the way that you loved mom. So completely.

We're going to get married. We have plans to start a new life, just me and my Anna Jean. But we have a job to do first. And it's a job that I hate.

I always tried to do the right thing. But doing right doesn't always give you the reward you need. Anna Jean has a deal set up for us. It's a one-time shot. We do this, and there are no more battles. No more crawling on my belly through the mud or the snow or the blood.

I'll be free.

There's a price to pay for freedom. I'm not proud of what I'm doing, but I want to give Anna Jean the life she deserves.

I won't be coming back. With what we've planned, I can't.

You were a good father.

I wish I'd been a better son.

"Sonofabitch," Trace whispered. His head lifted. He turned and met Skye's worried stare. "He was in on it. Tucker was working with Anna Jean. He betrayed us all."

***

Claire Kramer tip-toed down the stairs, her bag clutched tightly in her right hand. She didn't head into the main studio. She already felt like more than enough of an intruder in that place.

Her fingers slid over the knob at the back door. She opened it and eased outside as the alarm gave a reassuring beep. She took two steps—

"Going somewhere, Ms. Kramer?"

Claire screamed—and then she threw her bag at the tall, dangerous looking man who had been waiting for her.

The bag bounced off his shoulder, and Claire tried to yank open the door and rush back inside. But his palm flattened against the door, and his body slid behind hers. "Easy." He wasn't touching her, but he *surrounded* her. Too big and muscled. Fear and fury battled within her.

He'd been waiting for me.

Claire sucked in a deep breath. Then she attacked. Her elbow slammed into his solar plexus even as her fist flew up in a backhanded snap move. Her knuckles should've collided with his nose, giving a nice, satisfying crunch as the cartilage broke on impact.

But he caught her hand.

Claire stomped down with her left foot. He grunted.

That's right. I'm not easy prey. Not anymore. She'd spent years learning how to protect herself.

Claire spun around now, yanking her wrist free of his grip. She had keys in her left hand, and she brought them up, ready to shove those keys right into his eye—

He caught that hand, too. He didn't hurt her. He just held her, his strength undeniable. "You're good," he said, flashing a golden eyed stare at her. She planned to seriously damage those golden eyes. "But I think I'm a little bit better."

Those words infuriated her. He dared to taunt her? Hell, *no.*

Not again. Not again. The words rang in her head. They were Claire's vow to herself. She'd never be a victim again. She wouldn't be hurt.

He would.

Claire jerked up her knee, intending to hit him in the groin as hard as she could.

He pushed her back, flattening her against the door. A strong, muscular thigh pushed between her legs. "I think you need to settle down before someone gets hurt—"

She head-butted him.

"Dammit!"

His lip was bleeding.

Claire gave him a grim smile. "Looks like someone just got hurt. And guess what? More pain is coming."

He stepped back, freeing her and swiping at his bleeding lip. "*You?*" He tossed that out as if he were shocked. She'd shock him again with a punch to the face if he so much as inched toward her again.

"*You're* the grief-stricken sister that I'm supposed to be watching? I thought you needed a guard. No one told me you were so…" He waved his hand and drops of his blood fell on the pavement. "Violent," he finished.

You needed a guard.

"Who are you?" Claire asked him.

"Noah. Noah York." One dark brow rose as his eyes swept over her. His eyes unnerved her. She'd never met a man with golden eyes before.

"I'm not the enemy, sweetheart."

Her spine snapped straight at that.

"Delicate flower, my ass," Noah muttered. "Trace has you pegged all wrong. You'd think by now he'd be smart enough not to get fooled by a pretty face."

She swallowed and realized that she was choking back her fear. "Trace sent you?"

"Yeah. He had to leave town. Took Skye with him. Because you know, he can't breathe without her or some shit." Then he muttered, "Lovesick idiot that he is."

Her heart was starting to slow down, but she didn't trust the stranger. Not yet. "Give me proof."

"Proof?"

"How do I know you aren't lying?"

"Because I'm Noah York!"

"Is that supposed to mean something to me?"

His jaw dropped. That bottom lip of his—a sexy lip, despite the blood dripping from it—caught her attention.

Her gaze swept slowly over his face. The guy was handsome, and that put her on edge. She'd learned how dangerous handsome, lying men could be. His cheek bones were high, his nose a sharp blade, and his jaw was perfectly square and hard.

Too perfect.

Not for me.

He stared at her a moment, gazing deeply into her eyes, then he smiled. A dimple flashed in his cheek.

Not. For. Me.

"No," he said softly, "I don't think the name should mean a thing to you." He rolled his shoulders. "Tell you what, I saw Reese parked in front of the building. I'm guessing you met him already right? Trace's driver-slash-guard?"

Yes, she remembered Reese.

"He can tell you that I'm safe. Then maybe you'll stop trying to attack me."

She glanced down the length of the building. They were in the narrow back alley. It would only take a few moments to race to the front of the building and check out the guy's story.

Claire didn't move. "Why would Trace tell you both to guard me?" Suspicion had her eyes returning to Noah.

"I know, sounds like overkill, right? That's Trace." His smile invited her to smile back with him.

She didn't.

His smile slowly faded. "I see it," he said and his voice was grim now.

"What do you see?" Claire instantly demanded.

"Your pain, sweetheart. I see it in your eyes." He took a step toward her. "I'm sorry, I—"

"I don't need your pity." She'd seen pity more than enough times in the eyes of people she met. Pity. Anger. Hate.

Been there, done all of that.

She usually got those stares from most people, sooner or later. Except Skye hadn't looked at her that way. Skye hadn't judged her.

"Too bad," he snapped right back at her. "Because you're getting it. I didn't know Sara, not personally, but I've heard she was one hell of a woman. I'm sorry the world lost someone like her."

Her eyes stung. "R-Reese is around front?" She needed to verify who this guy was and get away from him, no matter what. Her stomach was in knots. Her heart twisted, and each time she looked into those golden eyes, Claire just felt...*off.*

"I'll go first," he said, his voice soft but deep. A rumble that got beneath her skin. "You'll feel better that way, won't you?"

She nodded. "I'm not about to turn my back on you."

"Then I guess I'm the one who has to show trust."

He marched ahead, moving easily through the narrow space.

She didn't follow, not at first. She let him get a few feet in front of her, then Claire scooped up her bag.

He rounded the corner and Claire quickly darted after him. Her gaze scanned the area. Sure enough, Reese was waiting by the studio's front door. He was leaning against his parked car.

When Reese saw them, he quickly straightened. "What are you doing here?" Reese demanded as he hurried toward Noah.

"Guard duty," was the instant reply, "same as you."

Reese's eyes widened. "Are you bleeding, man?" He advanced on Claire. "Are you okay, Ms. Kramer? Were you attacked?"

"No, she was the one doing the attacking," Noah said.

Reese's eyes widened, but he seemed to recover from his surprise quickly. "Good, that's—"

"I'm looking for Skye Sullivan." The voice—a woman's smooth, cultured voice—cut through Reese's words.

They glanced to the right and saw a redhead standing there. Her eyes were hidden by dark sunglasses, but her head was tilted toward them, and Claire could feel the weight of the woman's stare.

"You're not Skye," the woman said, as if dismissing Claire instantly. "I was told this was her studio."

"Skye Sullivan's not here now," Reese said. "Something I can help you with?"

The redhead laughed. "No, you can't help me at all. I'll come back for Skye." Then she turned. She had on shoes with three-inch heels. Claire wasn't even sure how the woman managed to walk in them.

Frowning, Claire looked away from the redhead. Her gaze focused on her real problem—*Noah.*

Noah's gaze was still on the other woman. His eyes were narrowed.

Right. Cue the lady in the tight skirt and low-cut shirt, and, of course, that guy would be all over her.

"She's familiar," he whispered.

The woman lifted her hand. A taxi jerked to a stop just two feet away from her.

"The nose is different...the lips are fuller. Hair's red, not blonde..." It sounded like Noah was just muttering to himself.

Claire rubbed her temples. They were throbbing again.

"Ms. Kramer?" Reese asked. "Were you going somewhere?" His eyes were on the bag that she still held.

"A hotel," she heard herself say. "I just can't impose on Skye. I need to—"

"It's all different," Noah snapped. *Still talking to himself?* "But the walk is the fucking *same.*"

He pushed past them, his arm hitting Claire's as he raced toward the taxi. He reached the curb just as the taxi sped away. His fists flew into the air in impotent rage. "*Fucking hell!*" Noah yelled. "It's not him. *It's her.*"

CHAPTER THIRTEEN

"I know what I saw." Noah's voice was grim as he paced in front of Trace's desk. "The woman always had a walk of pure sin. That was how she first caught Tucker's eye. She changed her hair, got a nose job, injected her lower lip with collagen, but she didn't change her walk."

Trace stared at him. He'd only been in town an hour when Noah had called and demanded this meeting. Noah had insisted they meet at Weston Securities, a private meeting — just Noah, Trace, and Drake.

Trace had told him to screw that "private" plan. Skye was with him. She stood at his side as he faced the two men who'd gone to hell with him.

I can't keep any more secrets from her. Because he knew that the secrets were the things that would drive her away from him.

With Skye, it was all or nothing. He was trying so hard to give her all he had.

"You're actually telling us," Drake said, voice grating, "that Anna Jean isn't dead? You saw her today?"

Noah rounded on him. "*You* tell me. I mean, you're the one who supposedly to kill her, right? But I got to thinking…you were sleeping with her. You admitted that. So maybe at that kill moment, you hesitated. Did you hesitate, Drake?"

Drake glared back at him.

"I don't hear a damn answer," Noah snarled. "Did you kill her? Did you stab her in the heart? Or did you hesitate?"

A muscle flexed in Drake's jaw.

"Stop, Noah," Trace said wearily. "I found out more about Tucker. You both need to know that—"

"Yes," Drake hissed.

The tension in the room kicked up about one hundred percent. Trace's hand dropped to his side. He focused totally on Drake. "What did you just say?"

"I missed her heart." All of the color had bled from Drake's face. "I couldn't do it. I know she was trying to kill me, but I hesitated, okay? I wounded her, but she wasn't dead."

"She died in Tucker's arm," Trace said. He'd been sure...the way Tucker had reacted...

Drake closed his eyes. "I've replayed those moments in my head a thousand times. I didn't remember hitting her heart with the blade. I didn't, but she still died, so I thought I was wrong. I thought I'd imagined—"

"She's not dead." Noah's voice vibrated with fury. "The bitch is strolling around Chicago, looking for Skye."

Skye jerked beside Trace. "Why would she be looking for me?"

"Probably because she wants to screw with your head," Noah fired out. "She likes playing mind games."

"Or because she wants to kill you," Drake said.

Neither would happen on Trace's watch. "You got the name of the cab company?" Noah had told him that he'd missed the cab by seconds.

"Yes," Noah replied instantly.

That was something. "Now tell me that you got the cab number."

Noah rattled it off.

Trace picked up his phone. In two minutes, he had the manager of that cab company on the line. Thirty seconds later, Trace said, "He dropped her at the Navy Pier."

Noah headed for the door. "Let's get her, let's—"

"I'll send a team," Trace said, working to keep his voice free of emotion. "They'll get her."

Noah stiffened. He swung back around to stare incredulously at Trace. "Are you kidding me? It's *her*. After all that's happened, you're just sending a team?"

"Yes." Flat. "That's exactly what I'm doing because I'll be damned if I walk into some trap that she's setting." He pulled Tucker's letter from his pocket. "Tucker knew, okay? He knew what she was doing. He knew that she was setting us all up, and I'm pretty sure he planned for the three of us—" His gaze hit on each man there. "To die during that last mission. Only we got lucky. We lived."

Drake's eyelids flickered. "He...knew?"

"That's what the letter says. He was finishing his job with Anna Jean, and they weren't coming back. They had a future all mapped out. They just didn't count on us fighting back so hard."

Noah looked shell-shocked. "Tucker? He was setting us up, too?"

Trace nodded. Rage had twisted inside of Trace. He knew just how Noah felt.

Skye's fingers curled around his shoulder. Some of the fury eased.

"Anna Jean wasn't working alone then. I don't buy for an instant that she's working alone now." This was the part that sealed the deal for Trace. "I saw the bodies at the morgue. Sharpe, Parker, and Sara. There were no hesitation wounds on Parker, but the killer paused when he was carving up Sharpe's throat and when he was slicing open Sara."

Noah cocked is head. "He *paused*?"

"The wounds were deep. Hard. Strong. Anna Jean is many things, but I don't think she could've inflicted those wounds. The angles would've been wrong. The depth of entry—none of it matches up to her." Anna Jean had been all of five foot three and one hundred and twenty pounds.

"Then Tucker's here, too," Drake said. He looked and sounded hollowed out. "We thought that we left them to die, but they've come back to kill us."

"Revenge?" Skye asked. "If that's what this is about, then why attack all the others? Why go after Sara?"

Trace told her the dark truth. He said, "Because lives don't matter to Anna Jean. They never did." She'd been willing to use anyone or anything in order to get what she wanted.

"They're pawns in a chess game," Drake explained. "She's the queen on the board."

Trace's hands slapped down on the surface of his desk. He fucking knew how to play chess. "We need to find her damn king."

And destroy him.

***

It was storming outside. Skye stared out at the pounding rain. Lightning lit up the sky.

Thunder roared.

"She wasn't at the Pier," Trace said as he came up behind her. The others had left. Noah had stormed away, no doubt headed out to search on his own. Drake had followed Noah out, but his steps had been much slower.

Was he in love with Anna Jean? There was just something about the way Drake looked each time her name was mentioned. Pain filled his eyes. Skye suspected that there was a whole lot more to Drake's connection to Anna Jean had he wanted to confess.

Trace's hands closed over her shoulders. "My men are talking with the vendors there. Someone had to see her. They'll find her."

Skye saw another flash of lightning. She waited for the thunder to rumble. "Have you told me everything?"

His fingers began to rub her shoulders. "Everything that you need to know."

That wasn't the answer she wanted to hear.

"Don't tense up on me like that," Trace said. "Baby, you don't want to know about every battle. About every life that was lost or about how I felt when I had to pull the trigger each time."

"I do," Skye told him. Didn't he understand yet? "Good and bad. Everything in between."

He bent his head. Because the office was lit and it was so dark outside, she could easily see their reflections in the glass. He surrounded her, so big and strong.

His lips brushed over her nape. "I don't like for that world to touch you. The more you learn about me, the more you realize you're too good for me. That I shouldn't even be touching you."

He was wrong. "I like it when you touch me."

His right hand slid down and curled around her stomach, pulling her back against him. She could feel his aroused length pressing against her.

"This nightmare is going to be over soon," he promised her as he pressed another kiss to her throat. "Now we know we're looking for Anna Jean. She's not getting away. And we'll find her partner."

"Tucker?"

He seemed to hesitate.

And she caught that telling sign. "You don't think Tucker is alive, do you?"

His head lifted, but his arm tightened around her. "I'm not like Drake."

Skye waited, her heart racing.

"I didn't hesitate at the last instant. I know my shot hit his heart." Trace shook his head. "He didn't get out of that frozen hell, but she did. She took the dog tags, and now she's got some other dumb SOB doing her dirty work."

She gazed down into the darkness of the city. "So her partner could be anyone." Any man that Skye passed on the street. Anyone she saw. Anywhere. Any time.

"I'm running down leads right now. The guy made a mistake when he hacked into my phone system. I've got my techs on it, retracing his steps."

"You said that it's been years since that attack in Siberia. Why are they after you now? Why wait so long?"

"Some people can wait forever for the right vengeance."

"And this Anna Jean…she and her partner want to hurt you."

By hurting me.

He pressed another kiss to her nape.

A shiver slid over her. "I would do anything to keep you safe. You know that, don't you?"

His muscles locked. She felt the tenseness in his hold. "I don't want you at risk, Skye."

"But she came looking for me. In broad daylight." That just didn't sound like a woman who was trying to come in for a slow, sneaky kill.

"Anna Jean is insane. You don't want to ever get close to her."

"I've been close to other insane folks." *Like my mother.* "I managed okay."

He turned her in his arms. His gaze searched hers. "I don't like to think of you in danger. I *can't.*"

His lips took hers.

She kissed him back eagerly, her lips opening beneath his. Trace lifted her up, carried her a few feet across the room. She felt the hard edge of the desk against her thighs. He sat her down there, right on top of his gleaming desk, and he slipped between her splayed legs.

"I have you, and I won't let you go." One of his hands rested lightly against the column of her throat, right over her frantically racing pulse. "I don't care which asshole from my past comes calling, no one will take you from me."

Just as she wasn't going to let anyone take Trace from her. Not when they finally had a chance together.

He lifted up her shirt. Tossed it across the room. His eyes were lit with a bright, burning fire. Lust. Need. The same need that pulsed through her veins.

His fingers brushed aside her bra. Her nipples were tight, aching, and when he bent his head and took one sensitive peak into his mouth, she arched against him.

Yes.

But he had on too many clothes. Way, way too many. Her fingers pushed between their bodies. She caught his belt. Yanked it aside. Jerked open his fly.

So her moves weren't as easy or seductive as his had been. Skye wasn't in the mood for easy.

"Trace." His name came from her as a sensual demand. "I want you. *Now.*"

His head lifted. His gaze met hers.

"Now," Skye said again. And, seeing that hot lust in his gaze, she told him, "I want you to fuck me hard, Trace. No control. No limits."

His hands gripped the edge of the desk. "Skye, baby —"

"Everything, Trace. That's what I want."

What she'd have.

Lightning flashed beyond the windows.

Skye kicked off her shoes. She slid off the desk, her body brushing against Trace's. Staring into his eyes, she stripped off the rest of her clothes. Her pants fell. Her panties — she threw those at him.

He caught them in a tight fist. "I never want to hurt you."

She stood before him, naked. "The first time I came to see you in this office, I was terrified."

His eyes blazed an even brighter blue. "The first time you came to see me, I wanted to strip you and fuck you on my desk."

Her hands tapped on said desk. "Right here?"

"*Yes.*" A hard growl.

"Then I guess you're about to get your wish, aren't you?" She smiled at him and she touched herself, letting her hands slide down her stomach. Down to—

Trace grabbed her. He spun her around, turning her toward that desk. Her hands flew out and this time, her palms hit against the hard surface.

He was behind her. Fully erect, the head of his cock thrust toward her. She spread her legs. She arched against him.

He held her easily. Didn't enter her yet, damn him. Just let her *feel* him, all around her. "If I get too rough," he rasped out, "tell me to stop."

"I'll scream it," she promised, her own breath panting.

His fingers stroked her. Pressed against her clit. Drove her insane.

"*Trace!*"

He plunged into her, slamming balls deep. *Yes!* He withdrew. Plunged deep again. Harder. The thud of flesh hitting flesh seemed to fill the room. Again and again.

She was so wet for him. So eager.

Thunder rumbled.

Deeper, deeper. She pushed back against each thrust, trying to take as much of him as she could. Her orgasm beat down on her. Her muscles tightened. So close. Just right—

"Ah, baby, you didn't think it would be that easy, did you?" Trace whispered against her ear. He stilled.

Her sex clenched tightly around him, holding him in a desperate grip.

His mouth slid to her neck. He licked. He kissed.

His teeth pressed against her in a sensual bite. "Now," he rasped against her skin. "You're going to give me everything."

He withdrew. She cried out. "No, Trace—"

In a flash, he had rolled Skye onto her back. The wood of the desk pressed into her. Her legs hung over the edge of the desk. Her legs were open, her sex desperate for him.

"Remember…tell me…" Trace gritted out.

That was all he said. Because as she stared up into his eyes, she could see his control break. The blue turned wild in its brilliance.

He thrust into her. Deep.

His hands caught hers. He locked them to the desk, holding them on either side of her. He held her, controlled her completely, and all Skye could do was take the pleasure that he gave to her.

Helpless, trapped.

Again and again, he drove into her body. She'd thought that she was slick before. Now — "*Trace!*"

He yanked her closer to the edge of the desk. Her legs lifted and locked around his hips. The orgasm was there, the pleasure already starting to crest through her.

Trace kissed her. His mouth was hot. Open.

She came around him, exploding on a release so powerful that she shuddered.

But he didn't stop.

His thrusts came faster. They were even harder, lifting her body. She tightened her hold around him, trying to catch her breath.

"*You're not done, Skye.*" He locked both of her wrists in one of his. Kept them secured above her head. His left hand slipped between their bodies. He stroked her clit again. Pushed her and pushed her until she screamed.

But she didn't scream for him to stop.

She screamed Trace's name.

He came, surging into her with a hot release that had him shuddering.

Only he didn't stop.

He kept thrusting. His release made her even more sensitive to him, and his cock stretched, filling her, sliding over flesh that was desperate for more.

Insatiable.

Only for him. Only for —

He lifted her off the desk. Held her in his arms. Lifted her easily. She'd always known he was strong. But this—

"Squeeze me. As hard and tight as you can."

Her inner muscles clamped around him.

"Yes!" His eyes were still wild. "Want...more...want...*all*..."

He took her against the wall then. Her shoulders hit the surface, but she didn't care. He'd freed her hands, and her nails scratched down his back.

He was holding her hips now, lifting her up again and again. Forcing her to match his rhythm, forcing her to take and take.

She didn't have the breath to scream when the release hit her this time. She shuddered and trembled in his arms. Then she fell against him, limp, as her heart raced.

He still wasn't done.

Trace kept thrusting. A fast, hard tempo that she couldn't match. The tender lover was gone. She looked up and saw that his face was cut in hard lines of need. Primitive lust. Her arms wrapped around him, and that was pretty much all her exhausted body could manage.

His cock was so full. Big and thick, filling every inch of her. Her sex was swollen from her orgasms. With every thrust, she was on the brink of more pleasure...or pain?

The line was there, so hard to determine. Because the feelings coursing through her were so strong. So dark and powerful.

He erupted. *"Skye!"* His orgasm went on and on, and she was lost as she seemed to fall into the abyss.

Not pain.

Only pleasure.

Only...Trace.

***

Navy Pier. The place was normally a tourist's dream, but, in the middle of a night-time thunderstorm, the place was deserted.

Drake stood at the end of the dock, staring out at the glistening water. Lightning flashed in the dark sky. Bright strobes that lit the waves.

Anna Jean.

She'd been his worst mistake.

And he hadn't even managed to kill her.

Drake turned away from the water, hunching his shoulders against the rain that continued to fall in heavy blasts from the dark sky. He'd screwed up back then—when he'd *screwed* her. But he'd never met another woman like Anna Jean.

She'd had a walk of pure temptation. Eyes that made him think constantly of sex and the pleasures found between lovers. She'd belonged to Tucker. He knew it, and he'd done his best to keep his hands off her.

But she'd come to him. They'd danced too much and drank too damn much in a godforsaken bar in Russia.

They'd fucked in that same bar.

When the booze had cleared from his head, Drake had hated himself for what he'd done. He'd wanted to tell Tucker about his mistake.

But Anna Jean had said that Tucker would never forgive. Or forget.

"Drake…"

He turned at the faint call. He could just see the outline of a person, walking toward him. He squinted, trying to see better in the storm.

"Drake."

A woman's voice. Drifting to him. He took a step toward her, focusing completely on her now.

So when the blow came from behind, he didn't have time to defend himself.

Something heavy and hard slammed into the back of his head. Then Drake felt himself flying to the side, and he crashed right into the icy water.

***

"Did I hurt you?" Trace stared down at Skye as a fist seemed to squeeze his heart. His body still shuddered with aftershocks of the most powerful release he'd ever had.

He'd gone damn blind there for a moment. He'd only been able to feel — *her*.

Her head tilted back against the wall, and she smiled at him. A slow, sensual smile that pierced straight through him. "Was that supposed to scare me?"

He'd been too rough. Too controlling, too —

"If so, then I think you should work real hard to scare me again. You know, every night or so."

The tightness around his heart eased. He lifted her into his arms. Her hands wrapped around his neck, and he carried her to the bathroom.

Trace sat her on the granite countertop. Carefully, he cleaned off the signs of their love-making from her body. And when he looked up, he found Skye staring straight at him.

"Every lover that I've ever had…he's been you in the dark." Her voice was soft and sensual.

Always tempting me.

He tossed aside the cloth. Trace put his hands on either side of her body. He didn't touch her, not then. *Try to go five seconds without touching her.* "No other lover could ever compare to you." After he'd had sex with them, he couldn't get away from the other women fast enough. *Because they weren't Skye.*

And he'd felt guilty, so damn guilty, for being with them. Even when Skye had been a world away.

"I never asked you for a list of lovers," Skye said.

That gave him pause. He'd asked for a list of her lovers, back when he'd been trying to figure out who was stalking her. He'd also been tempted to destroy every man on her list.

"I don't want to know about them," Skye said. "Because then I'll just have people to hate."

His breath burned in his lungs. "You're it for me. There can't be anyone else, not after what we've had."

Her smile grew then and lit her eyes. She leaned toward him. Her lips pressed against his ear. "Good," Skye whispered, "because I'd hate to hurt a bitch."

Her words surprised him so much—coming from his delicate Skye—*not* so delicate—that Trace laughed.

Skye didn't laugh. She kept gazing up into his eyes. "Oh, Trace," Skye said softly. "When are you ever going to realize the truth? You don't love me because you want to protect me. You love because you realize that, deep down, we're very much alike."

His laughter slowly faded.

His Skye.

If another man tried to come near her...

I'd destroy the bastard.

"Yes," Trace whispered, "we are." Then he kissed her once more.

***

Drake broke through the surface of the waves, his breath heaving out. He'd barely avoided slamming into the dock on his way into the blackness of the water.

"Over here!" A woman's voice shouted.

Her?

Someone was crouched at the edge of the pier. When lightning flashed, he could see the outline of a person's body.

He grabbed for the dock. Caught the wooden ladder that would get him out of the water.

Something dripped into his eyes. Water? Or blood?

Her hand reached for him. "Let me help you!"

He grabbed her and yanked her into the water with him.
She screamed. *Hell, yes, it's your turn to scream.*
She also...sank?

The woman disappeared beneath the waves. Swearing,
Drake dove after her. He caught her hair, long, spider-web
like tendrils that drifted in the water, and he reached lower,
grabbing for her.

They broke the surface together. She was gasping and
shuddering and clinging to him as desperately as she could.

"*Anna Jean?*" Drake demanded. No, that wasn't right.
Anna Jean could swim for miles. She'd gone swimming with
sharks for fuck's sake. Anna Jean had no fear. Anna Jean—

The woman was about to choke him with her death-grip
on his neck. "M-my...s-sister..."

He dragged her toward the dock. Hauled her up.
Dropped her like a sack of potatoes.

She pushed up to her knees. "Y-you aren't what I
thought..."

He still couldn't see her face. There just wasn't enough
light. Rain pelted down on them, hitting like hard spikes
against his skin.

But...her voice was wrong. Too soft and husky, and
tinged with the faintest of accents.

"Who the hell are you?"

She shoved wet hair out of her face. "I'm Piper, and I...I
believe you knew my sister, Anna Jean."

Believe? What the hell kind of game was this? "Where's
your partner?"

"I-I don't have a partner."

"Sure you do." And Drake yanked out his weapon. The
gun had been soaked, but there was a fifty-fifty chance it
would still fire at least one bullet. "The jerk who hit me and
threw me in the water. Now tell me...where the hell is he?"

She shook her head.

"Fine, I figure that answer means we get to do things the
hard way." He grabbed her and put the gun to her throat.

She screamed.

***

Trace answered his phone, stopping the peeling rings. "What the hell is it?" At this time of night, it had better be important.

"I've got her," Drake's growling voice said. "Get to your dancer's studio. I'm heading there now."

The line ended.

What. The. Hell?

CHAPTER FOURTEEN

"He's insane!" The woman screamed the instant she saw Trace and Skye. "He has a gun!"

Trace shoved open the door to Skye's studio. He made sure she got inside first, then he turned to confront Drake. "Have you lost what little sanity you had?"

"No, I found it...when I found *her*."

Drake pushed the woman inside.

Trace made certain that he secured the lock behind them all.

Skye hit the lights, and the illumination flooded down on them, giving Trace his first good look at the woman.

This just keeps getting worse.

The woman—a drenched redhead with flashing green eyes—was as pale as death. Her high cheeks gave her a hallowed out, frightened look—or maybe that look just came from the absolute terror that was reflected in her eyes.

"H-he tried to drown me," she whispered. "Then he put his g-gun to my—"

Drake shoved the gun into his waistband. "I found her at Navy Pier. Right before some asshole slammed a board into the back of my head and dumped me in the water. Now *she* won't tell me who her partner is, but the lady did confess to one thing. According to her, she's Anna Jean's sister."

Trace studied the woman's face. "Yes, I can see the resemblance." The eyes weren't the same shade of green, and her hair was the wrong color. Anna Jean's face had been more classically beautiful. Cold perfection—that was what he'd thought of when he saw Anna Jean.

"What in the hell is happening down here?" A snarling voice demanded. Then footsteps thudded down from the upstairs apartment.

And Noah appeared.

Noah?

Claire was right behind him, peering nervously over his shoulder.

Noah's gaze darted over to Drake and then that golden stare narrowed when he saw Drake's guest. "*You.*" He lunged toward the woman. "*Anna Jean.*"

"No!" The woman cried out as she tried to back away from him, and she thudded into Drake. "I'm not. My name's Piper! I-I'm her half-sister."

Noah's doubting gaze swept over her. "Nice trick. Got some collagen in your lower lip. A nose job. Died your hair." He peered at her. "And I'd wager those are contacts, just to make your eyes look a little different, right?"

"No!"

"Bullshit. I saw you walk away today. I know that walk. I know *you.* You always were a good actress, Anna Jean. Too good."

Her frantic green stare flew around the room and locked on Skye. "Help me," she begged. "This isn't why I came here. I-I needed to talk with you."

"So talk," Trace invited.

Skye edged around him. "Talk to *me.*"

The woman's chest shuddered. She glanced over her shoulder at Drake, then her terrified stare came back to Skye. "Y-you're in danger," she said. "I-I had to tell you. You needed to be warned."

Trace stiffened. "Did you just threaten her?"

"No, Trace," it was Skye who answered, her voice calm, "she didn't."

The woman — Piper or Anna Jean or whoever the hell she was — told Skye, "You have to get away from him."

Skye glanced back at Trace.

"He's a killer," the woman threw out, breath heaving.

Skye already knew that.

"He…he was my sister's lover. He killed Anna Jean, and I'm afraid he will kill you, too."

The hell, *no.*

***

All of the players were assembled. They'd gathered. Drawn in close.

Now it was time for the chaos.

Time for vengeance.

They were all to blame, so they would all suffer.

In the end, no one would be left.

I will win.

Trace Weston — oh, he would lose *everything.*

The bodies would start falling now. If they'd thought the blood ran heavily on the streets before…

It's nothing compared to what I am about to do.

***

"Hell." Noah sounded stunned. "You screwed her, too, Trace?"

Skye kept her eyes on the woman called Piper. "You're lying."

Piper shook her head. "No, I'm not! My sister was in a hospital, some hole-in-the-wall in the middle of Russia. I barely got to her in time. She was *dying.* He'd stabbed her and left her for dead — "

"I stabbed her," Drake said, his voice thick.

The woman stiffened. "Y-you?"

Skye watched as shock seemed to flare in the woman's eyes.

"I stabbed her, and I'm the one who left her for dead." He flashed her a hard smile. "And you know what? I'm the one who fucked her, too. So if you're looking for someone to blame for all that...look right here."

She slapped him. A hard, vicious hit that seemed to echo across the room.

Then the woman fell to her knees. She wrapped her arms around her stomach. Shuddered. "I-I found the dog tags. She had them. She told me..." Her head lifted. Her face was a mask of confusion and rage. "Trace. He was the one. He killed her. He screwed my sister and he left her to die." Tears leaked from her eyes as she looked once more at Skye. "And he'll do the same to you! He's a killer! A killer!"

Skye shook her head. "No."

"It was *me*," Drake said again. "*Me.*"

Claire tried to ease past Noah. He caught her arm and pushed her right back behind his body. "Don't get close to Anna Jean. She's a viper."

"*I'm not Anna Jean!*" The woman yelled. "Anna Jean died in a Siberian hospital. She lost her fingers and her toes to hypothermia. She struggled to live—for days and days, but the fluids built up around her heart. Or, around what was left of it. She died, broken and in agony." Now her gaze swung wildly around the room. "I-I thought it was just Weston, but it was all of you. *All of you!*"

Then she whirled around and grabbed at Drake. No, not at him. Her fingers latched onto the gun he'd tucked into his waistband. She yanked the weapon up.

Drake's fingers locked around her wrist. "Let go."

Trace flew across the room.

Skye didn't move. Her eyes were on the scene before her. Piper seemed so broken.

She came to warn me?

Piper let go of the gun. She whirled back toward Trace. "Y-you were going to do the same thing to Skye. I saw in the papers…you were with her. You were going to kill her, too."

"You're wrong," Trace said, his voice flat.

Piper flinched. "I wanted to help. I came all this way…to help…" Her shoulders sagged.

Skye's eyes narrowed on her. "If you thought Trace killed your sister, why didn't you go to the police?"

"Anna Jean died. Sh-she could barely remember what had happened to her. When she *could* talk, she told me that it was all white…snow and hell. A white hell, and that was *all* she could say." Piper drew in a shuddering breath. "But she had Trace's dog tags. She *had* them."

"And now they're in the city." Trace tilted his head to the left. "Want to tell me how that happened? Who'd you give the dog tags to, Piper?"

Piper seemed to pale even more.

Trace lifted his head. "Who was it?"

Noah stalked toward them.

"Y-you know," Piper whispered.

Skye frowned at her. Piper was shaking now. Trembling.

Piper glanced back at Drake. "I want to go. Please…please let me go…"

His fingers settled on her shoulder. "You had a partner at the pier," Drake said. "Is that the guy who had the dog tags?"

"D-don't…I'm afraid!" Piper cried out. Her stare slid toward Noah.

He'd halted a few feet from Piper. He stared at her, heavy suspicion on his face and in his eyes.

Skye's gaze darted between them. Something just wasn't right there.

"Who had the tags?" Trace demanded.

"*The cop!*" Piper screamed. Her hand came up and slapped over her mouth, as if she were horrified by the words she'd just said.

A cold chill slid down Skye's spine.

"What cop?" Trace asked, only now, his voice was lethally soft.

Piper's hands dropped to her sides. Her shoulders slumped, as if she were defeated, and she answered, "A detective came to see me in Atlanta. He found out about you and Anna Jean, and he told me that you were going to attack again. He said—he said we had to stop you."

"Describe this cop." The order came from Noah.

"E-early thirties. Blond hair. Dark eyes. Good-looking."

Alex? Skye's heart beat faster. "What was his name?" She asked.

Piper's lips pressed together.

"His *name*," Trace shouted.

Piper jerked. "He's a police officer," she whispered. "He wanted to help. He said that he'd investigated you. That he knew who you were, deep inside. He knew what you'd do." Piper's eyes gleamed as she cast a desperate glance toward Skye. "I just didn't want you turning out like Anna Jean!"

Anna Jean. A woman long dead, but haunting them all.

"Alex Griffin," Skye said softly, but...*this feels wrong.*

Piper's head moved in the slightest of nods.

Trace's face grew even harder. "You're telling me that you gave my dog tags to Detective Griffin?"

"He said he needed them for the investigation—"

"One of those dog tags turned up at a murder scene," Trace said, cutting across her words. "The dead man had been stabbed in the heart, and the knife wounds in his throat were so severe that he was nearly decapitated."

Piper gasped.

"The cop?" Noah edged toward Trace. "Are you really thinking it's him?"

A faint line had appeared between Trace's brows. "He was downstairs at my building when we got the call about Sara. He *couldn't* have killed her."

"If he'd had help, he could've done it." This flat response came from Drake.

"I'll be damned." Trace's eyes widened as something seemed to click for him. Then he said, "The wounds were different. There were hesitation wounds on Sharpe's neck and on Sara's neck. Those wounds weren't on Parker. I thought it was just easier for the killer to take out Parker but—"

"But it could've been two killers," Skye finished, understanding what he meant.

Trace nodded curtly.

"No!" Piper's high-pitched cry. "Cops protect people. They don't—they don't—"

"Give someone the right motivation," Claire's quiet voice was a direct contrast to Piper's, "and they'll do anything." Her lips twisted in disgust. "I've seen plenty of cops turn away from the law. I've seen them do things that would give you nightmares—and they did 'em just for a little money."

But Skye had been so convinced that Alex was a good cop. "He wanted to help me," she said. "He worked so hard to *help*."

"And he wants me out of your life," Trace told her. "Because he thinks I'm like the monster who killed his sister."

Skye wasn't so sure of that. Alex stuck to the law. He was a good guy, wasn't he?

Trace's phone rang then, startling her. Trace yanked it out of his pocket. "Look, Reese," he said into the phone, "this isn't a good time. I need to—*What?*"

Fear flashed across Trace's face.

"Where the hell are you? Yeah, yeah, all right, listen to me, okay? Stay there. No, don't try to face him yourself. This is personal. Stay there. I am on my way." He ended the call and his stare immediately locked on Skye.

"What's happening?" Noah's body was as tense as Trace's.

"Reese thinks someone tailed him back to his apartment."

Skye's breath caught. *Not Reese.*

Trace returned to Skye's side. "If you want to hurt me," Trace said, his voice a rasp, "you hurt the people close to me." His fingers slid over her cheek. "You and Reese. You two are my family."

She caught his hand. "I'm coming with you."

"No, hell, *no*." He gave a hard, negative shake of his head. "You might think Alex won't hurt you, but I know otherwise."

If they even *were* dealing with Alex. "Call him," Skye said, the words flying from her. "Call Alex. Find out where he is."

Trace dialed quickly. She barely breathed while she waited and —

"No answer, and I'm not wasting any more time — time that Reese may not have."

She was really supposed to what? Wait there? He could just get pissed. She was going with him. "*I'm coming.*"

"Skye —"

"Please!" Piper's desperate cry. More tears were on her cheeks. "I don't even know what's happening, but I'm scared to death. I-I don't trust them!" She pointed to Trace, to Noah, to Drake. Then her gaze came back to Skye. "I came here because of you. I wanted to help you, the way I couldn't help my own sister. Wherever you go, I want to go, too."

"No damn way," was Trace's instant reply.

Piper trembled.

"Stay here, Skye," Trace said. His voice lowered, "Please, baby, I'd go crazy if I thought he could get to you. Stay here and Drake — you protect her, understand? With your life."

Drake nodded.

"If Drake's got guard duty, then I'm your back-up," Noah said as he moved to Trace's side.

But Claire raced across the room then. She grabbed Noah's arm, leaned up, and whispered something into his ear.

His shoulders stiffened. He drew back and gazed down at her. After a moment, he nodded.

Skye didn't like this. Trace and Noah were headed for the door. Claire had wrapped her arms around Piper's shoulders as she tried to comfort the other woman.

Drake was still casting suspicious glances Piper's way.

"H-he put a gun to my head," Piper mumbled to Claire. "And he yanked me into the water."

That would explain her drenched clothing and hair.

But…a gun to her head?

Her gaze jerked to Trace. He was steps away from the door. "Come back to me!" She called out. He'd better. He *had* to return to her.

Trace paused at the door. "I'll be back, baby, safe and sound." He spared her a glance, giving her a hard nod. "Count on it."

Trace will keep his promise. He always kept his promises to her. She fought not to show the fear that clawed through her. "And you make sure that Reese is safe, too." Reese had faced too much danger on their behalf.

Then Trace was gone. The door closed softly behind him. The alarm reset with a faint beep.

Piper kept crying. Drake raked a hand over his face.

"Come upstairs," Claire told Piper. "I've got some extra clothes in my bag up there. You can dry off."

Piper let Claire lead her to the stairs, but she cast one more suspicious glance back at Drake. "You…you really killed my sister?"

His jaw hardened. He nodded.

"You bastard," she whispered and her face contorted with pain.

***

Sweat covered Reese's forehead as he glanced out of his apartment window. He was up on the second floor, and the street below him was dead quiet.

The storm had stopped. Finally.

But the danger hadn't passed.

He gazed down at the street. The street lamps barely provided any illumination, their glow was too weak. Shadows seemed to move down there.

His eyes narrowed.

Death was coming tonight. Hunting.

Hurry the hell up, Trace.

The phone behind him began to ring.

***

"I know someone was with her on that pier," Drake said, his shoulder brushing against Skye's arm. "The jackass knocked me in the head and dumped me in the water."

"But in all of the other kills, the attacker used a knife. No one drowned." The whole situation just didn't make sense to Skye.

Drake glanced up at the ceiling. "She knows more than what she's saying." He started to march for the stairs.

Skye stopped him. "You're the last person she wants to see now." There had been no missing the hate and fury on Piper's face. Skye gave a decisive nod. "I'll do it, okay? I'll talk to her."

"I don't think you should get anywhere near her," he snapped out. "Trace asked me to stay because he wanted you safe. If she's anything like her viper of a sister—"

"You loved her, didn't you?" Skye asked.

She heard a faint creak from upstairs, as if a door had opened.

Drake blanched. "What? What are you insane?"

"Maybe it wasn't love," Skye allowed. "But maybe it was as close as you'd ever come. You cared about Anna Jean, but you still had to kill her."

"She was going to kill me! She had a gun to my head!"

"And you had a gun to Piper's."

His eyes squeezed shut. "She's in my nightmares." All the emotion had drained from his voice. "Every night. I close my eyes, and I see her dying in that snow. An angel with blood for wings."

***

"Are we really sure a cop is the one we're after?" Noah asked.

Trace had the Jag's gas pedal shoved to the ground. "No, we won't be sure until we see him with our own eyes." Because all of the puzzle pieces weren't fitting for Trace.

The way the evidence had been planted at Parker's murder scene. Trace's shirt...the dog tag. All of that indicated that the killer had been trying to frame him, and a cop would know just how to set up a frame job.

But then something had happened. The killer had struck again. *Too quickly?* He'd gone right after Sara.

Why?

His hold on the steering wheel tightened. Maybe the cop had worried that Sara knew too much, that she'd turn on *him*.

So did you have someone else kill her? Someone who hesitated?

Trace raced through a yellow light. He needed to go *faster*.

***

"I should be in jail," Drake said. "That's where I belong. I fucking killed her." His breath rasped out. "That's what she tells me, every single night."

Did Trace have those same nightmares? Only, for him, was it the ghost of Tucker who came back and haunted him?

Another creak came from upstairs. Skye's gaze rose. *Is Piper listening?* Skye didn't want the other woman to hear anymore.

Her fingers slid down Drake's arm, and she headed for the stairs.

Sure enough, Piper stood at the top of those stairs. Her hands were wrapped tightly around her stomach.

Skye slowly climbed the stairs. Piper backed up, sliding into the apartment. She held the door open for Skye.

"All this time," Piper whispered, "and I blamed the wrong man."

"You didn't know," Skye told her as she closed the door behind her. She glanced quickly around the apartment, but she didn't see Claire. The bathroom door was closed. Maybe Claire was in there.

"You think you know everything," Piper continued, her stare glassy. "Then the truth comes along, and it rips your world right apart."

A muffled cry reached Skye's ears. She frowned. That cry had come from the bathroom. "Claire?" Skye called.

"She wasn't feeling well," Piper told her, blinking, and glancing toward the bathroom door. "She said she kept seeing *her* sister." A bitter laugh escaped her. "I guess they took both our sisters away, didn't they?"

Skye hurried toward the bathroom. She knocked lightly on the wooden door. "Claire?"

The floor squeaked behind Skye.

She lifted her hand and knocked on the door. "Claire, are you okay?"

Something sharp and hard—a knife?—pressed into Skye's back, freezing her. Terrifying her.

"I wouldn't worry so much about Claire. She's already dead but you...you still have plenty of time to suffer." Piper's breath blew against Skye's ear. "And don't even think about screaming, bitch. You raise your voice above a whisper, and I will slit your throat in an instant."

***

Trace slammed on the brakes. The Jag stopped with a squeal of its tires. "You take the back," Trace ordered Noah as they jumped from the car.

"And you storm the front." Noah inclined his head. "Just like old times."

Screw old times. Trace had taken his weapon from the car. After Sharpe's death, he'd made sure to keep the gun close. He checked the weapon. Loaded. Ready. Then he ran toward the apartment. Reese should be upstairs, waiting and—

Noah cried out, the sound sharp and full of pain.

Trace whirled around.

Noah was on the cement, sprawled beneath a street lamp. Blood poured from beneath his body.

"Noah!" Trace yelled. Then he realized what was happening.

Shooter.

Trace dove for cover, but he moved a second too late, and he felt the burn of the bullet slice across the side of his face.

A silencer. The SOB was up there, trying to kill them both without making a sound.

Trace ducked behind the Jag. This wasn't his first shoot-out. He might be rusty, but he knew this game, and he knew how to find the shooter. Based on the angle of those shots…his gaze swept up and to the left. Those bullets had come from the second story. Corner apartment.

Reese's apartment?

"H-help…" Noah gasped out the plea.

Trace jerked his gaze back to his friend.

Had the shooter heard that cry? If so, he'd know Noah was still alive. Alive and a sitting duck.

Another shot would end Noah.

Trace knew he couldn't just sit there and watch his friend die. Even if that *was* the killer's plan.

Trace glanced up at the apartment. *You want me? Then take your best shot.* He sucked in a deep breath. An image of Skye flashed before him.

Come back to me.

He would. He *would.*

***

"People have no defense against an innocent face," Piper said, sounding not the least bit shattered or scared any longer. Now, she sounded satisfied. Smug. "Men think you're weak, and they want to protect you, and women, well, they think you're a friend, so they let their guard down when you're close."

Skye was still facing the bathroom door. She'd heard no other sound from inside, but when she glanced down, she saw blood slipping from under the bathroom door.

Claire!

"Did you see her wrist?" Piper asked. "It looks like Claire tried to kill herself once. I noticed that right away. Weak bitch. I guess I helped her out this time."

Skye tried to keep her muscles loose. "You're not Piper, are you?"

Laughter.

And she had her answer. "You're Anna Jean."

The blade sliced across Skye's back. She cried out.

"Give the bitch a cookie!" Anna Jean jerked Skye around to face her. Skye's shoulders hit the bathroom door. "All I had to do was make myself look a little bit more like my goody two-shoes sister. Then they all stared right at me, and they believed every lie I told them."

Skye glanced over Anna Jean's shoulders. "Not everyone believed them." And that was why Trace had left a guard behind. Skye tried to act like she was looking at that guard right then.

Anna Jean's jaw dropped open. "Drake?" Then she was whirling around to face what she obviously thought was a new threat, her body vibrating with tension as she tried to follow Skye's stare.

Only Drake wasn't standing there.

Skye slammed her body into Anna Jean's and she screamed as loud as she possibly could. They hit the floor. Skye grabbed two handfuls of Anna Jean's still wet hair, and she slammed the woman's face into the floor. Once, twice.

But Anna Jean broke free. She slashed out with the knife, and it sliced over Skye's forearm. Skye jerked back, hissing out at the pain.

"That's just the start," Anna Jean promised.

Drake threw open the door. *"Skye!"*

Anna Jean grabbed Skye and put the knife to her throat. "Now the hero's here," she snarled.

The blade nicked Skye's throat.

"Anna Jean," Drake whispered. One of his hands held the gun—a weapon that was pointed at Skye and Anna Jean. "I see you now."

"And I see *you!*" Her words were a scream. "All this time, I thought it was Trace! I couldn't remember what happened to me—every time I closed my eyes, I saw the snow and the blood and I heard screams."

Drake took a step forward.

"I lost four toes, Drake! It was so cold out there. You left me in the cold."

Drake's face hardened. Emotion—emotion that Skye couldn't name—burned in his eyes.

"I was in that shit-hole of a hospital for months! Barely living, in pain every single day. And it was because of *you!*"

"Anna Jean—"

"Don't!" Anna Jean cried out. The knife sliced across Skye's throat. Skye felt the wet warmth of her blood sliding down her neck. "Take another step, and you know I'll cut her throat open. I'll enjoy doing it."

Drake didn't move.

"Trace's dog tags were left." Now Anna Jean's voice was hoarse. "The men who found me, they said he'd been the one."

"The men who found you," Drake repeated. In contrast to Anna Jean, his voice was thick with tension. Anger. No, rage. "They were your partners, Anna Jean. They were the men you sent to kill *us*."

Anna Jean laughed then. "But here you are, still breathing."

"So are you," he pointed out. He still had his gun up, but Skye knew he wouldn't take the shot, not while Anna Jean was using her as a shield.

This was insane.

"No thanks to you," Anna Jean said. For an instant, she sounded...lost. "I was going to let you live, Drake. Because I thought you were the one who loved me. But you — you're the one who left me to die?"

Red stained his cheeks. "You gave me no choice! You tried to kill me!" He sprang forward.

"And you just killed her," Anna Jean spat back. Her hold on Skye tightened as the blade dug into Skye's throat.

CHAPTER FIFTEEN

Trace grabbed for Noah. He expected to feel a bullet sink into him at any moment.

But it didn't.

He pulled Noah behind the Jag. His fingers ripped open Noah's shirt so he could see the damage. The bullet had gone straight through Noah's chest and out his back.

"Missed...my heart," Noah muttered. "Saw the glint of the weapon. Dodged just in time."

The street was still dead silent. Since the shooter had used a silencer, no one else had even been aware of the shots. Trace pulled out his phone and dialed nine-one-one. "You're going to be all right," Trace promised him. The guy was bleeding like a stuck pig, and he was as pale as death. Trace was afraid for him. Damn scared, despite his words.

"Nine-one-one, what is the nature of your emergency?"

"My friend's been shot," Trace told the dispatcher. "I need an ambulance, *now*." He snapped out the address.

"Have you seen the shooter, sir?"

Trace glanced up at the apartment. "He fired from one of the apartments. You need to get the cops en route *now*."

And if a cop already was on the scene?

"Get...him," Noah rasped.

Trace hesitated. "I'm not leaving you to bleed out on the street."

"What if..." Noah's breath heaved out. "Reese is dying, too?" Another breath shuddered from him. "I'm not...going yet," Noah promised and gave him a weak smile. "I...envied you too long. I'll get...what you have."

"Man, I think you're delirious." Trace pulled Noah's back-up gun from his ankle holster. He wasn't sure where Noah's other weapon was. "Can you hold this?" Because if he went up to find the shooter, then he had to know Noah was safe.

"Always." Noah's bloody fingers curled around the weapon.

Trace met his stare. "Don't even think of dying before I get back."

"It's not...that bad."

"No," Trace lied. "It's not."

Noah's lips curved. "Do me a...favor? No, two?"

Trace nodded.

"Kill the b-bastard."

"He's already dead." The guy just didn't know it.

"And then...tell Claire I was a fucking rock star...when I got sh-shot."

"Tell her yourself." Trace tightened his hold on his weapon. He'd keep covered as much as possible as he ran for the apartment building. But he had to hurry.

If the killer got away, there'd just be another attack. And another. It wouldn't ever stop. Not until *he* stopped it.

Trace kept his head low as he ran toward the building.

***

Skye didn't care about the pain. When the knife dug into her, she didn't scream or try to jerk away from the blade.

Instead, she lifted up her hands and she clawed at Anna Jean's eyes.

Anna Jean was the one to scream. The blade slipped, cutting Skye more, but she let her knees buckle and she fell right from Anna Jean's weakened hold.

Drake grabbed Skye and tossed her across the room. Then he lunged for Anna Jean.

But he staggered to a stop when she brought up her knife.

"Going to shoot me?" Anna Jean taunted him. "Going to leave me to die alone? Again? *You weren't supposed to be the one!*"

He circled her.

Skye put her hand to her throat. The wounds weren't that deep, and she pushed the pain to the back of her mind. After all, the pain didn't matter then. Stopping Anna Jean was all that mattered.

Why wasn't Drake firing at her?

"You were different," Anna Jean whispered. "I stopped him from killing you earlier because I always thought...*not you*, Drake. Not. You!" The knife trembled in her grasp.

He opened his hand. Held it out to her. "Give me the knife."

She laughed at him.

Screw this. Skye raced across the room. She yanked on the bathroom door. It flew open, but only just a few inches, because it hit Claire's prone body.

"Claire!" Skye sank to her knees beside the other woman. There was blood. So much. A growing pool of it. Not from a slit throat, but from a deep wound in Claire's gut. Skye's fingers covered the wound, pushing down as she tried to apply pressure.

Claire's eyes cracked open. Her stare was glassy, nearly blind with fear. "*Again*," she whispered. "It's happening a-again."

"No." Skye shook her head. "You're going to be okay. We'll get you help." She turned her head. Drake and Anna Jean were still facing off. *What the hell?* "Call an ambulance," Skye yelled at Drake. "Claire needs help, now!"

Drake's gaze jerked to Skye. He blinked as if waking from a dream. Or maybe a nightmare.

And in that one moment, Anna Jean attacked. She lunged
forward and drove the knife into Drake's stomach, and then
she yanked, jerking the blade to the right. He fell back,
stunned, his eyes wide.

"This time, you get to die," Anna Jean told him.

His knees sagged, and he hit the floor.

Anna Jean spun to face Skye. "Your turn."

Claire whimpered.

Skye kept applying pressure. "Claire has nothing to do
with this. Let her go." Drake wasn't making a sound. His
guilt had made him vulnerable. Guilt, love—they could wreck
a person.

"I don't give a shit about Claire," Anna Jean yelled. She
bent over Drake's body, and when she rose, she had his gun.
"Maybe he did love me," she said as she stared down at him.
"Because if he'd been smart, he would've shot me when he
had the chance. Instead, I had the pleasure of gutting him."
Her voice dropped. "That's what you get for leaving me in the
cold."

Drake's body was already covered in blood. So much
blood. But when Anna Jean moved to step around him, his
hand flew out. His fingers locked around her ankle. "No..."
Drake growled.

"Oh, darling, relax, I'll slit your throat and end things
soon." She lifted the gun. "But first, I want to make sure
Skye's dead. You were right, you know. I did have a partner.
And he's waiting for a phone call from me. One that tells him
Skye is dead." She smiled at Skye. "Who's going to save you
now?"

Skye stood up. She inched away from Claire, not wanting
the bullet to hit the other woman. "Why?"

"Because when Trace falls, we'll take everything he has.
All that money...mine."

This had been about money? "I thought this was for
revenge."

"Killing you…" Anna Jean shrugged. "That's for revenge. The rest is for money."

Drake was trying to heave himself up behind her.

Anna Jean's finger tightened on the trigger. "At least I'm being merciful. Good-bye, little dancer."

Skye flew forward even as—

Nothing happened?

Anna Jean's fingers squeezed the trigger twice more, but the gun didn't fire.

Skye slammed into her. They fell to the floor, landing right next to Drake.

"Stupid…f-freaking water…" Anna Jean snarled. "I'll just…do it…the old f-fashioned way…" Her fingers locked around Skye's throat and she started to squeeze.

Skye slid her own hands under Anna Jean's, and she shoved up, fast and hard, breaking the other woman's hold. Then Skye drove her fist into Anna Jean's face.

Again and again.

She was pretty sure that she heard bones crunch.

Anna Jean sagged back, unmoving.

Skye jumped up. Her hand throbbed. She'd probably broken some of her own fingers. She tried to grab for the phone that had been left on the little table near the door, but the phone fell from her now burning hand. Skye dove for it, and tried to dial nine-one-one.

Anna Jean yelled. *The woman just won't stay down.* Anna Jean pushed up to her knees. "B-bitch, you're done!"

And Drake drove the knife into her heart. Anna Jean gasped. Her eyes widened. She turned her head to look at him.

His face was ashen. His eyes appeared sunken. "I didn't…miss this time," he told her.

Anna Jean's lips trembled.

The nine-one-one operator came on the line.

Skye spilled out the emergency details as quickly as she could. When she looked back over at Anna Jean, the woman's body was ominously still.

And Drake was slumped over her.

Skye scrambled to them. She rolled Drake over. Checked his pulse. Faint, thready, but he was still alive.

"Hurry," she whispered into the phone. "Please, hurry."

She ran back to Claire.

"T-tell me she's dead," Claire whispered.

If Anna Jean wasn't dead yet, she would be soon. *And will Claire be gone, too?*

The phone in Skye's hands vibrated.

Another call was coming in. Skye was still on the line with the nine-one-one operator, but she glanced at the screen and saw the note for—

Unknown caller. The message flashed across the phone's screen.

The phone wasn't hers. It had just been tossed on the table.

Was it Claire's?

Or Anna Jean's?

Anna Jean's voice echoed through Skye's mind. *I did have a partner. And he's waiting for a phone call from me. One that tells him Skye is dead.*

Had the partner got tired of waiting?

Skye crouched next to Claire. She put one hand on the wound, keeping up the pressure. Her left hand held the phone. Her finger slid across the phone's screen as she took the call. "H-hello?" Her voice was a rasp. Lower than normal.

Static, then. "Is she dead?"

A tear slid down Skye's cheek because she *knew* that voice.

Frantic, she ended the call and immediately tried to get Trace on the line.

***

Trace bounded up the stairs. When he reached Reese's apartment, he didn't pause.

He kicked in the damn door.

Trace ran inside with his weapon ready, but he stopped cold at the sight of the body before him.

Detective Alex Griffin lay on the floor, face-down. Reese stood above him, a horrified look on his face. "I had no choice," Reese muttered. "No choice."

There was no weapon in Reese's hands. No weapon near Alex, either.

"He did it," Reese said. "He came here, with a knife, trying to kill me." Reese lifted his head. "Boss, dammit, *why?*"

Trace's phone vibrated in his pocket. He didn't answer it. Not yet. Carefully, he bent next to Alex. The cop's blond hair was matted with blood, and Alex's pulse was weak, but steady. "He's still alive. An ambulance is on the way."

Reese hadn't moved.

Trace looked up at him. "There was a shooter here."

Reese nodded frantically. "*Him.* He had me tied up, I got loose, we fought—"

Trace's phone kept vibrating. He rose to his feet. The gun was still in his hands. "We've been friends for a long time," Trace told Reese.

Reese nodded. He rocked back on his heels. "A cop...I can't believe...a cop..."

"I've trusted you with my life." The phone stopped vibrating. "More importantly, I've trusted you with Skye's life."

Reese's hand slid toward his waist. "You can always trust me," he told Trace, the expression on his face stark. "I've got your back. You've got mine."

Trace's jaw locked. "Right now, I'm wondering what the hell you *have* behind your back."

Reese's hand stopped its slow glide toward his waist. "Boss?"

"Alex was hit from behind. His head is matted with blood—blood that's already partly dry in his hair. If the blood had time to dry, that means he wasn't shooting at me. You were."

"What?" Shock slackened Reese's face. "How can you say that? I would never do that! We're friends!"

"Yes, we are." He didn't hear the scream of sirens yet. They needed to damn well get there. "But you're still the man who's been after me." Rage beat in his blood. "*You killed Sara.*"

Reese flinched. "No, no, it was the cop!" He took a lunging step forward.

"*Stop!*" Trace shook his head and aimed his weapon at Reese's head. "Another step, and I'll shoot you."

Reese's eyes narrowed. "The same way you shot Tucker? I guess you have a history of shooting your friends, don't you?"

"Only because my friends have a history of betraying me. I don't deal well with betrayal."

"I haven't betrayed you!" Spittle flew from Reese's mouth.

"You think I haven't checked on you?" Trace demanded, body tight. "Guess who didn't have alibis for the kills?"

His phone vibrated again.

Reese's gaze flickered at the sound. "Maybe you should get that call, boss."

"And maybe we should all just wait right here until the cops arrive."

At that, Reese laughed. "Like the great Trace Weston gives a flying shit about local cops. You do what you want, when you want. You always have."

And the mask that Reese had worn seemed to fall away. His face twisted with bitterness.

This was my friend?

"You climb out of hell, and you rise to heaven," Reese's voice was a grating snarl. His eyes flashed with fury. "That's your charmed life, isn't it?"

"My life's never been charmed." An alcoholic mother. A father who used his fists too frequently and forgot to even feed his son most days.

One war zone after another.

The phone stopped vibrating.

Reese shook his head. "You do have a weakness, though." Reese smiled at him. "And I can't believe you just left her alone…with Anna Jean."

In that instant, Trace's heart stopped.

"Oh, yeah, boss, it's her. New face. New contacts. New hair. But you—you're always so taken in by the innocent ones. The ones who look lost and scared, just like Skye."

Skye didn't look lost and scared. She looked like the most perfect thing in the world.

"Anna Jean came to me," Reese told him, smug now. "She told me about what you'd done. How you'd left her and Tucker to die. I'd heard the story before, of course. You'd told me *your* version, but this was different."

Anna Jean's story was bull. "You know Anna Jean betrayed the team."

"Like I gave a damn about that. I wasn't on that team." His smile stretched. "She wanted vengeance, and you know what I wanted?"

"No clue." Every instinct in Trace's body screamed for him to attack.

Alex still lay prone on the floor.

"I almost died for your girlfriend," Reese snapped. "When that freak of a doctor came after her, I wound up in the hospital. Collateral damage, right? Screw that!"

"You were not—"

But Reese cut right through his words and said, "I had your back day in and day out, but I got *nothing*."

Trace shook his head. "That's not true, you—"

"You saved my ass in battle, so what? I'm supposed to be your lackey forever? I want my share! Why do you get everything? *Why?*"

This time, Trace didn't try to talk. He knew Reese didn't care what he said.

"You were going to marry her. As soon as I saw the chunk of glass on her finger, I knew I had to act. I got Anna Jean in town, and we started our plan. Skye had to die, of course."

He fucking dared to speak so easily about her death?

"If you married Skye, then you'd change your will," Reese said, jerking a hand through his hair. "I couldn't let the money go to her. Not after all the time I'd put in to make sure I was the one closest to you."

Now Trace laughed. "You idiot. I never planned to change my will." Reese was so wrong. About so many things.

Reese blinked. "Wh-what? But...but I thought..."

"I was always going to take care of you, Reese. You were my *friend*." A lying, deadly friend. "But Skye, she was the one I loved. Even if I'd never gotten back with her, the bulk of my fortune was always set to go to Skye when I died." It had been his only way to take care of her.

Reese's jaw dropped.

"With the ring or without it," Trace said. "She was always mine. And I protect what's mine."

Trace's head tilted. Ah, he could hear the siren now. It was time to end this.

"You didn't protect her this time!" Reese's body vibrated with fury. "Anna Jean *killed* her. Your precious Skye bled out while you were on your way here. Anna Jean killed her the instant you left the studio. Then she killed Drake and Claire. They never even saw her coming."

Skye's alive. Skye's alive. He yanked out his phone.

Reese's hand flew up. He grabbed a gun—one that he'd had hidden behind his back—and he fired.

Trace fired at the same instant. The blasts thundered through the room.

Reese's lips moved. A weak gasp slipped from him.

Trace hadn't aimed for his heart. The bullet had blasted right through Reese's head.

Reese's body thudded to the floor.

Trace's weapon dropped. He pulled out the phone. Called back the number that had tried to reach him again and again. It wasn't Skye's number. It was a number he didn't know.

"Trace!" Skye's frantic voice shouted over the line.

She was alive.

"It's Reese," she told him, her voice warming him even as a chill seemed to surround his heart. "He's the one who's been after you."

Sirens screamed, coming closer.

"I'm on my way to you! Be careful, Trace, be very—"

"I love you," Trace told her as emotion rose up to choke him. "Always, you…"

"Trace?"

The phone slipped from his fingers.

Trace stared down at his chest. Reese had always been such a damn fine shot.

A good friend? No.

But a good killer.

I love you, Skye.

He just hated that he'd broken his promise to her. He'd said that he would return to her.

She'd asked for only one thing. *Come back to me.*

It was the one thing he couldn't give her.

***

Skye raced toward the apartment. Her breath heaved in her lungs even as her heart thundered wildly in her chest. She'd been disconnected. Trace's call had just ended and no matter how many times she tried, she couldn't get him back on the line.

"Ma'am, stop!" A uniformed cop appeared in her path. "This is a crime scene, you can't go in there!"

Police cruisers lined the street. Three ambulances — *three* — were there. "My fiancé is in that building! I've got to find him!"

"I'm sorry, ma'am, but no one is getting in there now." His face was grim but sympathetic. "Now just stand back."

"*Injured officer!*" Another voice shouted. "Make room!"

Her head snapped to the right. Two EMTs were pushing out a man on a gurney. They wheeled right past her, and she saw Alex's ashen face.

"Alex!" She rushed toward him.

His hand rose and caught her wrist. "So...sorry..."

An EMT pulled Alex's hand away.

But she grabbed it right back. "Where's Trace?"

Alex's eyes squinted up at her. "Was...watching Reese...caught him t-tailing me...thought Weston had...sent him..."

"Please, *where is Trace?*"

The uniformed cop wrapped his arms around Skye and pulled her back. The EMTs loaded Alex into the back of the nearest ambulance. The doors slammed shut and the siren screamed on.

"One fatality," a voice behind her muttered. "But did you see the blood in that place? It looked like something out of a horror movie."

Skye was glad the cop held her. Without him, she might have hit the ground right then. Her nails dug into his arms, and she turned to gaze up at the young officer. "Was the fatality Trace Weston?"

"I don't know who died, ma'am," he whispered back. "I wasn't cleared to go upstairs. I just know some guy took a detective hostage and started shooting people in the street." He pointed to the left, and she looked, gasping when she saw the dark pool of what had to be blood under a street lamp.

"They already took one man to the hospital. He had a gunshot wound to the chest." The cop's lips thinned. "I can't say anymore, okay? Go to the hospital. St. Mary's. Wait there."

She backed away from him, forcing her legs to move. *St. Mary's.* Claire and Drake had been taken to St. Mary's, too. The EMTS had arrived at her studio. They'd come with police.

The police had wanted to question Skye. They'd wanted her to go down to the station.

She'd just wanted to get away. She'd faked being sick and she'd darted to the bathroom. Then she'd climbed out of the window and grabbed the first taxi that she saw.

Her gaze flew around the scene. Trace's car was still there. Far too close to the ominous pool of blood. *It looked black. In the darkness, the blood looked so black.*

She didn't see Noah. She didn't see Trace.

"He's seizing!"

Two more EMTs ran from the apartment. A man was between them on the gurney. His hand fell limply, his fingers lax.

In that instant, everything stopped for Skye as she gazed at that hand.

It was the hand of the man who'd saved her from being raped when she was fifteen. That hand had struck out with vicious accuracy then, beating her attacker again and again.

That was the man who'd saved her from hell. He'd pulled her out of that terrible basement. Carried her. Held her close with that hand.

That was the hand of the man who'd proposed to her. His fingers had trembled when he'd slid the ring onto her finger. Weakness, when Trace was normally so strong.

Trace! They were loading him into the back of an ambulance, and she jumped inside with them.

One of the EMTs glanced up. "Lady, you can't—"

"I'm his fiancé." Oh, God, his chest. The blood. *"Help him!"*

The EMT jerked his head and went back to work. The siren screamed as the vehicle lurched forward.

Skye grabbed for Trace's hand. She held it like the lifeline that it was. She hadn't warned him fast enough. Reese had done this. The man they'd trusted.

Her hold tightened on him. "Come back to me," Skye whispered because she could tell — she could *feel* — that Trace was slipping away. His face was too still. Too pale. The life and energy — all that was Trace — *gone.*

"Please," she whispered while the EMTs hooked him up to machines and poked him with needles. "Don't leave me, Trace. I don't want to be without you." She'd tried that. And she'd felt as if she were only living half a life during those years.

"Come back to me," Skye said again.

But Trace didn't answer her, and a cold chill covered her body.

CHAPTER SIXTEEN

Skye walked into the morgue. The police chief was at her side. Because of this case, because of who was involved, she'd warranted attention from the man in charge.

Maybe that was supposed to make her feel better. It didn't. Nothing could make her feel better. Nothing could make her *feel* then. Her wounds were bandaged. The doctors had wanted to give her pain medication. She'd refused. There was no need for the drugs because a wall of ice surrounded her, numbing her. Each breath was an effort, sawing out of her lungs.

"I don't want to be here," Skye said. Her voice was wooden. As cold as she felt.

"We just need the identification process completed, Ms. Sullivan," he told her. His eyes and his face were sympathetic. Everyone kept looking at her that way. With sympathy. Pity.

She hated those stares.

The first body waited. She glanced down at it. Felt no emotion stir. Not even rage. She'd locked her emotions away. She had to lock them away, or else she'd go crazy.

I'm more like my mother than I thought.

Because she wanted to kill. Wanted to destroy everyone in her path.

Skye cleared her throat as she stared at the body. "That's Anna Jean Hurley. She was working with Reese Stokes. I believe they killed Ben Sharpe, Parker Jacobs, and Sara Kramer."

"You believe?"

"Yes. Anna Jean told me they did, so I believed the bitch."

He sucked in a sharp breath.

Skye glared at the body. For a minute there, rage had cracked through her surface. She couldn't have that. Because her pain was hidden just behind the rage.

Her gaze slid to the next slab. To the body that was waiting for her. Her lips trembled. Her hands clenched tightly into fists, and her nails bit into her palms.

"That's Reese Stokes." And he was missing part of his head.

The chief's shoulder brushed against hers. "Most people can't handle seeing a dead body, not one like this."

"Most people probably don't stare at the dead and wish that they'd been the one to do the killing." She looked up at him. "I do."

His eyes widened.

"Reese was Anna Jean's partner. I don't know why. Maybe because he was a psychotic jerk. Maybe because he fell for the wrong woman, and she warped his mind." Her gaze slid back to Reese. "I thought of him as family, and I hope the bastard is burning now."

She stepped back. "Now I need to get back to Trace." She'd been away from him too long already. Skye skirted around the police chief.

"I'm...very sorry, ma'am," he called.

Her fingers hesitated above the door.

"The doctors briefed me on Weston's injuries. I understand that he...he—"

Her spine snapped straight. "You don't know anything about Trace Weston. Neither do they. But I know plenty." She faced him. "He's the strongest man I know. And he's a man who keeps his promises. Trace isn't going to leave me. He's going to wake up. He's going to open his eyes *any* time." That was why she had to be there. "And he's going to make a full recovery."

The pity flashed in his eyes again. She *hated* that pity. She wouldn't look at it anymore. She left the chief, hurrying from the room and running back to the only man who mattered to her.

***

She was only supposed to stay with Trace for fifteen minutes at a time. That was the rule in the ICU.

Skye was breaking their rules, and the doctors hadn't tried to throw her out yet. Maybe they were afraid of the Weston name. Of the Weston money.

Or maybe…maybe they just had pity in their eyes, too, when they looked at her.

She stood by his bed. Stroked his fingers. They'd told her that machines were keeping him alive.

Skye wouldn't believe that. *He* was alive.

His skin wasn't warm to the touch, it was cool, too cold. So was hers. She rubbed his fingers, trying to force warmth back into him and wishing that she could be the one in that bed.

But she was there, at his side, helpless.

"Is this how you felt?" Skye asked him. "When I was taken and you were left behind, did you feel like this? Like you were being ripped apart, like you were losing your *life*…and there was nothing you could do but stand there and watch it all fall away?"

He didn't answer her. He couldn't. A tube was shoved down his throat. He couldn't breathe on his own. They'd operated on him — three times. He hadn't regained consciousness since the EMTs had hauled him out of that apartment.

It looked like something out of a horror movie.

"There's no one for me to fight." Her voice had gone hoarse. From the tears? Or from all the hours she'd talked to him?

Skye hadn't slept. She couldn't.

"I want to hurt the man who did this to you, but he's gone." And she was there. Holding him. "I need to confess something to you."

She heard the rustle of the curtain behind her.

Skye didn't look away from Trace.

"I would have killed Reese for you. I would have killed anyone to protect you." She swallowed, trying to ease the ache in her throat so that she could keep talking. "I was never afraid of the darkness that you carried. Because inside, I've got that same darkness. I think...I think I just hide it better than you do."

She hid her true self from everyone, but him.

"I would've killed them. I would've done anything for you." Her hand lifted. She brushed her fingers over his still cheek. "I still will. I'll do anything, Trace, just please, please come back to me. Because there is one thing I can't do...*I can't live without you.*" She didn't want to try.

A hand touched her shoulder. "Skye."

Alex's voice. He'd heard her confession. She didn't care. She didn't care about anything but Trace.

"Has there been any change?" Alex asked her.

Her fingers slid back down to hold Trace's hand. "Not yet. But there will be. He's coming back to me."

Alex's hand fell away from her. "I heard that..." He cleared his throat. "I heard that Claire Kramer and Drake Archer will be discharged soon."

Skye nodded. "That's good." They'd healed. Trace would, too.

"Noah York is improving. He lost a lot of blood, so the docs aren't ready to release him yet." Alex paused. "Noah said that Weston saved his life, and Claire...she said you are the only reason she's still here."

She still didn't look away from Trace. She just needed him to open his eyes. Once he opened his eyes, everything would be all right.

"I saw Reese following me when I left the station. I'd thought that Weston sent him after me."

She slipped her fingers over Trace's knuckles. Her engagement ring gleamed up at her. "You always think the worst of Trace."

"I *thought* he'd killed Parker because he loved you and wanted you safe." Alex cleared his throat. "But we found evidence at Reese's place. Photos. He'd been following Parker. Meeting with him."

"I guess they both wanted the same thing," Skye whispered. "To destroy Trace."

"Reese was…involved with Sara. We showed one of Sara's neighbors a picture of him, and the neighbor confirmed that he'd been there to visit her several times."

"He was just using her. He used her, and he killed her." And Skye had *trusted* him.

When you put your trust in the wrong person, you opened yourself up for all kinds of hurt.

Skye didn't think it was possible to hurt more than she did then.

"What I don't understand…" Alex's shoulder brushed against hers. "What I don't understand is why I didn't get killed, too. He had me. Reese knocked me out. He could've killed me at any point."

Skye blinked at that. Finally, she pulled her gaze off Trace. Focused on the detective. "He didn't kill you because *you* were going to be the killer."

Alex's brows rose.

"Anna Jean named you…she said that you'd come to find her in Atlanta. She was tossing you out to us all, setting you up as the killer." *Lying so easily.* "Then Trace ran over to Reese's place because Reese called and said that you were watching him."

"I—"

"It was your gun that Reese used to shoot Trace, wasn't it?"

He nodded.

That was what she'd thought. "You would've been killed, eventually. At the right time — a time that would match up with whatever scenario Reese planned to spin to the authorities. He would've killed you, no doubt with *Trace's* gun. That way, everything would end tied up nicely. You went after the killer — you shot Trace, but not before he fatally ended you."

Alex's gaze flashed to Trace. "Only the plan got fucked."

"Yes, but not soon enough." Because if she'd just reached Trace sooner, then he wouldn't be in that hospital bed.

Silence from Alex. The heavy, rough silence that seemed to push against Skye's skin. Then, finally, he asked "Is there anything I can do?"

She smoothed her fingers over Trace's. "He bounced back so quickly when Mitch shot him." *Just a few weeks before. Why — why couldn't they just have an easy life?* "But I guess Reese was a better shot." Damn the bastard. "They've operated on Trace so many times, trying to repair the damage from that bullet, but the doctors just —" She broke off and had to blink back her tears. "I don't understand why the doctors can't have more hope." She had plenty. There was no way that she would give up on Trace. "He survived before. He'll do it again." *Please, Trace, cheat death again for me.*

"I'm sorry, Skye."

So was she. "If you want to do something, then bring him back to me." Because that was the only thing that she wanted.

Alex pulled a chair closer to the bed.

A chair for her.

A chair for him.

"It looks like I owe that man my life," Alex said.

That man *was* her life.

They sat down, and they waited.

***

Skye was dead. Anna Jean had killed her. Sliced open Skye's throat. Let her blood drain out.

Skye was an angel with bloody wings. Dead on a snow covered field.

He'd left her behind, and she'd died.

Skye! Trace tried to scream her name. Again and again, but no sound slipped past his lips.

The cold froze him. Numbed him. And Skye was dead before him.

If she was gone, then he wanted to die, too. He couldn't, *wouldn't* go years without her again.

Skye had been his hope. His only dream.

She was gone.

And he wanted to be with her.

***

The machines started to beep louder. Faster.

Skye shot out of her chair. Her knees locked as she stood at Trace's bedside. "Trace?" Skye whispered.

He was coming back to her.

The beeping grew more frantic.

Alex rose from his chair. "Ah...Skye..."

A nurse and two doctors rushed into the room. They pushed Skye back.

"You have to go back to the waiting room, miss," the nurse told Skye as she blocked her path to Trace. "You need to go *now.*"

No way. Skye peered around the nurse's shoulder. "He's waking up! I'm not going anywhere!"

"Blood pressure's dropping...too damn low," one doctor muttered.

Alex caught Skye's hand. "We should go outside." He sounded so grim. So...sad?

"No!" Skye yanked away from him. "He's waking up!"

The nurse gave a slight shake of her head.

"You're wrong!" Skye jumped around the nurse. She shoved at the doctors. Fought to get to Trace. "*Come back to me! You promised.*" Her hands grabbed him. "Don't you do this! Don't do this to me!"

One of the doctors tried to pry Skye's hand away from Trace. He'd have to try a whole lot harder than that.

"Ms. Sullivan, you have to leave. He's…" The doctor's voice hardened. "We're trying to stabilize him!"

"No!" Skye yelled right back. "You're waiting for him to die, but I'm not." Her hold on Trace was desperate. "Don't go where I can't follow. Do you hear me? Don't you dare go where I can't follow. You promised me forever, Trace. That was your promise. But it hasn't been forever. It's been *weeks.* You. Promised. Me!"

The cold had cracked around her.

The rage had bled out.

There was only pain left. So much anguish. So much grief. And it was tearing her apart.

***

Skye's body vanished. The snow vanished.

Only the blood remained.

Skye? He tried to call out again, but his throat felt twisted. His speech was gone.

He couldn't hear anything around him. The silence was so complete.

And the blood began to darken.

"*…Promised me!*"

In the middle of the silence, her voice was deafening.

Skye's voice.

She was close to him. He just had to find her. She was close. She was alive.

"*…Forever!*"

The darkness deepened. It grew. So complete. So total. So—

Trace's eyes flew open. A room of white surrounded him. So bright.

"*Trace!*" His head jerked at Skye's cry.

She was there. A man in white — a doctor? — had his arms around Skye as if he'd been pulling her back.

Trace tried to call out to her.

She tore free from the man's hold. "You came back!" Tears were on her cheeks. Her eyes were so big and wide and so full of love. "You…came back!"

"I'll be damned," someone muttered.

Trace's gaze flickered to the left. Alex stared at him, a wide smile on his face.

Trace didn't smile back. Everything hurt too badly right then.

"You're going to be okay," Skye whispered. She pressed a kiss to his check. "Everything's going to be okay again."

Skye was alive. She didn't have a trail of bloody wings in the snow. She was right next to him. Staring at him with love in her eyes.

"You're with me," she said, smiling at him. A smile that lit up his whole world.

No, *she* was his world.

The doctors worked on him, but Skye stayed close. She held his hand. He wouldn't let her go.

He heard the doctor talk about breathing machines. Blood loss. Surgeries.

They took out the tube that had been in his throat. They poked him. They prodded him.

Skye stayed with him.

And when the doctors were done, she bent toward him and pressed a kiss to his lips. She still tasted like every dream he'd ever had. The good dreams. The dreams that made a man want to live, even when death called to him.

"You kept your promise," Skye whispered.

His throat felt as if it had been cut open. He swallowed. Once. Twice. Then he managed to say, "Had to…keep." Hell, that had sounded like he was spitting out glass. Trace tried again and managed, "Was…mine…to you…had to…keep."

But Skye shook her head. Her smile came again. The smile that told him everything was going to be all right.

Reese was gone. The betrayal, the pain, would always be there, but Trace didn't have to worry about the past coming back.

The threat was over. Dead.

Just like Anna Jean.

It was time to leave the dead behind. Time to focus on the living.

"It was your promise," Skye said. Her lips pressed lightly to his once more. "But you, Trace, you're mine, and I was ready to fight heaven and hell to keep you with me."

His promise. Her love.

Trace tried to sit up, to get closer to her, but he was so weak.

So Skye came to him. Carefully, slowly, she curled her body around his.

She held him. He held her.

The love that they had would keep them strong. Through whatever came in the future.

But he was damn well tired of death and danger. He was also sick of getting shot. He never wanted to see another hospital again.

He was ready for the promise of happiness that they deserved. And, for Skye, he'd make sure they got that happiness.

Another promise for him to keep.

Trace stared into her eyes. "I love you."

And he saw love shining in her eyes, an endless love that stared back at him.

A love that would last forever.

I always keep my promises to Skye.

Always.

###

COMING IN OCTOBER OF 2013...

MINE TO HOLD — NOAH AND CLAIRE'S STORY

HE WILL NEVER LET HER GO...

AUTHOR'S NOTE

Thank you so much for reading Skye and Trace's story. I hope you enjoyed MINE TO KEEP. If you would like to learn about my upcoming releases, you can subscribe to my newsletter (http://www.cynthiaeden.com/newsletter/). You can also visit my website (http://www.cynthiaeden.com) for information about my books.

HER WORKS

"Mine" Romantic Suspense Series

- MINE TO TAKE (Book 1)
- MINE TO KEEP (Book 2)
- MINE TO HOLD (Book 3 - Coming in October 2013)

"Deadly" Romantic Suspense Series

- DEADLY FEAR (Deadly, Book 1)
- DEADLY HEAT (Deadly, Book 2)
- DEADLY LIES (Deadly, Book 3)

Harlequin Intrigue Shadow Agents

- ALPHA ONE (Shadow Agents, Book 1)
- GUARDIAN RANGER (Shadow Agents, Book 2)
- SHARPSHOOTER (Shadow Agents, Book 3)
- GLITTER AND GUNFIRE (Shadow Agents, Book 4)

"Bound" Paranormal Romance Series

- BOUND BY BLOOD (Book 1)
- BOUND IN DARKNESS (Book 2)
- BOUND IN SIN (Book 3)
- BOUND BY THE NIGHT (Book 4)
- BOUND IN DEATH (Book 5)

Additional List of Cynthia Eden's Paranormal Romance Titles

- THE WOLF WITHIN
- HOWL FOR IT
- ANGEL OF DARKNESS (Fallen, Book 1)
- ANGEL BETRAYED (Fallen, Book 2)
- ANGEL IN CHAINS (Fallen, Book 3)
- AVENGING ANGEL (Fallen, Book 4)
- NEVER CRY WOLF
- ETERNAL HUNTER (Night Watch, Book 1)
- I'LL BE SLAYING YOU (Night Watch, Book 2)
- ETERNAL FLAME (Night Watch, Book 3)
- HOTTER AFTER MIDNIGHT (Midnight, Book 1)
- MIDNIGHT SINS (Midnight, Book 2)
- MIDNIGHT'S MASTER (Midnight, Book 3)
- IMMORTAL DANGER
- WHEN HE WAS BAD (anthology)
- EVERLASTING BAD BOYS (anthology)
- BELONG TO THE NIGHT (anthology)